"What's wrong, Shay?" Julia scanned the room. "What are you looking at?"

"There . . . there in the far corner of the greenhouse ceiling. Just past that last white pipe."

Julia's high heels clicked across the brick floor as she approached them. "What is it? Did someone climb up from your patio, Liam, to spy on us or worse yet, break in—" She screamed, and her oversized handbag thudded to the floor.

Shay choked on the deep breath she'd sucked in. "Julia, remember earlier when you told me that if I find any problems to let you know and you'd have someone on your staff take care of it?"

"Uh-huh."

"You weren't talking about body removal, were you?"

Books by Lauren Elliott

Beyond the Page Bookstore Mysteries
MURDER BY THE BOOK
PROLOGUE TO MURDER
MURDER IN THE FIRST EDITION
PROOF OF MURDER
A PAGE MARKED FOR MURDER
UNDER THE COVER OF MURDER
TO THE TOME OF MURDER
A MARGIN FOR MURDER

Crystals & CuriosiTEAS Mysteries
STEEPED IN SECRETS
MURDER IN A CUP

Published by Kensington Publishing Corp.

LAUREN ELLIOTT

Steeped in Secrets

Kensington Publishing Corp.
www.kensingtonbooks.com

Steeped in Secrets

Chapter 1

Shayleigh Myers or Shay, as her friends and family called her, hopped out of the black Explorer into what was a typical cloudless California late August morning. She gazed at her surroundings, finding it hard to believe she was actually back in the small town she thought she had left behind forever. But sixteen years and one failed marriage later, here she was again.

At first glance, she couldn't see that much had changed. The entire town of Bray Harbor, but especially High Street, was still the same. The Victorian-styled streetlamps; colorful, historic buildings in wood-clad, brick, and stone; and the cobblestone roadway always reminded her of a picture straight out of a storybook. Today . . . well . . . it allowed her to linger comfortably in the past—even for a split second—and forget all the heartache she had endured since she had last set foot on the redbrick sidewalk leading down High Street.

A revitalizing energy coursed through her as she stood appreciating the sights. Here she was again, that once precocious teenager who was going to go out and conquer the world. For that instant, there was no sign of the broke midthirties divorcée she had become. The forces surging through her were like soap bubbles that magically washed all those heartbreaking years away.

Then her daydream bubble burst.

"What in the world happened to Molly's Tavern?"

Instead of the familiar Molly's sign, a marquee advertising Madigan's Pub stood in its place. Her heart sank further when she took a closer look and realized that many of her other favorite shops were also gone—like Gertie's Grounds, the coffee shop where she and her high school friends used to hang out. All those comforting thoughts she had about how nothing had changed—except her—quickly faded. It was clear that time had not stood still here while her life had gone on. Like it or not, this was her new reality.

She tapped the documents she had tucked in her handbag. It was apparent that today was going to need a good kick start if she was to make it through, and that would begin with a coffee. Yes, a large mug of strong, dark coffee. She judged by the image on the sign, a steaming cup and the name Cuppa-Jo, in the old Gertie's location, that they still served the elixir of the gods. Her gaze darted to the MADIGAN'S PUB sign across the road from it, and she shivered. Yup, if she ever needed some fortification to make it through the day, she was going to need some, and now.

As she made her way down the sidewalk toward the coffee shop, light coastal breezes tickled her cheeks, and the briny air left a hint of sea salt on her lips. The forgotten taste stirred warm memories of her childhood and her once carefree life in this little artsy town just down the coast from its sister city, Carmel-by-the-Sea. She mentally crossed her fingers in the hope that the coffee shop still had the same fifties décor that Gertie's had, which was like a set out of the *Happy Days* television show. She desperately needed the comfort of knowing not *everything* in her world had changed.

Shay dropped into a faux-wicker chair on the coffee shop's street-side patio and closed her eyes, reveling in the smell of fresh sea air and the sun warming her face. If she had been born a cat, she'd have started purring. These were all the little things she'd taken for granted growing up on the West Coast and forgotten about while living in hot, dry New Mexico for the last decade and a half.

"Would you like a menu?"

Shay sat up and shielded her eyes from the sun, cursing herself for having left her sunglasses in the SUV. She squinted into the face of a young platinum-blond woman sporting a tousled asymmetric haircut, and winced at the sparks of light glistening off her diamond nose ring and eyebrow studs that made her entire face appear to glow. Was it the sun, or was Shay glimpsing the girl's feelings? Sometimes Shay couldn't tell the difference between what she thought and the feelings she had when something stirred within her.

"The sun's right in your eyes, isn't it? Here, let me tilt the umbrella a bit for you." The server started to make an adjustment to the pole, casting shade over Shay.

Shay thrust out her hand and stopped the girl's final adjustment. "Honestly, it was fine, and I'd rather keep it the way it was." She gazed into the girl's face, noting shade had also been cast over her, and she no longer appeared to be glowing. Shay always did have what some people called uncanny heightened senses. Not many people she met were empathic enough to sense other people's energy like she did, and what she saw in her dimming aura and felt from the girl right now definitely were no longer rays of sunshine.

"Fine, whatever." The young woman thrust out one hip, pulled a pen from behind her ear, and suspended it over an order pad. "Coffee?" she asked, obviously forcing a smile across her black-lipstick-covered mouth.

"Please," Shay said. "Just cream, thanks," she added quickly, anticipating the young woman's next question.

The server gave her a curt nod, turned swiftly on her heel, and headed for the shop door. Shay flinched from the trail of fiery vibrations the girl produced. Certainly, Shay couldn't have been the cause of the young server's dark explosion of energy. She thought she had handled the umbrella incident and the shade being cast over her rather well. She tried to shake it off. The girl was most likely just having an all-around bad morning, and what Shay thought she saw when she first looked at her was clearly only the sunshine glistening off her diamond facial adornments.

When the door closed behind the server, the energy in the air rapidly shifted. Shivers prickled at Shay's skin. She glanced around. What she was sensing now wasn't related to the young server. Someone was watching her.

She scanned the street but couldn't see anyone who might be focused enough on her to induce her tingling sensations. Then an unseen magnet pulled her gaze across the road to a sign that read CRYSTALS & CURIOSITEAS, and her chest constricted with uneasiness.

The red banner over the shop entrance was faded and weatherworn, but the storefront was still in fairly good condition. The old rustic wooden benches she remembered sat on each side of the door under the bay windows. An array of summer flowers spilled out of large ceramic pots at each end. The shop really didn't look like it had changed much over the years. Nothing about it stood out as being the potential source of the heightened ripples of unrest rolling through her. Then the ripples swelled. Their intensity grew into a tidal wave that shot a tremor through her.

Sitting, unmoving in the doorway alcove between the two bay windows, was a pure white German shepherd. At least, she hoped it was a dog because based on its size and build, it could easily have been a wolf.

Their eyes locked, and a shockwave surged through her. The dog stood up. Its gaze never wavered as it stalked across the road and sat back on its haunches at the edge of the outdoor patio. The stare from its crystal-blue eyes overpowered her. It was as if he could see into the depths of her soul. Despite the warmth of the morning, she shivered with the surging pulses of electricity racing between them.

"I see you've met Spirit." A woman's voice broke through her thoughts, severing Shay's connection with the dog.

Shay jerked and swung around, coming face-to-face with a woman sporting short salt-and-pepper hair, which showed her to be slightly older than Shay's own thirty-five years.

"Joanne?" Shay leapt to her feet.

She couldn't believe that the first familiar face she saw in town was her sister Jen's oldest and dearest friend. Although Shay was two years younger, Jen's friends had always treated her as an equal and had been her friends too.

"I knew it had to be you." Joanne embraced Shay in a bear hug. "I'd know that long red hair anywhere, but I never thought I'd see the day you'd come back to town, Shay Myers."

"You didn't think *you'd* see the day?" Shay replied with a short laugh.

Joanne grabbed her hand and pulled Shay back down into her seat and took the chair beside her. "So, what brings you back to Bray Harbor? You couldn't get out of here fast enough when you left."

"I know." Shay chuckled uneasily, recalling the dark days after her parents were killed in a boating accident the summer just before her eighteenth birthday. "But you remember what it was like when my aunt came to stay with me and Jen. Jen was starting at the college in the fall, but I had one more year of high school." Shay hung her head and whispered, "It was just a tough time. Grief can be complicated, all the emotions, pain, anger . . ."

An image of her aunt's face popped into Shay's mind. Their aunt, bless her heart, really did try to step in and mother the two headstrong young women, but to eighteen-year-old Shay, she was a constant reminder of what they had lost, and she resented her for it.

"Yeah." Joanne nodded, her eyes softening. "It was a difficult time for both of you, but especially for you, I guess, because besides college, Jen had started dating Dean, so she had him to help her through it." She pinned her gaze on Shay. "You know, I always thought you and your best friend Adam Ward would marry after high school. I was shocked when you suddenly packed up and left the next year right after you graduated."

"Adam?" Shay tossed her head back, laughing. "No." She struggled to compose herself with the thought. "That wasn't *that* kind of relationship." Joanne's words brought back the memory of her old friend and how they had drifted apart in high school when Shay started to hang out with Jen and her friends.

"Really?" Joanne said in awe. "I always thought your leaving had something to do with him, because he moped around for over a year after you left."

"You're kidding!"

Joanne shook her head.

"No, as far as I was concerned, Adam and I were just friends, and with Jen making a life of her own, going away to college in New Mexico seemed to me like a good alternative to living in that house with our aunt and the family ghosts. Anyway . . ." Shay shifted uncomfortably in her chair. "Tell me about the dog. You called him Spirit." Shay looked back to where the German shepherd had been sitting. "That's weird." She looked up and down the street. "Where did he go?"

Joanne eyed her curiously, very likely because of the abrupt change of subject, but reached over and patted Shay's hand. "Don't you go worrying about him," she said with a reassuring smile. "He has a habit of doing that. Here one minute and gone the next."

"But don't *you* worry about him?"

"Not mine to worry about."

"He's not yours?"

"He belongs to no one. Comes and goes as he pleases."

"Really? He's a stray? But he looks so well taken care of. Surely someone must look after him."

Joanne shook her head. "The only person he ever took to was Bridget Early. He kind of adopted her one day, and the two became inseparable. As a matter of fact"—Joanne leaned closer, tucking breeze-blown strands of her short bobbed hair behind her ear—"the day she disappeared, he did too. This is the first time I've seen him around since then. Although, I heard that the day her body washed up on the beach by the pier, he was seen standing guard over it until it was found, and then he disappeared again, at least, until today."

"How long ago was that?"

"Maybe about a month ago. I'm not really sure."

Shay frowned and studied Joanne's face. "What can you tell me about Bridget?"

"Not much to tell, really. You knew her too."

"Not really. I remember her vaguely. I went into Crystals & CuriosiTEAS a few times when I was a kid, but she said something strange to me the last time I was in there, and it scared me."

Shay couldn't recall now exactly what the tea shop lady had said to her, but she did remember going home and telling her mother what happened and how dark her mother's face grew. Then all she said was, *You shouldn't go there. It's not a place for children, and you'll see things that you won't understand.* Her mother's words were all she needed at the time to confirm her own feelings about Bridget and the shop, and she soon forgot about it. It was funny how the recollection came back to her now though.

"So I never went back," Shay added. "I used to see Bridget around, but she was always staring at me." She shuddered with the memory. "From then on, I avoided her as much as I could."

"I remember how oddly she treated you when we'd all go in and poke around all the weird stuff she sold in there. It was like something out of this world to us kids, wasn't it? We couldn't resist it." Joanne faintly smiled at the recollection. "And let me tell you, neither she nor her shop ever changed over the years. She was a strange duck, that's for sure. The only person I knew she ever mixed much with was Pearl Hammond, two of the most unlikely people you'd ever think of as being friends. You remember Pearl, don't you?"

Shay shook her head.

"She lived next door to Bridget and runs the ice cream shop down on the boardwalk?"

"Oh right," Shay said with a chuckle. "I vaguely remember *her*, but I'll never forget her homemade ice cream."

"How could you? I think we all lived on her sprinkle cones more than one summer, as I recall," Joanne added with a soft laugh. "Actually, I heard through the grapevine that Pearl came across Bridget's body under the pier. I guess it must have really freaked her out because we don't see much of her on High Street these days. She sticks pretty close to home and her ice cream shop now. You might go ask her about Bridget if you're that interested." She eyed Shay curiously.

"Thanks, I will." Shay smiled and glanced at her cell phone to check the time. She pushed it to the side and sighed. She'd forgotten that driving anywhere in Bray Harbor took only a few minutes instead of the hour or so Santa Fe and Albuquerque required. There was still thirty minutes until her appointment with Julia, another old high school friend of her sister's and now a local real estate agent. She surveyed the open seating area. "I like the changes out here. This outdoor patio is a great idea."

"Thanks." Joanne beamed.

"Your idea?"

"Yup, after Gertie passed about four years ago, I bought it from the family. None of them were interested in keeping Gertie's dream going, but I was. This place held a lot of special memories for me." Her gaze dropped, and a soft smile formed on her lips. "Did you know my husband, Gary, proposed to me right there"—she pointed to the window—"at that table?"

"I remember you waving your ring finger in our faces when you met us all later at the beach party," Shay said with a laugh.

"Yeah, that was a great night." Joanne gazed wistfully at the café window. "Anyway, after I bought the place, I decided that after forty years of the same old, same old, it needed to be brought into the twenty-first century, and I made a few changes. I even got cappuccino and espresso machines. Go ahead and order any of those big-city Frappuccino, mochaccino blends you want. We can make them." She grinned.

"Congratulations, I'm happy for you." Shay squeezed her hand. "I can't believe that Jen never told me. I had no idea when I sat down that you were the Jo in Cuppa-Jo." Shay laughed and stared at the CuriosiTEAS sign.

"How rude of me to sit here gabbing and not get you a coffee." Joanne began to stand up.

"That's okay." Shay placed her hand on Joanne's arm. "Your server took my order."

"And she hasn't brought it yet?" Joanne glared at the shop door. "I'll be right back after I deal with that girl."

"No, don't worry about it. Maybe she got busy inside with a customer or had to brew a fresh pot. I still have half an hour till my appointment. Sit and relax. It's great catching up."

Joanne dropped back down in her chair. "I really

am sorry about the service," she said, glancing back at the door. "Tassi, the server, is my sister Karen's daughter, and wow, is she trouble. I thought it was challenging enough with a teenage boy; Caden's sixteen now too, you know."

"Is he really? Wow, I remember when he was born. It was just before I left. I can't believe he's sixteen now though. Where have all the years gone?"

"I know, right. So now I have two teenagers to raise." Joanne shook her head, clearly showing her frustration.

Shay looked questioningly at her.

"For the past couple of years, Tassi had been coming from Carmel most weekends and holidays, but about six months ago Karen sent her here to live with us full-time. In the hope I'd be able to turn the girl around. It seems she was at her wit's end with her. What else could I do? Karen's my sister, and Tassi's my niece, so I couldn't really say no, could I?" She glanced back over at the door, and dropped her voice. "Ever since Karen and her slimy lawyer husband's divorce was finalized last year, Tassi's a girl-gone-wild, I'm afraid."

"I take it your sister was married to Brad too?"

Joanne's eyebrows shot straight up to her hairline, and then she snorted, stifling a giggle. "Trust you to lighten the mood. It's refreshing to see that you haven't lost your sense of humor." She placed her hand on Shay's and gave it a gentle squeeze. "Jen told me what happened to your marriage too. I'm so sorry."

Shay had hoped to get through what was bound to be a surreal morning without reliving her past with anyone. However, Joanne's words ignited a spark of her suppressed rage at Brad. Her scumbag accountant ex-husband—as she *fondly* called him—had taken everything she owned in his swindle of her gemstone and jewelry company. The company she started just before she met him. When they married he said, as her husband, he would come on as a silent partner and work behind the scenes as her financial consultant and accountant, but that it would remain *her* company. Ha, that was a good one. Love certainly is blind, and she'd been so naive in her belief in a happy ever after that she'd ignored the red flags. It seemed he had different plans from the onset and cooked the books accordingly.

She didn't even want to dredge up the two-year affair he'd been having with her assistant. Shay took a deep breath and crammed her thoughts back into the box in her mind and shoved it high up on a shelf to be dealt with another day.

"What's that old saying?" Shay waved off the look of sympathy in Joanne's eyes. "When life gives you lemons . . . blah blah blah." A fleeting smile touched her lips. "So, here I am back home squeezing those lemons, hoping something wonderful will come of it."

"I admire your resilience," said Joanne, her fingers tightening around Shay's. "I know it can't be easy for you to have a successful career pulled out from under you and having to start all over again."

Tassi appeared over her aunt's shoulder, placed two cups on the table, and smiled at Joanne. "I guessed you'd want one too."

"Thank you." Joanne nodded. "And you'd be right." She flashed an apologetic glance at Shay.

"But I wish you'd serve the customers as quick as you do me."

Tassi's gunmetal-gray eyes darkened, matching her charcoal eyeliner, and locked with Shay's. "I was brewing a fresh pot." She spun around and headed toward a young couple who had just sat down.

The chill in the air Tassi left behind her made Shay edgy. She shifted in her chair, sensing that the disturbance she felt from Tassi went deeper than a girl-gone-wild.

"See what I mean?" Joanne laughed.

"Shay!" A tall, professionally dressed, flaxen-blond-haired woman dashed across the narrow street. "You're over here? I expected to meet you at the shop." The woman flashed a nod of acknowledgment toward Shay's table companion. "Joanne," she said with a frosty edge to her voice as she pulled a chair closer to Shay's.

"Julia." Joanne acknowledged her with a bob of the head and returned an equally cool greeting as Julia made herself comfortable at their table.

"I'm guessing that this is an exciting day for you, isn't it?" Julia said, shoving a large brown envelope across the table toward Shay. "These are the land title transfer documents." She glanced coolly at Joanne as she clasped her hands in front of her. Her blood-red manicured fingernails contrasted against the white tablecloth.

Joanne glanced questioningly at Shay. "Why, what's happening? What land is she talking about?" She looked at Julia. A knife could have sliced the tension-filled air. Julia ignored Joanne's questions, turned her chin to the side, highlighting the back s-waved bun of her coiffured hair, and gazed down the street.

"I'm really not exactly certain of the details right now." Shay tapped the envelope. "That's why I'm meeting with Julia." Her heart sank at the look of betrayal on Joanne's face. "Joanne, it's just that—"

"Never mind," Joanne said with a wave of her hand. "It's none of my business anyway. It's not like you and I have kept in touch over the years." She shoved her chair back, causing Julia to jump. "I'll leave you to it then. I have to get back inside anyway. Drop by again soon, Shay." She smiled, and then her normally soft-chocolate-brown eyes glowered at Julia as she stood up and turned on her heel.

Julia opened her mouth to retort but quickly snapped it shut when Joanne stalked off.

Shay blew out a deep, noisy breath, hoping to dispel the bristling air that surrounded their table. She knew that despite whatever else had transpired between these two old friends, she was partly to blame for the negativity engulfing them now. Shay wanted to run after Joanne to explain why she couldn't answer her question and let her know it had nothing to do with not *wanting* to tell her about the land title and the real reason she was back in Bray Harbor.

The fact was, Shay didn't know how to explain any of what was going on now to anyone. Even her own sister was oblivious as to why Shay had returned to her hometown. She couldn't explain it to Jen last night when she showed up unannounced on her doorstep. Nor again, this morning when Jen grilled her over coffee. Shay had feigned being late for an appointment, grabbed her sister's keys to the Explorer, and took off to meet Julia in the hopes of finding some answers for herself.

She barely knew how to process the news of receiving a mysterious inheritance from Bridget Early, a woman she scarcely knew in her youth. It must be an error. She'd already told a team of lawyers that, and they assured her it wasn't. Until she knew what was going on, there was nothing she could tell anyone that would satisfy them or make them understand any more than she did. It was all weird and mysterious, and hopefully the woman sitting at her elbow could shed some much-needed light on the subject.

Julia pasted a saccharine smile on her ruby-red lips. "Shall we get on with our business, then?" Her chair grated on the patio surface as she pushed it back.

"Yeah, good plan." Shay wedged a five-dollar bill under the sugar jar on the table, hoping the breezes wouldn't snatch it away, and followed behind her sister's old friend.

She recalled how Jen, Julia, and Joanne were fondly known in high school as the Three J-Birds. However, after the exchange she had witnessed between two of those so-called old friends, she had her doubts that the once inseparable threesome answered to that anymore. She bristled with curiosity to find out what had happened and how this affected her sister's relationship with them. But she couldn't let their issues concern her. She forced herself to breathe deeply as she followed the lanky woman across the street and focused on the reason for her relocation back to the town she swore she'd never set foot in again.

Shay's knees trembled as she drew closer to the overhead CRYSTALS & CURIOSITEAS sign, and the sun-faded gold lettering on the bay windows became clearer. One window advertised TEACUP READINGS and the other promised PROTECTIVE AND HEALING STONE TREATMENTS. Sickness spread through her—no—terror. She stumbled and nearly tripped on the sidewalk curb.

"I'd forgotten what services Bridget offered her clients," Shay cried, grabbing Julia's navy jacket sleeve. "I'm a gemologist. The stones I know, but protection and treatments?" Her head shook with the force of the bobblehead figure on her sister's car dash. "I don't even know anything about teas, let alone readings." Shay's hand gestured to the window lettering. "How can I do all this?"

"I think that stuff is all hooey anyway." Julia flicked her hand in a dismissive gesture and turned away. "Just fake it. I'm sure Bridget did."

Shay gasped at Julia's declaration, and a low growl resounded behind her. Goose bumps exploded on her bare arms. She slowly turned her head. Spirit sat behind them on the curbside. His top lip pulled back in a snarl. His crystal-blue eyes fixed on Julia as she muttered to herself and fished around in her oversized bag, seemingly oblivious to the dog's threatening growls.

"Where are they? I was just in here yesterday making certain that the company I hired to take care of the place for the past month had been doing their job. I didn't want us to be surprised with a roomful of cobwebs this morning. I'm sure you know how difficult it is to get good help these days. You have to keep on them to make sure they're actually doing what they are paid to do, and . . . ah-ha!" She pulled a brass key ring from her bag. "It appeared that everything was in working order for you yesterday. But if you do find *any* problems, just let me know, and I'll have someone on my staff take care of it." Julia jiggled the key in the lock until it clicked.

Shay glanced back at the now vacant curbside. She shivered and scanned the street but saw no sign of the hulking canine. Had she just imagined the dog?

The shop door swung open, and the tinkle of bells pulled her from her chaotic thoughts.

Julia handed the keys to Shay and waved her inside. "Welcome to your future, but be prepared: it might be more than you're willing to take on."

Chapter 2

Welcome to your future . . .

The rest of Julia's words were not lost on Shay, and along with the visions of a phantom dog, Shay's already frayed nerve endings bristled on high alert. Was she ready to step into an unknown future? Panic set in, and Shay stood inside the doorway unable to move. Common sense reminded her that she needed a new career since Brad had abruptly ended her last one by casting a shadow over her reputation. But were her so-called *heightened* senses enough to make a go of operating a tea and psychic shop? Did she even want to?

Her mouth hung slightly open as her gaze flitted around the store. Where would she even begin to make some kind of sense out of all this in the large congested room? "I guess it wouldn't take too much to learn about teas, and then I could renovate it and turn it into a regular tea house, couldn't I?" she said quietly, almost speaking to herself as she scanned the large space.

Julia glanced sideways at her. "That might be a bigger job than you're willing to take on."

"It appears that I would just need to clear out some of this clutter and—"

"Hold that thought. We haven't even started the tour yet."

"What do you mean?"

"You'll see." Julia's china-blue eyes sparkled with mischievousness.

Shay's chest tightened, but the mixed aromas of pungent earthy smells and seductive spice fragrances inundated her senses, sending an envelope of calm over her. A glass-enclosed sales counter, doubling as a display case, ran almost the entire length of the back wall. She moved toward it, making her way past short wooden shelving units packed with various assortments of cups, teapots, statues, odd-looking trinkets, and books about mystical topics. Her hand rested on the spine of one entitled *Discover Your Psychic Powers* by Tara Ward. This was one book she would have to remember to read if she decided to try and make a go of this.

She smiled at the book's neighbor, Carolyn White's *A History of Irish Fairies*. Since she was little, she'd always felt an affinity for Irish folklore, especially fairies. She could never understand why, given that both her parents were of Scandinavian descent and not from the Emerald Isle. Her sister was a clear testament to the family heritage with her blond hair and blue eyes.

Shay's fingers trailed over the top of the book-shelf. She noted the sidewall shelves packed with gold-foil bags in varying sizes all bearing the Curi-osiTEAS red label. When she reached the sales counter, she studied the large wooden bins set out in a row against the wall behind it. The overhead shelves behind the counter contained large glass jars filled with brown and green leafy substances.

This was way more than she'd bargained for. What on earth was half this stuff, and what would she do with it? She leaned against the counter and released a pent-up breath, fighting back a sob. Then she noted the shelves inside the glass case under her elbow, which held displays of assorted gemstones. There were dozens of trays labeled with tags identifying rose quartz, fluorite, amethyst, and other gems. Finally, something she was familiar with.

With more confidence, and the gut-wrenching reality that she had nothing left of her past and this might be as good as it gets, Shay surveyed the shop again in its entirety. "It doesn't look like it would be much of a problem to renovate." Shay glanced over at Julia. "It appears it just needs a good cleanup, and after I get rid of things I wouldn't use I can add some chairs and tables, and voilà! A nice cheery teahouse, especially with those double bay windows."

Julia shook her head and cleared her throat. "Okay. Are you ready to see the rest?"

"Yup." Shay smiled, feeling better about her new acquisition, and made her way past a display rack of small packaged herbs and spices. "I hope by the rest of it you mean the living quarters?"

"You didn't know?" Julia glanced over her shoulder and bumped into a wooden barrel labeled Dried Sage.

"Know what?" An edge of panic threatened the calm that the heady scents in the shop had induced. "The terms of the will stated that I inherited the shop *and* the living quarters?"

Julia stopped outside a door in the corner of the back wall. She slowly turned around.

"I sure hope that was right." Shay's voice quivered with tears. "Because I can't afford my own place right now, and I don't want to impose on Jen and her family any longer than I need to."

"So, you didn't know then?" Julia's eyes flickered with amusement as she studied Shay's face. "The living quarters are a two-bedroom cottage on the beach."

"An entire cottage?" Shay's already wobbly knees buckled, and she grabbed at the wall for support.

"Yes—I took it for granted your lawyer explained that."

Shay shook her head. "No, no, he didn't. Wow, I had no idea. That's the best surprise I've had all day."

"I'll warn you though. It's fairly small and very old, so it might not be to your taste. If not, don't worry, I can sell it in a heartbeat, and then you'll have enough money to buy something more to your liking."

Shay's face lit up. "No, small is fine. I'm sure it'll be perfect, but what's on the second floor of this building, then? I always assumed that's where Bridget's apartment was."

"We'll get up there in a few minutes. First, we'll finish our walk-through of this floor, okay?"

"There's more to the store?"

"Oh, yeah." Julia chuckled. "Follow me. Like I said, renovations might be a big job here. Remember, Bridget was in this space for over thirty years."

Shay's mind conjured up images of dusty boxes and junk-cluttered storage rooms behind the wooden door. She shuddered at the thought of having to sort through them before she could clear them out to start renovating and making money. Although, knowing she would have her own *paid for* seaside cottage did help take the stress off her lack of funds. In a pinch, she could always impose on Jen for meals. Yes, she had to think positively—something she'd forgotten how to do over the last few years. Maybe it wouldn't be as bad as she pictured, and there would be some real gems behind that door she could sell. Eagerly, she stepped toward Julia.

The wooden door swung open with an eerie moan that sent a shiver up Shay's spine. The sound echoing in her ears now was uncannily similar to the noise she swore she had heard when the lawyer in Santa Fe removed an aged document from a folder and read the terms of the will to her. When their meeting had ended, he abruptly shuffled out the office door, leaving Shay lost, numb, and stunned as to who Bridget Early was to her or why she was the woman's sole beneficiary. The same resonating sound now made her wonder what exactly lay behind *this* door. She took a deep breath and started forward behind Julia when the door chimes jingled. A puff of fresh, tangy sea air filled the store.

Shay turned, and a small gasp caught in the back of her throat. Never in her life had she seen such a set of electric-blue eyes. Of course, they were made more so by the frame of raven-black hair dangling over the man's tanned forehead. Her gaze darted down his tall, athletic body to the red, formfitting T-shirt covering his broad chest, then to his thigh-hugging blue jeans. She was quite certain all the heady scents in the shop had induced a hallucination because he was too perfect and there was no way he could be real. On the other hand, if he was real and was an example of the customers she could expect, then studying all those books on the shelves would be a pleasure and not an impossible chore.

"Liam?" Julia cried out over Shay's shoulder. "I didn't expect to see you here today."

A shy smile graced his lips, but his piercing eyes remained focused on Shay's. "I couldn't miss the opportunity to welcome my new neighbor, now could I?"

Shay detected a sing-song Irish lilt to his voice and gulped. "Your neighbor?"

"I'm sorry." Julia stepped forward. "Shay, this is Liam Madigan. He owns the pub next door. Liam, this is my old friend Shayleigh Myers."

"Shayleigh, is it?" His smile broadened as did his Irish brogue. "Has anyone ever told ye that ye have the most amazing topaz eyes?" he said, his unwavering gaze still holding fast on hers.

Heat rose from under Shay's collar and crept across her cheeks.

"I'm afraid," said Julia, "the shop isn't open for business yet. As a matter of fact, we were just going to do the initial walk-through of the rest of the shop." She gestured to the door and glanced from her flushed-faced friend to the bemused smile on Liam's lips.

"Could I join you, please?" He clasped his hands in a prayerful gesture. "When you mentioned to me that the new owner was coming in today, I thought it would be a perfect time to check out the place with the new-owner tour. I've always wondered what secrets Bridget kept locked up behind that door."

"I guess there's no problem with you tagging along . . . that is, if Shay agrees?"

His gaze still locked with Shay's. His blue eyes lit up, and he flashed her a dazzling smile. It was enough to melt any woman at the knees, and she simply nodded her agreement.

"Brilliant!" He rubbed his hands together and stepped toward Shay. An impish sparkle in his eyes joined his smile. "After you." He waved her ahead of him.

Shay smiled shyly and took one more fleeting glance at Liam as she skirted past him, in part to make certain he was real but mostly because he was easy on the eyes, especially when he flashed her that toothy grin that highlighted his dimples. Perhaps learning about the psychic trade wouldn't be as bad as she thought. "So you've never been back here?"

"No," he said, his gaze holding hers a moment longer. "I wasn't a customer, so I never had the privilege of being invited into the inner sanctum."

"Sorry." Her heart plummeted to the pit of her stomach, and she paused in the doorway. "But I assumed that you were one of Bridget's regulars." She hoped her disappointment wasn't telegraphed by her voice. "I . . . I guess you weren't a customer because you don't believe in all the other stuff Bridget did?"

He lifted a brow, appearing amused at her reaction. "I'm Irish and from the same county as Bridget, so I believe. But I only came in for teas and cooking herbs. As for the other *stuff* she did here, I see me gran for that." He gave her a cocky wink.

Julia popped her head out the door. "Are you two coming? We have to finish here, then I have to show you the cottage, and I have a one o'clock. Let's get a move on."

Shay stepped into the back room. Unlike the front of the store, this area was uncluttered and sparsely furnished, but the sight of hundreds of strings of crystal pendants hanging from the ceiling rendered her speechless. A heavy black drape was drawn across the back wall and continued along the side walls, cocooning the entire area. The only furnishings were a small round table with two chairs in the center of the room, and a wooden

cubby shelving unit near the back side of the curtain enclosure. The shelf cubbies contained size-
able uncut gemstone rock chunks, different colors
and sizes of candles, and a large crystal ball.

"This," Julia said, "as you can see, is where Bridget conducted her private and group readings,
and this"—she grabbed the edge of the curtain to
their left and walked it back toward the rear wall,
revealing a small kitchen—"is where she brewed
her teas and dried her herbs and spices." She
pointed to a large countertop food dehydrator.

"Kind of disappointing, isn't it," Liam whispered in Shay's ear.

"What do you mean?" She glanced at him over
her shoulder. "Look at all the pendants strung
from the ceiling. It's breathtaking."

"I guess I was expecting more . . ." He raised his
hands beside his face, wiggling his fingers. "Woo-
woo." His eyes widened with his feeble ghostly impersonation.

"Then see if this is more to your liking." Julia
yanked on the corner edge of the back curtain
and revealed an ornate wrought-iron spiral staircase.

"Now that's what I was waiting to see," Liam
said. "Access to the second floor."

"Why?" Shay eyed him warily. "Are you hoping
it's filled with the bodies of her customers?"

"Now that would make a good tale to tell
tonight in the pub, wouldn't it?" With a flash of
humor in his eyes, he shuffled past her toward the
staircase. "Actually, I have a rooftop patio on my

second floor, and at night I could hear her singing. When it was a quiet night in the pub, I would
just sit for hours, listening to her Irish songs. She
had quite the voice, sad but really good." He stepped
up onto the first metal stair. "Always wanted to see
what she was working on up here till the wee hours
of the morning."

"What's that?" Shay pointed to the wall behind
Liam.

"What?" Julia looked to the spot Shay had indi-
cated.

"That, poking out from behind the edge of the
curtain." Shay whipped the drape back farther.
"Wow. Look at that. The colors are so vivid; the picture could be alive."

Liam stepped down and stood back to get a full
view. "Wow is right. That's a painting of Titania,
queen of the fairies, and the fairy princess."

"How do you know that?" Shay glanced at him.

"It's in an old book of Irish folklore that my
gran has." Liam stood back and studied the large
framed print. "You know, if I didn't know better,
I'd say ye posed for this, Shay. The model has the
same long, wavy red hair and the same delicate
features that you do."

He thinks I have delicate features! Heat from her
blush spread across her cheeks. She touched her
fingers to her face to make sure she hadn't sponta-
neously combusted.

"Did you ever do any modeling in Santa Fe?"
Julia stared wide-mouthed at Shay.

"Not for this one at least," Liam interrupted

over Shay's head. "Unless she's over a hundred years old. I can't remember who the artist is, but my gran's had her book since she was a wee babe."

Shay leaned closer to the picture. "What's that she's holding in her right hand and giving to the princess?"

"It's bluish-red, whatever it is," said Julia, squinting as she leaned closer. "Just looks like a glowing ball of blue light to me."

"Yes, it does, doesn't it?" Shay's knees began to give way. She had seen that same glowing light image somewhere before but couldn't remember where. The memory swirled around in her head like a thick fog, and she grabbed on to the wrought-iron railing beside her.

Liam's hands grasped her shoulders and steadied her. "Are ye okay?"

She nodded. Her eyes remained steadfast on the print. "Yeah, I think all the scents in here are just getting to me." She weakly smiled up at him.

His eyes narrowed as he studied her face, then his lips turned up ever so slightly at the corners. "Okay, if ye say so." His smile broadened, and he released his hands.

The air crackled and filled with the spine-chilling howls of a dog. Shay jerked. All three of them spun toward the open back-room door that allowed a clear line of sight to the glass-front entryway.

"My word!" Julia patted her chest as if she were trying to halt the same palpitations that sent Shay's heart hammering. "It's only Spirit." She laughed.

"I haven't seen him around for a while." Liam looked down at Shay. "Must be something about this shop he's attracted to." He arched a sly brow and grinned.

Julia shivered. "Well, now that we all have our hearts back in our chests, shall we take a look at the pièce de résistance?" She climbed up the circular stairs.

Shay glanced back at the now empty front doorway alcove and then at the print on the wall. A shiver rippled across her shoulders. Out of the corner of her eye, she caught Liam watching her, a puzzled expression on his face. She flashed him what she hoped was a smile worthy of an Oscar and headed up the stairs behind Julia. With Spirit's howls still fresh in her mind, her insides churned more with each rung of the metal stairs.

When Shay reached the top, a heady, earthy scent tickled her nose, and she grinned with delight. Aside from a small alcove office near the top of the stairs, the remainder of the entire second floor was bathed in brilliant, warm sunlight. This definitely was not what she expected to find up here.

Liam reached the landing and whistled. "Now I get it."

"Pretty awesome, isn't it?" Julia made a sweeping motion around the room. "This is where Bridget grew some teas and all the herbs and spices she used in her shop."

"Pretty unexpected." Shay stepped farther into the massive greenhouse. "The entire ceiling has been replaced with glass, and look at the back wall. The original brick has been removed, and it's glass too." She scanned the rows and rows of waist-high wooden box planters filled with vegetation. Her fingers toyed with a spiked marker labeled Thyme.

"Look at that." Liam pointed upward. "There's even sprinkler heads over each row."

"That answers my question about the humidity level in here." Shay's gaze traced the intricate system of overhead water pipes, and she stood in awe of the hanging irrigation system Bridget had installed. "This must have taken years of work to complete."

"I did remind you she was here for well over thirty years." Julia winked.

"Yeah, it's pretty amazing." Shay scanned the breadth of the large space and gasped. Her heart thudded to a near stop and then galloped in her chest.

"What?" Liam's eyes narrowed as he looked in the general direction she gestured toward.

"What's wrong, Shay?" Julia scanned the room. "What are you looking at?"

"There . . . there in the far corner of the greenhouse ceiling." The fine hairs at the back of Shay's neck prickled. "Just past that last white pipe. From here you can just make out a pair of—sprawled legs." Wide-eyed, she looked at Liam, who had already set off, skirting his way around the rows of planters. Shay darted after him and skidded to his side when he stopped short to retrieve his cell phone from his jeans pocket.

Julia's high heels clicked across the brick floor as she approached them. "What is it? Did someone climb up from your patio, Liam, to spy on us or worse yet, break in—" She screamed, and her over-sized handbag thudded to the floor.

Shay choked on the deep breath she'd sucked in. "Julia, remember earlier when you told me that if I find *any* problems to let you know, and you'd have someone on your staff take care of it?"

"Uh-huh," grunted Julia, backing away.

"You weren't talking about body removal, were you?"

Chapter 3

Shay leaned forward from her perch on the outside bench. Her elbows rested on her knees. Her hands clasped around a take-out cup of Jo's coffee, which someone had kindly handed her in the blurred chaos that followed the gruesome discovery. Her gaze drifted from the herringbone-brick sidewalk to Frank Burrows, the local sheriff. His face looked grim, and his narrowed beady-marble eyes showed that his attention was focused elsewhere. It was clear that he wasn't listening to Julia as she explained that she was just in the store yesterday, and that there had not been a dead body on the skylight then. When she finished her statement, he placed a large, liver-spotted hand on her arm, nodded, and stepped around her to where Shay's brother-in-law, Deputy Dean Philips, stood, taking a statement from Liam.

As Burrows walked toward them, a large blue

vein throbbed at his temple. He unclipped his handcuffs from his police belt, whispered something to Liam that Shay couldn't make out, and then waved the cuffs under Liam's nose. Liam jerked and snorted a reply. The sheriff grabbed Liam's arm, swung him around, and slapped the cuffs on him, yanking him toward his patrol car at the curbside. Shay gasped, jumped to her feet, and started toward them. A hand gripped her arm and spun her around. Dean's eyes flashed a warning as he pulled her back toward the bench.

"Dean, stop it," Shay hissed between clenched teeth and tugged her arm from his clutches. "Why has the sheriff arrested Liam?" Her mind raced back over the events that had just occurred. "Oh no!" Her eyes widened. "Do you think *he* could be the killer?" She plopped down hard on the bench.

Dean shook his head. "I really doubt it."

"Why not? Think about it. His roof apparently has direct access to the greenhouse roof, and he seemed awfully anxious to go upstairs when Julia was giving me the tour. A tour, by the way, that he crashed in on, totally uninvited." She gave Dean a smug glance.

"Did he say why he wanted to get up there?" Dean asked, taking a seat beside her.

"He just said he'd often hear Bridget singing from up there and had always wondered what she was working on until the late hours of the night." She leaned closer to Dean. "But I'm thinking now maybe he wanted to distract us so we didn't see the body because he hadn't had time to get rid of it yet," she whispered.

"Do you really believe that?" He pinned Shay

with a look. "If he had killed the victim, would he have wanted to be up there if his devious ploy didn't work and the body *was* discovered?"

"Maybe. You know, to establish innocence."

"He didn't tell you, then?"

"Tell me what? We really didn't have time to talk. He said he just dropped in to meet his new neighbor, and I guess to see the second floor and—"

"Look, Shay. Liam is one of the good guys."

"Everybody is capable of committing murder given the right circumstance," she said, shooting him a side glare.

"Yeah, I guess so." Dean stiffened. "But I like to think that most people won't cross that line."

"So, you don't think your smooth-talking blue-eyed friend—" Her words caught in her throat at the memory of his caressing gaze. She brushed it off. "You don't think Liam could or did cross it?"

"Not for one minute."

"How can you be so sure?"

"The story really isn't mine to tell." Dean toyed with the sheriff's department hat in his hands. "You should ask Liam about it."

"No, you tell me now. I need to know if the sheriff has evidence to prove that the guy I just spent the last half hour with"—*drooling over*—"could be a killer."

"Trust me, you didn't, and he's not."

Shay sat back and crossed her arms. "Explain then."

Dean slapped his hat on the bench between them. "Because . . . he was a detective with the San Francisco Police Department for over ten years."

"I see." Shay's arms dropped to her sides as she shifted on the bench.

Dean rubbed his hand down his face. "But I bet ten-to-one that your first scenario is the same one Burrows will be repeating to the district attorney's office later."

"Why?" She studied Dean's strained face. "What does the sheriff have against him?"

"Liam left the SFPD because he was forced out. He caught on to a group of dirty cops and his investigation of them led the Internal Affairs Department to file charges. Six of them are doing prison time now."

"But he was just doing what every good cop would do, right?"

"Some fellow cops don't see it that way. They don't take kindly to one of their own turning on them. There's kind of an unspoken 'blue wall of silence.' An unwritten code among cops and, well, he broke it . . . and that led to a lot of problems for him. No one wanted to work with him, and when they were forced to, they wouldn't have his back like a partner should. He got shot in the line of duty, although it was suspected his so-called partner actually shot him. Liam would never say though."

"Oh my God!" Her hand shot to her mouth.

"Yeah, it was just a shoulder wound, but a clear warning that he had a target on him and was on his own, because if his partner at the time didn't shoot him, then he let him get shot."

"Is that when he quit?"

He nodded. "Yeah, he moved down here a couple of years ago to start a new life. When Molly decided to retire, he jumped at the opportunity to buy her pub. Back to his roots, I guess." Dean chuckled. "His grandparents own a pub in County Clare, Ireland."

Shay recalled what Liam had said about seeing his gran for all the other *stuff* and smiled at the vision she had of him as a little boy, toddling around a pub while his gran was doing psychic readings in a back booth, and she started to giggle but caught herself when Dean flashed her a questioning glance. "Anyway, so, why does Burrows think Liam—oh. Burrows knows what happened in San Francisco."

Dean nodded. "Burrows has had it in for him since he set foot in Bray Harbor."

"In what way?"

"It started with little things. Before he bought Molly's, it was a barrage of parking tickets and pulling him over without cause. After he set up shop, Burrows started generally harassing pub patrons for things like parking too close to the sidewalk. He forced us deputies to set up regular check stops out here on the corner." Dean motioned with his head to the intersection a few shops down to their left. "Then he made sure the health inspector would conduct continual *surprise* visits by reporting made-up health department complaints Burrows claimed he received from customers. Which were all bogus, by the way." He glanced at Shay. "Then when Liam started construction on the rooftop patio, Burrows paid off the building inspector to harass Liam every step of the construction process, delaying the final approval for the entire busy tourist season last summer. It almost ruined Liam financially with all the extra non-code items the inspector insisted on before he would sign off on it."

"So now, with this murder on the roof next door to the pub, Burrows has one more thing to add to his list of harassments."

"It looks that way. But even if I can prove Liam couldn't have possibly done it, Burrows will just find something else to go after him on."

Shay sensed that for Dean his dedication to Liam was more than just doing the right thing for a member of the Bray Harbor community, and she placed her hand gently on his arm. "Liam's also your friend, isn't he?" she asked, already knowing the answer.

"Yeah, I guess my only friend. You know how it is after high school. People get married, have kids. Life gets busy, and me being in law enforcement . . . well, people just kind of drifted away. Then Liam came to town, and we hit it off and . . . he's a good guy. I can't sit back and let that old coot railroad him for his own personal reasons."

"Do you think that the sheriff is so jaded that he'll falsify evidence just to charge Liam with murder?"

"You bet. Burrows wouldn't think twice about it, so I just have to do my darnedest not to let that happen."

"Okay, Deputy, what can we do?"

"You? Nothing. Me? I have to solve this and prove my buddy's innocent."

"Come on, there must be something I can do to help out. After all, it was my shop roof the body was found on."

Dean adamantly shook his head. "Unless you got some sort of crystal ball in there that can point me to the real killer, stay out of this." He grabbed his hat, shoved it on his head, and rose to his feet. "But *you* keep out of it. We don't know what or who we are dealing with yet," he said, pushing strands of light brown hair up under his hat brim. "Anyway, I'd better get down to the station and make sure that Liam doesn't *trip and fall* on his way into a cell."

Her eyes widened. "Would the sheriff really do something like that?"

"I don't know. I just know he holds a real grudge against Liam."

"Why?" She stood up and stared into Dean's darkening brown eyes. "I get the feeling that there's something more you're not telling me about the connection between Burrows and Liam."

Dean blew out a noisy breath and rubbed the back of his neck. "The sheriff's brother was one of the crooked cops convicted."

"I see." A wave of unease rippled through her. "Could the sheriff be the killer?" She swallowed hard at the vile taste in her throat. "You know, to finally vindicate his brother by setting Liam up and sending him to prison?"

"I don't know, but if he is, I'll make sure he pays for it." Dean turned on his boot heel and headed for his cruiser.

Shay squeezed the bridge of her nose and tried to make sense of the jumble of thoughts and feelings all muddled inside her. Why did she feel so compelled to be dragged into the middle of this?

It just couldn't be because of Mr. McHeart-Flutter, could it? Pfft, no!

Shoving that thought from her mind, she reviewed the information Dean had given her. She really couldn't let an innocent man go to prison if an obviously biased and corrupt sheriff got his way. But there was something else gnawing at her. Julia told her and the sheriff that she'd checked the shop yesterday and there had been no body. Then why did one show up the very day she took possession of the store? Was it a coincidence or a warning? After all, everything about Bridget's disappearance and ultimate death and the inheritance of the woman's possessions was all rather mysterious, wasn't it?

Chapter 4

Shay knew one thing. She was going to have to get up to the pub's patio to check out the access to her rooftop to see with her own eyes how easy it would be for someone to dump a body up there. The questions burning inside were simple. Could the body have simply fallen onto her glass roof from a fight in the pub, or would someone have had to deliberately place it on her rooftop—or worse yet, have actually murdered the victim there?

However, first, she needed to figure out how she was going to slip past the diligent-looking female deputy posted guard outside the pub entrance. The questions racing through her mind weren't urgent by any means. They would eventually come out in the police report, but that was only if Burrows was forthcoming, or—she shuddered—honest about the results of his investigation. No, she needed to see the crime scene herself to act as an impartial set of eyes just in case it didn't go Liam's way, as she feared it might not after hearing what Dean had to say.

The increasing murmurs from the gathering onlookers in the street told her that at least half the townspeople had turned out to see what had happened in their usually sleepy little village. Maybe she could find a way to use them as a distraction for the deputy.

A friendly voice broke through the whispering crowd. "Shay! Hello! I'm here."

Shay grinned as her sister burst through the mob and ducked under the police tape. Jen wrapped her long slender arms around Shay and pulled her close.

"I knew you'd come," Shay said, squeezing her tight.

"I jumped on Hunter's bike as soon as Dean called to tell me what was going on."

Shay pulled back and stared at Jen. "You rode a ten-year-old boy's bicycle all the way down here?"

"Of course, I did. I knew you'd need me. Besides, you took my car this morning, remember?"

"Yeah." Shay sheepishly grinned. "I guess I did."

"What's going on here? Dean was kind of short on details."

"Did he tell you about the dead body we found?"

"Yeah, and he babbled something about ligature strangulation resulting in a broken neck, but they wouldn't know anything conclusive until the autopsy was complete. Then he said something about a glass ceiling, which didn't make any sense, but just before he had to hang up, he said you,

Julia, and Liam were all being questioned about it." Jen's eyes widened. "What do you know about this?"

"Nothing. Honest. I have no idea who the guy is. Did Dean tell you anything about him, his name, maybe?"

"No. He said the victim didn't have a wallet or anything on him."

"No ID? That's weird, don't you think?"

"I guess, but the motive could have been robbery so maybe not. Although he did say they thought the guy might be European."

"How can they tell?"

"All his clothes, including his shoes, were European labels, nothing American."

"Hmm." Shay glanced at the shamrock on the pub sign. "Were they Irish clothing labels by chance?"

Jen's eyes widened. "You're not suggesting Liam *did* have something to do with this, are you?"

"No, no, Dean told me his history." She glanced at Jen. "I just thought when you said he might be European that maybe it was someone from his past with a score to settle with him, and that's how the guy ended up in Bray Harbor in the first place."

Jen tossed her head back and laughed.

"What's so funny?"

"It's just that—" Jen tried to stifle a laugh. "Not many people have a score to settle with a twelve-year-old."

"What do you mean?"

"Liam was twelve when his parents immigrated to America. His father was an inspector with the Gardaí, as the police are called over there. He took a detective job in San Francisco to investigate an Irish mob ring that was operating out of there at the time."

"But Liam has a full Irish accent like he came over more recently."

"Only when he's trying to charm the ladies or when he's angry. That's when the full brogue surfaces. The rest of the time he just speaks with a slight accent, somewhere between American and Irish." Jen grinned. "Obviously, he was trying to spellbind you with his best Colin Farrell impersonation, and judging by the splotches on your cheeks, it worked." Jen gave her sister an exaggerated wink.

Shay swatted at her sister's arm. "Don't be silly. He's . . . well, he's not bad to look at, but I'm off men right now, remember?"

"If you say so," Jen said with a teasing lilt in her voice as she studied Shay's matching flaming-red complexion and hair. "But I think the lady doth protest too much," she added with a laugh.

Shay gave an involuntary eye roll. Reminding her sister of all the heartbreaking details of her bitter divorce was the last thing she wanted to do right now, and she quickly diverted the conversation back to the present.

"You said his father came over to work on a case involving the Irish mob. Maybe it was someone from back then, wanting to get even with the family. Mobsters are known to carry grudges."

"You seem convinced that this *does* have something to do with Liam."

"No, maybe, yes, not directly, but—" Shay scrubbed her hands over her face. "Oh, I don't know. I guess I'm just trying to make sense of all the whirling thoughts and crazy feelings going on inside of me right now."

"Come on." Jen draped her arm around Shay's shoulder as if she sensed her sister was in no mood for any more teasing. "You look exhausted. Let's go over to Jo's and grab a coffee, and then you can tell me exactly what happened."

"The police have just cleared the inside of the tea shop as a possible crime scene. Would you mind if we go in there instead?"

"No . . ." Jen's arm dropped to her side. "But why would you want to? Considering—"

"I think I need to right now." Shay turned and looked at the tea shop door. "Something about the scents in there really helped me focus and calmed all the crazy feelings I was having today about taking this place over and . . . well, I think it's good for me."

Jen grabbed Shay's shoulders and spun her around so Jen's nose was no more than an inch from Shay's. "What do you mean, taking over this place?"

Shay didn't miss the raised eyebrows and gasps from a few of the closer onlookers at the shrillness of her sister's tone. She grabbed Jen's elbow and tugged her toward the shop door. "We can discuss this in here." She yanked the door open and propelled Jen past the greeting of the overhead tinkling bells.

"Okay, enough of all this mystery stuff." Jen pulled her arm free and glared at Shay. "First you arrive at my door unannounced, and then I hear about a murder that you're being questioned about, and now you tell me you *own* this stuffy old place." She crossed her arms. Her normally forget-me-not pale blue eyes flashed with sapphire sparks. "Now, spill!"

"There's no cloak-and-dagger stuff going on, if that's what you think," said Shay, her eyes avoiding her sister's. She scuffed her foot over a smudge on the wide-planked wooden floor. "It's just a series of unexplainable events that happened so fast. As for me not telling you that I was coming, I thought that since you and Julia were friends, she would tell you about the shop and my coming back. After I got here, I would then explain the whole story to you."

"So Julia knew? Typical." Jen snorted. "No, she never mentioned a word because we're not friends anymore. That woman doesn't value friends. If she can't make money off you, you're useless to her."

"I had no idea."

"How could you? In the last two years, I've barely heard from you."

"I guess I deserve that." Tears pooled in Shay's eyes. "I just didn't know what to say half the time. I felt like such a failure."

"Do I need to remind you that what happened wasn't your fault?" Jen's face softened and she rubbed Shay's arm.

Shay nodded. "I know. Brad is the one who cheated on me and stole everything out from under me. What I didn't tell you in the end was that he not only stole my business and the home we built together, leaving me with nothing, but he also made my clients believe I cheated and stole from *them*."

"What?"

"Yeah, he's completely destroyed my professional reputation as a gemologist, leaving me holding the bag for *his* criminal acts with the expectation of—"

"You cleaning up after *him*. Right?" Jen pulled her sister close and squeezed her shoulder.

"Right, and it took every dime I had to pay my clients back the money *he* stole." Shay tilted her chin up and sniffled.

"So you're broke too?"

Shay hung her head. "Yeah, but the way I look at it now is that Brad was the one left holding the bag."

"How's that?"

"Because . . . the bag he's left holding is named *Angela Powers*, my so-called assistant."

Jen's laugh was muffled by the hand she'd clasped over her mouth, but the smirk she was trying to suppress sparkled in her eyes. She managed to choke out, "Did you ever see the witch again since the day you came home and found her with a measuring tape in *your* condo?"

"No, but Brad took to phoning daily after that to make sure I still planned on being out by the end of the month. He told me that if I had time to change *Turner* back to my maiden name, then I had more than enough time to find someplace else to live. And *then* he reminded me that *Angela* was getting impatient because her apartment sold, and she was chomping at the bit to get in there to start redecorating so *they* could move in."

Jen leaned back against a bookshelf, her eyes sympathetic. "Oh, honey, you're not a failure, no matter what you think." She searched Shay's face. "Just look how you've landed back on your feet." She gestured around the store.

Shay sputtered out a husky laugh.

"But now you have to tell me what this is all about and how in heavens you ended up owning this . . . this . . . this esoteric emporium passing as a tea shop." She stopped and sniffed the air. "But you know, you're right. About the scents in here, I mean. It just kind of"—she fanned the fragrances toward her nose—"they flow over you and . . . and it's a lot like the feeling you get after a good yoga session, don't you think?"

"Yoga?"

"Don't tell me you're not into yoga?" Shock and then disappointment flashed through Jen's eyes as she gaped at her sister.

Shay chuckled. "Yeah, sure, every day! Whoopee." Shay twirled her finger in the air. "Lots of fun to be had by all."

"So much for us doing something fun together as sisters."

"Yeah, no, it's not my idea of a good time."

"Well, I love it and I go to yoga classes twice a week." Jen wrinkled up her nose and pulled a childish face at Shay.

"Each to their own." Shay gave Jen an exaggerated eyeroll and perched her backside on the edge of a wooden crate of dried flowers. She took a deep breath and brought Jen up to speed on the events of the past two weeks leading to her unplanned return to Bray Harbor. "I really had no other choice. I had nothing left and no place else to go." Shay swatted a tear from her cheek like it was a mosquito.

Jen also wiped tears from her own eyes. "And"— Jen sniffed—"you still have no idea why Bridget left you this or her cottage?"

Shay shook her head.

"There must be a reason." Jen pressed her lips tightly together and scanned the shop. "Did you find any clues when you were touring with Julia before the whole dead body thing?"

"Nothing, but I was thinking. Do you still have that trunk of Mom and Dad's?"

"Yeah." Jen tucked behind her ear a lock of hair that had escaped her ponytail. "But I haven't looked in it for years. Not really since . . . the accident."

"You were always braver than me, that's for sure. Just being near it gave me . . . you know . . . that feeling I sometimes get. I couldn't bring myself to open it."

Jen nodded. She was well acquainted with her sister's *funny* feelings about people and things. "I'll get Dean to haul it down from the attic, and I'll go through it for you."

"Great, thanks. Love you," she said, smiling.

Jen leaned over and touched her fingers to Shay's cheek. "Love you too, but what exactly am I looking for in the trunk?"

"See if you can find any papers or anything that mentions Bridget. I have to find out who she is to us and how well Mom and Dad knew her, or what Bridget Early was to me, if anything."

"Yeah, that's the million-dollar question right

now, isn't it? What do you have to do with the old tea-shop lady?"

"Exactly, and maybe it can give us a clue as to why a body showed up on my roof the day I took possession of her store. There was nothing in the news Mr. Byren delivered to me when he read the will that screamed 'warning, warning, future murder scene' or how I might be dropped right in the middle of it all because of a pair of the most amazing—"

"A pair of what?" Jen asked with a sly curl of her lips.

"A pair of electric-blue eyes." She couldn't get them out of her mind, so, like a five-year-old, she stuck her tongue out at her big sister, who already seemed to know what she was going to say. That was one of the downfalls of the close bond between them.

"Shayleigh Myers, you have fallen under the Madigan spell, haven't you?"

"Who, me?" Her hand went to her rapidly pounding chest, and she frantically shook her head in denial.

"I hope not, because there's a long line of eligible and some not-so-eligible women, if you know what I mean, vying for his affections."

"You can rest easy. I won't be one of them." Unless, of course, he smiled at her again. "Wanna see what I've inherited?" Shay looked at Jen and hoped she'd take the hint at the sudden change of subject and wouldn't pursue the Liam thing any further. It appeared as if the mere mention of his name induced a skin-burning attack of her red-mottled-monster disorder. She wished she was a pretty blusher like Jen. But no, she was cursed with alabaster skin that transmitted her emotions in flashing neon.

"Of course, I do." Jen tilted her head, a look of anticipation on her face. She uncrossed her arms and launched herself from her resting place against the bookcase. "This will be interesting. I don't think I've been in here since we were kids."

Shay pointed out the racks and shelves of knick-knacks and trinkets, noticing for the first time that many of them depicted ancient Celtic symbols. She moved on to the bookshelves and rationalized that a number of the assorted metaphysical topics might help her learn what it was that she was supposed to do here to keep customers rolling through the door. However, by the time they got to the back of the shop, Shay was in a full-blown panic about the various herbs and spices sealed in the bags along the sidewall shelves, the ones in the wooden bins, and the even more mysterious leafy and stemmed substances in glass jars behind the counter.

"I have no idea what any of that is or what I'm supposed to do with it! I'm a coffee drinker," Shay exclaimed. "I don't know the first thing about teas other than the orange pekoe brand I pick up occasionally at the grocery store when I have a cold. How on earth am I going to run an entire shop devoted to tea?" She stabbed her finger on the glass above the gemstone tray in the display case. "Can you believe these are the only things in this entire store that I'm comfortable with?"

"It's clear this is all out of your area of expertise. So what do you plan on doing with the store?"

Shay fiddled with her hair, twisting it into an unfastened spiral that hung loosely over her shoulder. "Honestly, I don't know. I need to make a living, so when I first came in, I thought I could clear a lot of this out and turn it into a regular teahouse or bistro. I even had the momentary idea of having Jo supply finger sandwiches for lunch and getting Muriel Sykes, over at the Muffin Top Bakery, to supply some of her dainties. Then I discovered there's a small kitchen in here." She flung the back-room door open, hoping if it opened quickly, she could avoid hearing that nerve-prickling noise again. It paid off. The only sound was Jen's gasp at the sight of the sparkling ceiling. "As I wouldn't be looking at making this a full industrial kitchen, I don't think it would be too hard to turn this into a sandwich and dessert prep area." She gestured toward the counter and stovetop. "I think I could make it work . . . in time."

"In time and *money*." Jen shifted her focus to Shay instead of the dancing rainbows the hundreds of suspended pendants produced. "Which, if I might point out, you don't have."

"Maybe I can find an investor?"

"Don't look at me." Jen held up her hands. "I haven't worked since Maddie was born, and she's twelve now."

"Then it would be the perfect way for you to get back into the working-mom thing. We could be partners. That way we could work shifts around your mom-duty schedule."

"No, no, no," Jen said, backing away. "I've been out of that world too long and have no intention of going back at this point. Between Dean's crazy shifts and two active kids, I have my hands full. Besides, I know as much about tea as you do." She cocked her head and studied Shay's face. "But it sounds to me that you're maybe thinking of finding a way to make this work."

"I don't know. I keep going back and forth." Shay tapped her fingers on the top of the food dehydrator. "Those were my thoughts before"—she pointed up the spiral staircase—"seeing the *welcome* decoration on the roof. Now I think maybe selling it, taking the money, and starting a little handcrafted jewelry business down on the Boardwalk for tourists might be a better idea. I could still keep the cottage. Although I haven't seen it yet, I'm sure there would be space enough for a work area, and it would still give me a place to live."

"Now, that sounds more realistic. As you said, you don't know the first thing about all this." Jen pointed to the crystal ball on the shelf. She blew out a noisy breath and looked up the staircase and then back at Shay. Her eyes darkened, and she pointed her finger and motioned up. "Do you think the body is gone now?"

"I don't know. I only know that Burrows told me inside the shop has been cleared for now since there is no evidence of any crime happening in here."

"Is it a storage room up there?"

"Not exactly. That's the area where, if by some miracle I do decide to keep the place and renovate it into a teahouse, I would really need your interior decorator touch."

"I just told you I'm not interested in going back to—"

"As a sister," Shay quickly added. "Not as a partner. Don't worry. I heard you loud and clear."

"Good. If your common sense does fly out the door, I can give you a few ideas once I see the space, but . . . other than that, I'm out." Jen started toward the steps and visibly shivered. "But if you ask me, selling the place seems like the more responsible thing—"

A loud crash from above split the air.

Shay's ears pricked as a rapid *click . . . click . . . click* resonated down the stairwell. "Someone's up there," she whispered.

Chapter 5

Shay pushed past Jen, who stood, feet frozen in place and her mouth wide-open, her words left hanging in the air.

Jen tugged on the back of Shay's blouse. "Where are you going?" Her voice was barely a whisper.

"I have to see who's still up there. Burrows told me they were done in here."

"But . . . but what if it's the murderer?"

"If I'm not back down in five minutes, then call the police." She crouched and crept up the stairs.

"Are you crazy? You can't leave me down here by myself! What if someone else is hiding behind these curtains?"

Shay ignored the hysterics behind her and kept climbing. A low groan of protest escaped Jen's throat, and she sprang up the steps on her sister's heels.

Shay softly laughed. "You've been married to a cop too long," she said under her breath.

"It's at least taught me caution," Jen hissed. "Something you need to learn."

Shay stopped on the top step and peeked around the corner of the wrought-iron rail.

"Can you see anything?" Jen whispered in her ear. "Who is it?"

"Shh!" Shay swiped her hand back, pushing Jen away to put some space between them. "I can't see, and I want to see him before he sees us."

"Maybe I should call Dean?"

"And tell him what? That you're a scaredy-cat?"

"That's exactly why cats have nine lives. I'd at least like to have one good one."

Shay stiffened and stood straight up. "Julia? What are you doing up here?"

Jen huffed and scooted up the last two steps, coming to a halt beside Shay. "Yeah, what she said." She cocked her head toward Shay and thrust her hands on her hips. "It was my understanding you turned over the keys to the shop, so I guess that means *you're* trespassing." Jen shot Julia one of her best piercing mother-looks.

"Not really. I was doing you a favor, Shay," Julia snapped, completely ignoring Jen. "I thought that someone better supervise the body removal to make sure *they*"—she pointed to the three figures on the overhead glass—"don't do any damage."

Shay looked up just as a stretcher was being lifted onto her roof.

"After all, if I'm going to sell this place for you, I need to know if repairs will be needed first." Julia looked up and winced when a fourth man joined the others on the glass.

"What do you mean, sell this place for me?"

"Surely, you can't possibly be thinking of keeping it after—" She pointed up and pursed her lips. "This whole murder thing on the property will no doubt ruin my agency's reputation. Full disclosure and all that crap." A clipboard slid off the gurney and thudded onto the glass. Julia jumped and cursed.

"But I haven't decided what I'm going to do yet."

"Come on, Shay," Julia said. "What other options do you have now? You know how locals talk, and the last thing you need after the tourist season is over is to have *no* customers because people around here have long memories, especially when it comes to murder."

Shay glanced at Jen, her eyes pleading for her support.

Jen stepped forward, crossed her arms over her chest, planted her feet firmly, and stared down her nose at Julia. "I think that's a decision Shay needs to make *after* she thinks about it a while and not one that she should be pressured into by a money-hungry Realtor. You know exactly what I'm referring to."

Julia flinched and her eyes darted to Shay. "But I have a lot of out-of-town buyers who will snap this up in a heartbeat. They've just been waiting for an opportunity to get a foothold in the lucrative Bray Harbor market, and more than one expressed disappointment that this prime property was not for sale as the beneficiary had been found."

"I don't understand," Shay said, rubbing the back of her neck. "When we did the tour, you were all gung ho about me keeping this place as is. So, what's changed?"

Julia put her hands up. "Okay, in the interest of full disclosure, I'll tell you. I *just* had a call from an interested buyer who is willing to pay above market value for the shop *and* the beach cottage and is willing to waive a property inspection. You stand to make a lot of money from this deal."

"Which means you do too"—Jen's brow rose—"especially if you're double-ending it by representing both buyer and seller?"

"Well . . . yes." Julia shrugged. "But Shay is the one who will make out like a bandit."

"Who's the bandit?" Jen all but spat out.

Julia's jaw tightened. "Look, Shay, think about it. You really didn't want a tea and psychic shop to begin with, did you?"

Shay scanned the greenhouse and then glanced up to the four men above her head, hunched over the corpse. This complete about-face by Julia sent Shay's BS radar buzzing. "No, I'm keeping it. Tell your buyer to invest in something else."

A soft gasp escaped Jen, but she remained silent.

Julia's cheeks took on a crimson hue. "You know what I'm going to do? Just because you've always been a *good* friend to me"—she shot Jen an icy glare—"I'll hold him off as long as I can today, and we'll hope he doesn't walk away from his offer. Then you sleep on it, and we'll talk tomorrow first thing in the morning." She pasted an unnatural smile on her lips, one that didn't quite reach her eyes. "How does that sound?"

"No need." Shay crossed her arms and mimicked Jen's stance. "I've made up my mind. I'm not selling."

"But—"

"You heard her." Jen cut in, showing her solidarity with her sister. "It's not for sale, not the business, and definitely not the cottage."

"And speaking of the cottage, can I have the keys, please?" Shay held out her hand.

Julia stiffened. Her tongue flashed out and licked her ruby lips. "Okay, if you really have made up your mind, there's not much I can do now to change it, is there?"

"No, this is what I want."

"You might feel differently about it after you don't see any money coming in, which I know you sorely need." Julia's mocking eyes stabbed Shay's confidence.

Jen stepped toward Julia and pinned her with a glare. "Actually, she'll be just fine. I'm going to be her partner *and* investor."

Shooting daggers replaced the derisive look in Julia's eyes. "We'll see." She fished around in her large bag, holding Jen's gaze. "You both might end up broke, and then you'll be begging me to take this off your hands, and this buyer and his offer will be long gone."

"That's a chance we're willing to take." Jen nudged Shay's shoulder. "Aren't we?"

"Yes. Yes, we are. Now for the keys." Shay thrust her hand toward Julia.

Julia huffed and dropped a key ring into Shay's open palm. "Think about it, Shay." She pressed Shay's fingers closed over the three keys. "But I'll call you tomorrow, anyway, just to make sure you haven't changed your mind once you've had time *alone* to think about it." She shot Jen a look that said it all. There was no love lost between these two former best friends.

"It's cottage number five on the far end, tucked in at the base of the hill with all the trees behind it," Julia said. "You can't miss it. It's the one separate from the other beachside cottages. I also had my people clear out all Bridget's personal belongings. They're in a storage rental unit, paid up until the end of the month at Gilmore's Storage up by the highway. That's what the larger key is for. The third smaller one?" She shrugged. "I have no idea what it opens. I'm sure you'll figure it out though. Oh right, and I almost forgot in all the commotion"—she pulled a small brown parcel out of her bag—"a courier delivered this to my office yesterday. It seems that the lawyer forgot to give it to you when you were in his office."

Shay took it from Julia's hand and turned it over in hers. "What is it?"

"I have no idea. There was just a note along with it that said to give it to you when you arrived."

"Thanks." Shay tossed it in her bag.

"Aren't you going to open it?" Julia's voice quivered with excitement.

"I will later. I've had enough surprises for one day." *Besides, it's probably something else you'll want to sell out from under me.* She glanced at Julia, whose disappointment was clearly evident in her eyes.

"But, Shay . . ." She groaned.

Shay shook her head.

Julia could plead all she wanted to. Something told Shay there was more going on here than Julia was saying. This buyer seemed to have appeared rather quickly, and him being so willing to pay above market value told Shay to be careful. Until she figured out what was really going on with the shop and the cottage, there was no way Julia was going to see what was in the lawyer's latest surprise package.

Julia blew out an exasperated breath when the text alert on her phone pinged. "I have to go," she said, glancing at it. "Karl's outside waiting for me. We were going to go out for cocktails to celebrate the sale." She glared pointedly at Jen and then Shay. "But now . . . he's going to be furious, and we won't be celebrating anything." She waved her hand in the air as she walked away on her clickety-clackety heels. "Going back on my word to the buyer is going to ruin my business."

"We all know your word isn't worth much around here anyway," Jen snapped.

Julia gasped and muttered something inaudible as she marched down the stairs.

"And maybe you should have talked to Shay *before* you gave him your word!" Jen called out.

"Just looking out for my client," Julia hollered back up the stairs. "Something you should be doing for your sister and not letting her make the biggest mistake of her life." The bells tinkled over the front door, sounding Julia's departure.

"That woman." Jen stomped her sandaled feet.

"Ten-to-one the buyer is one of her husband Karl's sleazy business friends."

"What kind of business is the old high school star quarterback in these days? I think I remember hearing from you that after a pro-ball career didn't work out, he went to work at his father's company, Fisher's Insurance?"

"Yeah," Jen said, leaning against a planter. "That lasted long enough for him to realize if he wanted to keep his greedy wannabe pro-ball-player's-wife happy, he was going to have to go into a much more lucrative line of work."

"What's he into now?"

"Who knows? I only know he made a lot of connections while in insurance and has used those to broker some pretty big deals. I guess he's an agent of sorts. He hears about a business opportunity and then finds the right people or person to invest in or buy it. I'm not sure that kind of position even has a title. Business consultant or investment broker, maybe?" She shook her head. "But it really doesn't matter. I only know he spends a lot of time with some pretty shady types."

"What does Julia think about that?"

"She doesn't care as long as the money keeps rolling in, and it seems to be. You should see their house now, a real Hollywood-type cliff-top mansion." Jen rolled her eyes. "The sweet little cheerleader we all knew and loved in school has really climbed up the social ladder, mostly due to her and Karl stepping on everyone else as they did it and not caring who they hurt in the process."

"You've mentioned something to that effect a few times now. Care to elaborate?"

"Maybe later." Jen ran her fingers through her hair. "I'm just too mad at her right now to talk about it. Any more would really get my blood boiling."

"I found her sudden about-face from earlier interesting. First, she basically encouraged me to keep the shop, and then, out of the blue, she has an eager buyer for it. It makes me wonder what's actually going on here."

"*Her* sudden about-face?" Jen stared at her. "You really threw me with yours. I hope you were just being stubborn with her because she made the assumption that you would sell because of—" She motioned toward the ceiling. "But you're really going to be finding another agent to sell it, aren't you?"

"I thought you were supporting me in this. You told Julia that you were going to be my partner and investor."

"Pfft, that was just for the Julia Show. I couldn't let her score another win on the back of a person I care about. She definitely has something up her sleeve that will no doubt be in her favor. But, seriously, you can't really be thinking of making a go of this place, can you?"

"Why not?" Shay stood, hands on hips, and surveyed the greenhouse. "This space could be developed into a nice, sunny tearoom with large potted leafy plants and ferns scattered throughout. I could leave the downstairs as a tea store, the kitchen area could be expanded, and I could add a take-out counter back there too."

"There's still the question of money. In case you forgot, I don't have any. We live off one salary and have two kids. I can't help you out. Sorry. I didn't mean for my outburst in front of Julia to get your hopes up. I was just—"

"I see that now." Shay sighed. "You were just trying to get under her skin." She smirked and glanced sideways at Jen. "But if your offer is not to be, then I guess I'll have to keep this space up here as is for now, start with smaller changes to the main floor, and continue to work toward my overall vision."

"What about the vision you had not fifteen minutes ago about a jewelry shop on the Boardwalk?"

Shay arched a sly brow and grinned.

"Sometimes when I think I have you all figured out, you go and surprise me with something like this. You are a true mystery, little sister." Jen shook her head and wrapped Shay in a hug. "Sorry, I would help financially if I could. You know that, right?" She gave her sister's shoulders a tight squeeze. "And remember, whatever you decide to do, you can at least depend on my emotional support."

"Yeah, I know." Shay squinted at the officers on the roof. "Who's that blond guy wearing the coroner's jacket up there?" She blinked, then blinked again. "He looks kind of familiar?"

Jen looked up as the gurney was being lifted off the glass. "He should. You two were stuck together like glue all the way through elementary and middle school."

"What?" Shay snapped her mouth shut. "That can't be coke-bottle-lenses, geeky little Adam Ward, can it?"

"Yup, not so much of a geek anymore, is he?" Jen laughed.

"No." Shay chuckled. "He sure isn't."

Jen's text alert sounded, and she fished her phone from her purse. "It's Dean. He had to drive the kids to their swim camp this morning because I didn't have a car." She flashed a cheeky grin at Shay. "And he's stuck at the station. Something about 'Liam protection duty'?" Her brows rose. "Anyway, he can't go back and pick them up and camp's done for the day." She dropped her phone back in her handbag. "This means I have to find a way to get them from the pool."

"Here." Shay pulled the car keys out of her cropped jeans pocket. "Leave me Hunter's bike. I'm going to stop by the cottage, and then I'll meet you at your place later."

"Sounds good. Where's it parked?"

"Just down the street in front of the Crafters Corner Market."

"I'll find it then. I could come back after I pick up the kids and get you and the bike."

"No, that's okay. A bike ride right now might help clear my head."

"If you're sure?"

Shay nodded. "Go, you can't keep the kids waiting."

"Okay, I left the bike beside Jo's door, but I'll put it by one of the benches out front." Jen snatched the keys from Shay's hand, kissed her cheek, and headed for the stairs. "We can talk later about all this, and don't open that parcel until you come home. After today, I'm dying to see what surprises *it* holds." She laughed and disappeared down the stairs.

Shay had forgotten all about the parcel. She glanced at it in her bag and dropped the cottage keys in the purse.

The keys *thunked* on the package and sparked.

Shay jumped and almost dropped her bag. She rubbed her eyes and stared at the keys and package lying dormant and sparkless at the bottom of her purse. *I'm going crazy!*

Chapter 6

Shay locked the front door of CuriosiTEAS and turned in time to see the disappearing taillights of the coroner's van closely followed by a deputy's cruiser. Her lip curled up in disgust as she eyed the yellow crime-scene tape still fluttering in the wind around her storefront. With the departure of the coroner and police, the crowd on the street appeared to be slowly moving on as it became clear that the show was over for the day. She glanced at Madigan's Pub, still cordoned off but now deputy-free. With the crime-scene tape still up and the deputy gone surely it would be locked up tight, but something pulled her toward the door.

"Heck, why not." Her gut feelings—when she chose to follow them, that was—hadn't let her down in the past. She shouldered her bag and headed for the door, fully expecting to find it locked, but to her surprise, it opened freely in her hand, and she stepped inside.

"Sorry, we're closed," a woman's voice called out in the faint light.

"I know," Shay replied as she blinked repeatedly, willing her eyes to quickly adjust from the bright sunshine before she tripped over a chair leg on her way toward the faceless voice. "I'm Shayleigh Myers. I own the tea shop next door." Her vision finally adjusted to the dim light, and she stood, speaking over an ornate oak bar at a woman with silver spiked hair and a face deeply etched by too many years spent in the sun.

"So you're the new mystery owner, are you?" The woman eyed her as she methodically dried a shot glass from the bar sink in front of her. "Not much of a welcoming first day, was it?" She set the glass on a rubber runner along the bar edge. "Sorry, where's my manners." She dried her hands and reached for Shay's. "I'm Carmen, one of the bartenders here."

"Nice to meet you."

"It sucks being shut down for your first week, doesn't it?"

"A week!" Shay gasped and perched on the edge of a bar stool. "But the sheriff told me my place was cleared."

Carmen let out a chesty laugh that matched her husky voice. "He said the same thing to me, which is why he let me stay to clean up the glassware and dishes from last night." She retrieved another shot glass from the sudsy water. "But, he told one of the deputies to tell me after he hauled Liam away that *both* sites will remain closed for at least a week, or until *he* decides to take down the police tape."

"Another week? That doesn't make sense if they've cleared the scenes."

"It'll be longer, I'm sure, if he can get away with it."

Shay remembered what Dean had told her about the ongoing harassment and shook her head. It appeared Burrows was going to do everything in his power to destroy Liam and his business, and she was being included in that vendetta.

"Unbelievable," muttered Shay as she glanced around the bar, noting that it had gone through a lot of changes since it was Molly's. The old rickety tables had been replaced by new sturdy oak ones. In addition, whitewashed walls covered the old drab bricks, smoke-stained from years of smoking patrons before it was banned. The back wall that had once housed the dartboards had also been removed, exposing the now open staircase that used to lead up to Molly's office and a storeroom. "Is that the access to the rooftop patio?"

"Yup, that leads to the scene of the crime." Carmen leaned across the bar. "Wanna see it?" she whispered.

"Yes!" Shay replied and winced at her all too enthusiastic outburst. "I mean, I'd like to see how easy it is to access my roof from there."

"It's not impossible, but it seems weird that someone would go to those lengths to dispose of a body." Carmen tossed the dish towel on the counter and came around the end of the bar. "I'll show you what I mean. Follow me." She trotted up the wide wooden stairway and turned right at the top.

The patio was like most rooftop ones Shay had seen in California and New Mexico. The front wall had been lowered to a height that still acted as a safety barrier but allowed for somewhat of a street view below. There were about a dozen round tables with umbrellas scattered over the space, and around the perimeter were flowerpots and leafy plants—similar to what she envisioned for her greenhouse renovation. The back brick wall facing the alley and the two side walls remained intact, creating a wind barrier for patrons. The hallway behind her housed what she assumed was still Liam's office on the left side of the staircase as they came up, with this half, the old storeroom, developed into the open patio. Directly across from her on the far side would be her adjoining wall. She headed across the patio for the iron ladder bolted to the side and to what must be the access to her greenhouse roof, and climbed up.

Sea breezes whipped through her hair, lashing it across her face. She swept it from her eyes and examined the expanse of the greenhouse roof. It appeared it was a series of smaller glass panels locked together by rods that fed into steel beams, where they were joined to Liam's brick wall. There was another steel rod running the length of the greenhouse at the rear, which secured the glass panels on the roof to the ones that ran up the back wall of her greenhouse.

Shay wasn't certain if it was the sun's reflection or if one of the larger bolts on the back beam appeared to be more scarred and weathered than the others were, but she could clearly see that it had deep scratch marks on it, even from this distance. However, Julia did mention that Bridget had this built nearly thirty years ago, so that might be the reason. Perhaps the others had been replaced over time. She squinted and peered closer. Yes, even though the panels appeared secure, she mentally put an entire roof inspection on her to-do list, just to be certain. All she needed was a lawsuit if one of the glass panels crashed to the alley below.

As the roof appeared to be solid, and secure in the thought that there had been four good-sized men on there not that long ago, she tentatively hoisted herself over the edge of the brick wall and rose shakily to her feet on the first glass panel. From this angle, she could clearly see where the body had lain.

Despite the crime scene investigators' attempts to remove evidence at the scene, there were still smudges and faint impressions of footprints left behind from whatever it was the crime team had used to dust for evidence. She judged the area to be about four feet over from the top of the pub wall. Which meant it was highly improbable that the body *fell* on her roof from a bar fight gone too far. It would have had to be hoisted up the six-foot ladder and tossed over the edge to hide it from eyes below on the patio. No easy task, she guessed, and not one that could have gone unnoticed by other pub patrons, which meant the actual murder itself must have occurred on her roof. Which brought to mind her next question: What was the dead man doing up here in the first place?

Shay hesitantly took a step to get a better look to help piece the chain of events together. A solid thud beneath her foot halted her. She bent down and tapped against the glass only to discover that it was thick layers of acrylic safety glass, which made sense given the vicious winds and rainstorms the West Coast often experienced.

"Did you find something?" Carmen popped her head over the top of the brick wall.

"Just that I can breathe a little easier knowing this is safety glass and not real glass." Shay frowned.

"What's wrong?"

Shay looked back at the spot she had rapped on and then slowly turned toward Carmen. There it was again. Something shiny between the glass and the steel bar flashed in the sunlight. She ran her fingers over the groove between the two construction materials. "Yes, there's something wedged in here."

"Can you get it out?"

Shay ran her finger over the small object and shook her head. "It's in too tight. I need something to pry it out."

"I got just the thing. There's a first aid kit behind the bar."

"Ooh, maybe there's a pin or a needle in it that I can use."

"Something better, I think." Carmen disappeared down the ladder to the patio below and returned a few moments later out of breath and grinning. She crouched down beside Shay, who was busy snapping photos of where the object was embedded, and held out her hand. "Will this work?"

"Needle-nosed tweezers. Perfect!" Shay shoved her phone back into her bag, took the tweezers, and began to pry at the target. "I can't believe the crime team missed this."

"Whatever it is, it seems like it's wedged in there pretty good," said Carmen. "My guess is if the sun hadn't hit it just right earlier, then they wouldn't have seen . . ."

Shay swatted impatiently at her windswept hair flying in her eyes.

"Here, let me get that." Carmen held Shay's hair off her face. "Can you tell what it is yet?"

"Just about have it." Shay's lips pressed tight in concentration. "There!" She sat back on her heels and held a small round object between the tweezers' tips.

"A button?"

"Yeah, but not any old button," Shay said, twisting it around. "See how the sun brings out the luster when the rays reflect off it. A regular plastic button would have a flat white color. This one has more of an incandescent hue. My guess is it's mother-of-pearl and probably off a man's high-end dress shirt."

"Or a woman's blouse?"

"I don't think so. If it were from a woman's blouse, it would likely be more rounded on the surface and probably larger. More decorative, but as I'm not a fashion diva, I'm not sure. It was once attached to a blue shirt. See the threads still attached in the buttonholes." She pointed. "And this looks like it might be a tiny shred of material attached to the thread ends. If so, that means it was torn off the shirt and didn't just fall off."

"How do you know all this? I mean about the difference between it being plastic and mother-of-pearl and what a woman's shirt would be like compared to a man's?"

"I was a gemologist and jewelry maker in a previous life. I guess I picked up a few fashion tidbits along the way."

"And now you own a tea and psychic shop?" Carmen's brows rose. "How did that happen?"

"It's a long story." Shay chuckled. "Maybe over drinks one day I'll tell you all about it." She twisted the tweezers in her hand and examined the button. "Does Liam ever wear a blue dress shirt when he's working?"

"Never! Jeans and T-shirts always. He keeps it pretty casual around here, as we all do," Carmen said, gesturing to her own jeans and tank top. "I mean, I do have some dressier blouses, even a blue one, but never wear them to work. Like I said, Liam prefers the vibe in the pub to be pretty laid-back."

"Hmm." Shay inspected the button again. "Julia told me she was in the tea shop yesterday and clearly, there was no body there then. So . . ." Shay studied Carmen's face. "Do you remember seeing anyone wearing a blue dress shirt recently, like perhaps last night?"

"I was off at six and didn't notice anyone who stood out as being overdressed. Kenny worked the evening shift. I can call him and ask him if he saw anyone."

"Since autumn is just around the corner, I'm sure there are lots of tourists still in town, making the best of this incredible summerlike weather. It might be a dead end, but ask him anyway. Maybe someone stood out in his mind for some other reason." Shay looked carefully at the button again. "I don't think this alone will help prove Liam's innocence, but you never know. Which means, I need something to put this in just in case the police can get any prints or DNA from it."

"I've got a tissue." Carmen stood up and tugged one from her front jeans pocket. "It's clean, just a bit scrunched."

"That'll do." Shay took it, wrapped the button, and shoved the wadded tissue into her front pocket. She scanned the rooftop. "I think I have all I'm going to find up here. Except for the crime team missing the button, they seem to have done a fairly good sweep of the area."

"You know, the button might not have anything to do with the murder. It could have come off anytime, maybe during construction or—"

"How many construction workers do you know who wear a dress shirt with mother-of-pearl buttons on it?" Shay grinned and glanced sideways at Carmen. "No, I'd say this button came off a high-end silk shirt by the look of the threads and material scrap."

"You're probably right. Let's hope after you give it to Burrows, it will help clear Liam. Because anyone who knows Liam also knows he's never dressed like a lounge lizard in his entire life." Carmen laughed.

"I'm not giving it to Burrows."

"But . . . you just said."

"I'll give it to my brother-in-law. He's one of the deputies."

"Who's he?"

"Dean Philips."

"You're Jen's sister?"

"Yeah, do you know them?"

"Sure do," Carmen said, chuckling as she started down the ladder to the patio. "They come in here from time to time for their date nights."

"Glad to hear they still have some fun in their lives. To hear my sister moan some days about how hard-done-by she is, you'd think life ended as soon as she got married and had kids." Shay laughed, descending the ladder behind Carmen.

"Let me tell you, life is far from over for them. When they're in here, they kick up their heels with the best of them. You should see Dean and Liam after a few drinks. I don't think I've ever laughed so hard watching two grown men dance an Irish jig. They're hilarious."

"That is something I'd like to see." Shay stepped off the last rung of the ladder onto the patio.

"I'll let you know the next time they're in, and you can see for yourself." Carmen's chesty laugh echoed down the stairs into the empty bar.

"Thanks, I'd like that, and thanks for your help up there today."

"No problem. It was nice to meet you and fingers crossed that Burrows, the old goat that he is, doesn't keep us shut down too long. I don't know about you, but I can't afford another forced week off," said Carmen as they made their way downstairs to the pub.

"It's a regular occurrence from what I heard."

"Too regular." Carmen slapped her hand on the bar. "Someone needs to stop that man." She leaned toward Shay and pinned her smoky-blue eyes on

Shay and hissed, "I hope the discovery of a stranger's body on the roof was only a dress rehearsal for the real intended victim, Frank Burrows." Her lip turned up at the corner.

Shay flinched with the flatness of Carmen's voice and the sudden shift in the woman's demeanor. "You'd better be careful what you say. If someone overheard you"—Shay glanced over her shoulder—"it might not go so well for Liam." She dropped her voice. "Or you, for that matter."

"Yeah, you're right. I'm just frustrated with all this. It seems we're shut down every other week, and it puts a financial strain on all of us. No work, no pay," she said, resuming her glass washing. "Burrows has to be breaking a lot of laws with his harassment, and I hope he gets locked up himself."

"If that's true, I'm sure he will . . . eventually. But I'd better call Dean to tell him what we found."

"Nice meeting you." Carmen examined a glass under the overhead light. "And good luck with your shop. I only hope that you're a better *seer* than Bridget was."

"What do you mean?" Shay's voice wobbled, and she stopped short, bumping against the door.

"That her gift didn't help save her in the end, did it?" Carmen arched a knowing brow.

"No, I guess it didn't, but I thought her drowning was ruled accidental."

"That's what Burrows reported." Carmen shrugged. "But who knows." Her chuckle did nothing to dispel the ominous ring in her voice. "If she'd been a real psychic, wouldn't she have been able to see that she was in danger that day, and prevented the accident?"

What was it that Julia had said? All the psychic stuff was hooey anyway. Maybe she'd been right, and Bridget did just fake it. There was no evidence of foul play, and the cause of death was reported as accidental.

Carmen set the glass on the bar top. "If you ask me, I think she *saw*"—she hooked her fingers in air quotes—"something that somebody didn't want her to and killed her to shut her up." She leaned across the counter and motioned up the stairs. "Maybe that's why that guy was killed too. I get the feeling there's something bigger happening here and that our beloved sheriff is involved somehow. He was too eager to arrest Liam and shut both our businesses down, don't you think? Anyway—" She picked up another glass. "Have a good day and *welcome* to Bray Harbor," she said and tossed her head back, releasing a caustic laugh that split the air.

A cold shiver snaked up Shay's spine, and she glanced toward the staircase. Whatever had happened here, Shay knew she needed to purge herself of the ominous fog that Carmen's words filled the air with. *Keep breathing, you need to breathe.* Shay slowly backed toward the door. Carmen's words—*I hope you're a better seer than she was*—echoed in her mind as she flung the door open and stepped into the street. Sucking in a deep, cleansing, sea-air-filled breath, she wrestled with Carmen's abrupt energy shift, wondering if she might be right. That there was more going on here than seen at first glance.

Shay studied the gold lettering across her store windows, TEACUP READINGS and PROTECTIVE AND HEALING STONE TREATMENTS. Could Bridget have managed to keep this shop open for over thirty years by faking it? Shay shook her head. There was no way. She couldn't have been a con woman all those years. There had to have been something to the powers she was reported to have had. But if so, as Carmen had alluded to, why had they failed her in the end? Shay spun around when the air surrounding her shifted and a whisper-light breeze caressed her cheek.

"Tassi! Are you looking for me?"

"Yes." The server girl from that morning stepped up onto the curb. "Is it true?"

"Is what true?" Shay stepped toward Tassi and eyed the elusive Spirit standing motionless beside the young woman.

"That you're the new owner here?"

"Yes . . ." Shay studied the anxious look on the girl's face. "I guess I am." Her gaze returned to Spirit, who had neither moved nor taken his eyes off her.

"Are you as good as she was?"

Shay was taken aback and hoped her tendency toward splotchy skin didn't give away uneasiness. "Were . . . were you a customer of Bridget's?"

"Yeah. She was a pretty cool lady and my friend." Tassi's dark eyes darted to the ground, and she rubbed her red Keds shoe over a pebble on the sidewalk. When she looked up, tears glistened in her eyes. "She was actually my only friend in town."

"I'm sorry for your loss." Shay chewed her lip. "Her passing must have been hard on you."

Tassi's shoulders stiffened, and she locked eyes with Shay. Her bottom lip quivered. "Will . . . will you find out who killed her?"

"Killed her?" Shay's eyes widened.

"Yeah, you know, like the guy they found up there." She pointed to Shay's second story. "Murdered her."

"You think she was murdered?"

"I know she was. Promise me you'll find out who did it." She turned and hurried across the road.

"Wait, Tassi! What makes you think someone murdered Bridget?"

Tassi picked up a bike leaning against the short iron railing in front of Cuppa-Jo, hopped on, and began peddling down the street. "I have to go," she called over her shoulder. "My aunt will have a fit if I don't get back to her place now."

"Tassi, wait!" Shay shouted, but it was no use. The girl disappeared around the next corner.

Shay sucked in a deep breath. Could there be any truth in what she said? "What do you think, boy?" She looked at Spirit, sitting motionless at the curbside. "Was Bridget murdered or did she accidentally drown like it stated in the police report?"

The hulking dog lay down, rested his head on his front paws, and whimpered so woefully that shivers raced up and down Shay's arms. She crouched beside him and looked up at the storefront—the enduring legacy of a woman. A woman Shay knew nothing about, but who had for some unknown reason seen fit to bequeath it to her. Lacing her fingers through his warm, silky fur settled her nerves. He wasn't a phantom. He was real, and so was his pain. Tassi wasn't the only one mourning the loss of Bridget. "I'll find out what really happened to your friend. I promise." Her whispered words were met with warm, wet strokes as Spirit lapped his tongue across her hand.

Chapter 7

Shay gave Spirit one last scratch behind his ear and made her way to the bike leaning up against the bench exactly where Jen had promised it would be. She struggled to pull her arms through each of the handles of her large handbag, hoping to carry it backpack-style in order to keep her hands free to maneuver. Ending up as roadkill really wasn't in her plan for the day. Steering this pint-sized bicycle was going to be an adventure all its own. There was no reason to tempt fate even further.

She hopped on the bike, and when she glanced back at the dog still lying prone on the sidewalk, her heart ached. There was no taking away his grief, but if she could, she would find out the truth behind Bridget's death. It wouldn't bring his friend back, but maybe finding the answers would help ease his and Tassi's pain. She pedaled north on

High Street, wondering if Pearl's grief also ran as deep. Was that why she didn't come around the neighborhood anymore? There was only one way to find out. According to Joanne, if Shay wanted to learn more about Bridget, then Pearl Hammond, who ran the ice cream shop on the Boardwalk, was the one to speak to.

The fastest way to the beachfront cottages was to head over one block to the beachside Boardwalk. It would give her the opportunity to talk to Pearl, and the direct route would get her to the cottage quicker. She could easily look at what else she'd inherited and still be back at Jen's in time for dinner. Just as she was about to turn off High Street, her gut instinct told her *no!* It was midafternoon, and with the tourist foot traffic the waning summer's end brought with it, bicycle riding on the Boardwalk could quickly become an accident in the making.

Instead, she powered down on the pedals and headed straight up the road, dodging around opening car doors and midday traffic. As hard as she tried to scrunch up her five-foot-seven-inch frame, her knees couldn't escape banging against the handlebars. She awkwardly spread her legs farther apart, trying to avoid ending up covered with black-and-blue marks. Cursing ten-year-old boys and their short legs—at least, in her nephew Hunter's case—she wobbled along the roadway. It appeared that an accident might be in her future anyway.

Each rotation of the tires was accompanied by an odd swishing sound. Shay glanced at the front wheel, half expecting to find one of Hunter's sports cards pinned to the spokes for effect, but nothing appeared to be causing the noise. When she glanced back at the rear tire, she spotted the source. Spirit was loping along the road right behind her. She laughed, as the large animal clearly was not running to his full stride but instead keeping his gait checked in time with her feeble attempt to ride an undersized bike.

When she reached the side street that led down to the pier at the end of the main boardwalk, she planted her feet firmly on the pedals and skidded to a stop. Spirit came to her side, cocked his head, and studied her. "What's wrong, boy?"

He whined and looked straight up the street they had been traveling on.

"I know exactly where you want to go, but I need to talk to Pearl Hammond." Her heart sank at the large group of people lined up at the small ice cream shop's take-out window. "But it doesn't appear that right now is a good time for that. So, you win." She looked back to find the dog gone. Shay chuckled and shook her head. "You were named well, my friend." She pedaled straight up the road that led to the access street for the Crystal Beach Cottages.

The ten seafront cottages at the far north end of the beach were set out in two rows on a gently sloping hillside. The front five all had direct beach access, and the second row, slightly higher up the hill, were offset between them. This design ensured that all the cottages had a sea view. However, beach access for the back five was limited to the tiered stairway that flanked the south end of the development. A gravel alley ran behind the first row, giving residents rear access and parking. It also served as the front approach and parking access for the back row of cottages.

Shay scanned the cove and smiled. The founder of Bray Harbor, John O'Toole, a fisherman from Howth, Ireland, had chosen well when he selected this area back in 1854 to build his little fishing community. If memory served her correctly, the cottages originally served as fishermen's cottages when the area was first settled. It was said that during that time, fishing was a strong industry on the Monterey Peninsula, where he started off working. On one of his fishing excursions, he discovered this small harbor just south of Monterey, and it reminded him of Bray Harbor, an area close to his home in Ireland. John settled and built the first whitewashed cottage on the beach, and if Shay remembered her local history, that cottage was none other than the one she was heading for now, number five. It was the one farthest away, set off on its own, and tucked up against the windswept semi-forested hillside.

When she came to the top of the terraced stairway that led down to the narrow wooden sidewalk running along the front of the five beachfront cottages, she hopped off the bike, smiled, and lifted her face to the warm afternoon sun. Shay drew in a deep breath and filled her lungs with the freshness of the briny sea air, and recalled that growing up she'd always thought this end of the beach was magical. When the sun or moonlight caught the small pebbles mixed in with the sand, at just the right angle, it gave the impression of millions of diamonds having been sprinkled over the shoreline.

Seeing it again after all her absent years, she recalled the legend she had grown up with. According to folklore, this stretch of beach did hold mystical properties, which was why the town's founding father, John O'Toole, was drawn to it in the first place. Today was no different than when she was a little girl, the first time her parents had ever brought her here. It truly was magical to see the beach laid out before her in an explosion of shimmering crystals. She pinched herself. She couldn't believe she was actually going to live in one of these cottages.

Before she made her big move to New Mexico, it had been near impossible to buy one of these coveted cottages as they had been passed down from generation to generation and seldom went up for sale. However, Jen informed her a few years ago that Julia's real estate company started to scoop them up one by one. She had offered the owners above market value, and she was now making an absolute killing financially in the local tourist rental market.

Shay knew she should consider herself lucky that Bridget had held out against Julia dangling the carrot of monetary greed, and, by a strange twist of destiny, Shay was going to reap the rewards. As hard as it was to believe, she did actually *own* one of these charming getaway oases.

Her grin widened as she picked up the bike by the crossbar and hauled it down the first step. She pushed it across the flat section of the boarded walkway and lifted it again to navigate down the next set of stairs and jumped when a car horn beeped from the road behind her. The bike slipped from her hands. As if in slow motion, it bounced down the steps, wobbled across the level section, bounced over the next step and the next, and came to a crash at the bottom.

"Is that my son's bike?" a voice bellowed behind her.

Not believing what she had just seen, Shay turned and shrugged her shoulders. She winced and nodded at her brother-in-law, who strode toward her from his parked cruiser. "I'm so sorry." Her voice cracked in a whisper.

"He'll never forgive his favorite aunty if you've destroyed his pride and joy." Dean chuckled as he bounced past her and headed for the tangled heap at the bottom.

"His *only* aunty," she called after him.

He picked up the blue-and-white bicycle. "He won't have any then, if that's the case," he said with a chuckle as he inspected it.

Shay trotted down the stairs. "So, what's the damage?"

Dean shook his head. "Nothing as far as I can see." He straightened up and pinned her with a stare. A glint of amusement filled his eyes as he studied her face. "I guess it's safe to say you'll remain on his Christmas gift list."

"Phew, I wasn't looking forward to spending the rest of my life nephewless. It would have been really awkward when I showered Maddie with gifts." Shay laughed and took the bike from Dean's hands and looked up at him, brushing windswept strands of hair from her eyes. "Did Jen send you to pick me up? I haven't even had time to check out my new home yet."

"I have no idea what you're talking about. I didn't even know you were down here until I saw you on the stairs." His brows creased, showing his confusion. "What new home?"

"Jen didn't tell you about my other inheritance?"

"No, we haven't talked much this afternoon. I was on Burrows-and-Liam watch duty, remember."

"Right, Liam." Shay winced. In her excitement over the events of the day and in her eagerness to set eyes on her new home, she had forgotten all about Liam's arrest. "How is that going? Has he managed to avoid any *accidents* while behind bars?"

"As a matter of fact, the charge against him was stayed for now because Liam has an airtight alibi for last night. Much to Burrows's dismay, I'll add."

"That's great news!"

"Yeah, I was just dropping him off at home." He gestured toward the cottages.

"What?"

"I said—"

"I heard what you said. He lives here? At Crystal Cottages?"

"Yep, number six, up on the back row."

By the hot spots erupting across her cheeks, Shay knew full well that her blotch monster had reared its head once again with the mere mention of Liam's name. She turned away quickly and started to push the bike toward the cottages, hoping that Dean's far too observant eyes missed her reaction.

"Wait," he said, clasping his hand around her upper arm. "You never told me how you came to be the owner of one of these."

"Right. I got sidetracked, I guess," she said, still avoiding a face-to-face. While she wrestled with her stream of internal dialogue about the mixed emotions she was having knowing that *Mr. McHeart-Flutter* was not only her work neighbor, but now, her home neighbor too.

She inwardly moaned at the idea of never again being able to stop her face-monsters from reappearing, even when she went home. After all, she was bound to run into Liam in the cottage community, wasn't she? Yes, well, unless she spent her life in semi-seclusion except for interactions with her customers. Somewhat like—from what she could tell—Bridget apparently had. Was that the reason why her benefactor rarely engaged with anyone? Was she also trying to avoid her own *Mr. McHeart-Flutter?*

Shay took a deep breath and focused on a glistening pebble in front of her on the wooden sidewalk and, in one breathless rant, relayed the information about her cottage inheritance. Her brother-in-law whistled but didn't utter a word. She could feel his eyes boring into her as if he was waiting for something else. "The cottage came with the tea shop. Pretty cool, hey?" She kicked the pebble aside with the toe of her white slip-on Keds.

"Yeah, very cool. Wow. I can't believe that you actually own one of these."

"Yup, I do." She beamed, looking up and surveying her new community. "But it's getting late, and I don't want Jen to have to hold dinner for me, so I better get a move on." She started walking the bike again.

"Are you okay?"

She stopped and stared straight ahead. "Yes, it's been a long day, that's all, why?"

"Well, ever since I told you Liam lives here too, you got kind of weird. Is him being your neighbor going to be a problem?"

She bit down on the inside of her cheek to keep her monster in check and glanced back at him. "No, I just was surprised, that's all."

"Lots of surprises today for everyone, I think." Dean chuckled as he headed back up the staircase. "Call if you decide you don't want to ride the bike back," he called back to her. "One of us can come and pick you up."

"Thanks." She waved and walked along the wooden plank path. As she passed each cottage, she noted that they all held their own personal charm and features. Whether it was a vibrant paint color over what would have been a basic white-wash, or a pot of bright summer flowers set on the front stoop or porch, the ambiance reminded her of an Irish fishing village. She made her way past numbers one, two, three, and four. All previous thoughts about her surprise neighbor vanished. Her gaze focused on the whitewashed cottage at the far end of the row, and the hulking white form perched beside the dark green door on the wide front porch.

Shay rested the bike against the bottom of the handrail and trotted up the three steps to be greeted by the wagging tail of her new friend.

"This is a welcoming surprise." She bent down and gave him a scratch behind his perked ear. He turned, pawed at the door, and then looked back up at her. If dogs could smile, he was. Shay slipped her bag from her shoulders and fished out the key, jiggling it in the sea-weatherworn lock until it clicked. She closed her eyes and slowly inhaled a deep breath. For the second time today, she was about to walk through a door into her new future.

"Well, my friend." She looked down at Spirit, his focus on the door and his hind end wiggling, obviously anticipating her next move. "I hope I'm ready for this." She flung the door open and stepped inside.

Chapter 8

Like everything else that day, the inside of the cottage held a number of surprises that caused Shay to gulp in hopes of squelching the lump growing in the back of her throat. First off, it was much larger than it appeared from the outside. The small front hallway was flanked on Shay's right by a double-wide entrance surrounded by rough-hewn beams, which led into a comfortable-sized living room. The real eye-catcher for her was the large stone hearth and chimney on the opposite wall. Visions of cool winter evenings spent curled up in the cozy periwinkle-blue overstuffed chair by a blazing fire had her rubbing her hands in anticipation.

As if reading her mind, Spirit bolted past her and made his way around the end of the pale yellow flowered sofa that backed onto the entrance-way. He let out a low yelp, collapsed onto a snug dog bed in front of the fireplace, and dropped his head onto his front paws, releasing a throaty noise that sounded like a sigh of contentment. "I guess that means you're glad to finally be back home, doesn't it, boy?"

Shay's smile broadened as she scanned the room. On either side of the wood beam mantel were built-in bookcases. The same detailed craftsmanship continued around the corner of the wall and merged with a wide window seat covered in blue-and-yellow cushions perfectly positioned for her to spend time daydreaming while watching the waves crash onto the beach.

Along the back wall of the main room was a snug nook, complete with a well-worn brown leather chair and ottoman. A fringed Victorian floor lamp and a small round side table sat at its right, all of which created a perfect reading retreat. Everything about this room—right from the vintage trunk doubling as a coffee table to the faded area rug covering the center portion of the wide-planked floorboards—was perfect! The entire room felt as though it had wrapped Shay in a warm, welcoming hug. Never in her life had she felt more at home.

With the house's continued welcoming embrace, Shay dropped her handbag on the end of the sofa, glided across the room, and poked her head through the arched doorway beside the reading nook. Her eyes widened in disbelief at what she was seeing in the kitchen.

The bright afternoon light poured through not only a back window but also a side and front window, filling the room with a golden glow that enhanced the age-darkened butcher-block counter tops and the planked cupboards, which appeared to have recently received a coat of bright white paint.

There was even room for a small round dinner table and four chairs tucked into an alcove with windows on two sides. The one along the back gave her an amazing view of the forest-covered hill that the cottage nestled up against. The window on the far side of the table gave her a clear view of the garden and carpark and was situated next to an additional entrance to the cottage. Because of the angle her cottage was on, she also had a direct line of sight to the cottage behind hers on the second row. Fingers crossed that it wasn't *Mr. McHeart-Flutter's.* But she'd worry about that later.

Right now, she wanted nothing more than to explore her new home and pinch herself. Yes, this was all hers, and she had the papers to prove it. *Wow!* She glanced around and couldn't stop grinning. It was all so perfect. She practically skipped across the living room to the entrance hall to check out the bathroom and bedrooms.

Shay had already decided that no matter what she found down the hallway, it would definitely be better than spending the next few months on the pull-out sofa in her sister's basement den. She peeked into the bathroom as she passed and noted the fresh beachy colors of seafoam green and blues offset by what appeared to be an original white porcelain pedestal sink and clawfoot tub. Much to her delight, there was even an overhead shower with one of those circular shower curtain bars to help keep the spray in check.

Giddy with excitement, she decided that the small bedroom next to the bathroom would be a perfect craft room if she ever got back into making jewelry. That only left one more room to check out. She crossed her fingers for something a little larger than the single-bed-sized one and stuck her nose into the second bedroom. Her heart did a backflip. It was perfect. There was more than enough space for the vintage nightstand, large dresser, and the ornate cream-colored porcelain finished metal-framed double bed.

She wrapped her arms around her middle and squeezed. Was this all hers? Nothing in the cottage so far mirrored the same mishmash clutter of Bridget's shop. It was clear to Shay that at home Bridget had been a very different person. This revelation only enticed Shay to learn more about the mysterious Bridget Early. Who was she really? Was she the woman who dabbled in the shaded mantle of psychic mysticism or was she truly the carefree and charming soul depicted by her cottage?

Shay jumped at the sound of a thud from the other room. She darted back to the living room only to find her handbag on the floor and Spirit standing over it with the small parcel Julia had given her clutched between his jaws. She laughed and patted her pounding chest with relief. In all her excitement, she had forgotten completely that he had accompanied her into the cottage.

Although he appeared docile, she wasn't completely confident in how Spirit might react to any given situation given his earlier growls and howls. Tentatively, she removed the package from between his sharp white teeth. At the touch of the manila envelope in her fingers, the sensation of a slow-burning fire spread through her, setting her nerve endings sparking. The foreboding sense that the fire raging inside her was going to backdraft at any moment cinched around her heart like a vise grip.

Shay stared at the envelope. With blazing nerve endings, she struggled against the urge to run, but she sucked in a deep breath for courage and stutter-stepped to the sofa. She glanced at Spirit, who had not moved nor taken his eyes off the parcel. When she was seated, he lay down and rested his head on his front paws, but his eyes never wavered from the package, and she gave a small involuntary shiver. It was as though he knew what the contents were, and he was going to make sure she opened it.

She glanced at him again, nodded her understanding, and then with shaking hands, tore the bulky envelope open. Out into her lap tumbled a worn brown leather pouch. When she picked it up, the skin on her fingers tingled. Something akin to a weight shifted inside her, and she clasped the pouch like a life preserver.

Spirit sat upright. His tail thumped on the floor, and his eyes fixated on the pouch as though he were waiting for a treat. Shay took this as a sign to continue, and since his hairs weren't standing on end, she brushed away her peculiar sensations. With uncooperative fingers, she managed to undo the leather tie binding the pouch and shook out what appeared to be a small dark-blue perfume bottle into the palm of her hand.

As the glass touched her skin, a flash of blue light illuminated the room, and the screech of a rusted door opening echoed in her mind. The fine hairs on the back of her neck prickled, and the air around her crackled and groaned. There was another spark of light and everything around her took on a crystalline appearance. Colors became so vibrant that they took on a scent. She could taste and feel the texture of them on her tongue.

Shay tossed the bottle and pouch onto the carpet and hugged her arms tight around her knees. She'd always had what some called heightened senses, but this went beyond anything she had ever experienced.

Mesmerized, she stared at the bottle lying on the carpet. The glow had faded, but the memory of its transformation and the uncanny sensations that flooded through her when she held it were forever sealed in her mind.

Spirit dropped the leather pouch on her lap, and his cold, wet nose urged her to pick it up. She gulped back the lump lodged in her throat. With numb fingers, she fished through the small pouch and slid out a single piece of paper, unfolded the page, and read the cursive script out loud.

"Gaze upon this magic bottle to determine what healing methods to prescribe. Do not follow your ancestors and bury this bottle under a fireplace, floor, or inside a wall, but always wear this bit of fairy magic close to your heart as a protective charm against spells, evil spirits, and magical attacks from those who wish to do you harm."

Spirit's single howl sent a quake through Shay as she finished reading. In that split second, she knew her life had changed forever.

With eyes fixed on the bottle, she stood up, and gingerly stepped around it. After grabbing her handbag off the floor, she retrieved her cell phone from her purse and dialed the number for the only person who might be able to explain what all this meant.

"Good afternoon," a woman's small voice answered. "Offices of Byren & Brin . . ." The woman sniffled. "May I help you?"

"Yes, it's Shayleigh Myers. I was in a few weeks ago to see Mr. Byren in matters regarding the estate of Bridget Early in Bray Harbor, California. I was just wondering if I could speak to him for a moment."

"Miss Myers?" There was a long pause. "Yes, um . . . I'm afraid . . . Well, you see." Her voice seemed strangled with suppressed tears. "I'm sorry. Mr. Byren was taken to the hospital not long ago, and it seems, well . . . it seems . . . he died."

Numbed by the words, Shay stared at the phone in her hand until it slid through her fingers and tumbled onto the carpet. Her eyes burned. She dug through her purse, searching for a tissue, and blew her nose. She did recall throughout their brief meeting that the elderly white-haired man had coughed repeatedly. When he had removed the aged documents from the folder and begun reading, he had hacked, wiped his mouth with a handkerchief, and then dabbed it across his perspiration-beaded brow.

Shay had thought that his breathing seemed

strained because his shoulders shook with each inhalation. But he'd forged on and continued to read aloud in a raspy, monotone voice. She sat patiently, listening to the strict terms of what sounded like a will. A hundred questions raced through her mind. When he finished, she opened her mouth to speak, but without looking at her, he raised his hand and reached into the top drawer of his desk and retrieved a large brown envelope.

She had been so taken aback by what he read that her mind flitted from one thought to the other, and she couldn't focus on anything except what Brad had put her through and the fact that she needed a new career and a new life, and it appeared all that had dropped into her lap, literally.

She had stared at him, unable to speak as his trembling hand slid the envelope across the desktop toward her. When he stood up, his knees buckled, and he gripped the desk edge and shuffled out of the office side door. She knew she had lost the opportunity to sort everything he had said in her mind, which might have been for the best because at the time she had been a bumbling idiot and couldn't string two thoughts together. Little did she know that day would spiral out of control, leaving her in Bray Harbor with new questions piling on top of her still-unanswered questions.

Now as she gazed at the bottle on the floor, she realized that the one person who might have given her a clue who Bridget Early was to her, or why she was the woman's sole beneficiary, was dead. She would have to figure this out on her own. But how?

Her heart wrenched, and she dropped onto the sofa. Spirit padded toward her, rested his head on her lap, but when she went to stroke the fine hairs behind his ear, he nudged her hand toward the bottle still lying on the floor at her feet.

Hesitantly, with Spirit's nose guiding and encouraging her movements, she reached for it. When her fingers wrapped around the small bottle, it was as though someone else's hand had replaced hers.

A velvety whisper brushed across her cheek. *"Look beyond the amber veil."*

Spirit let out a low, mournful bay that shot a shiver from the base of her spine to the top of her head, culminating in an explosion of blue light.

Chapter 9

Shay jerked and looked around. She squinted and tried to make out the obscure images in the murky light. The banging sound came again except this time it was closer and sharper. A dark figure by her knee moved. Her chest tightened as it skirted past her. Out of the corner of her eye, she caught sight of a darker shadowy figure in the window and heard a rapping on the glass.

"Shay, are you in there?"

"Jen? What the heck?"

She scanned the dusky lit room, and the realization of where she was hit her. From the moonlight backlighting the hazy window figure, it was clear that it was late evening. "But how?"

She heaved herself off the sofa and staggered past Spirit, who, except for the comforting thump of his tail on the hall carpet, sat as a silent sentry beside the door. "What are you doing here?" she asked, struggling to understand the horror in her sister's eyes.

Shay fixed her gaze on two dark figures behind Jen, reached beside her to the switch plate, and flipped on the porch light. "Dean? Liam? What's going on? Did something happen? What's wrong?" Her voice teetered on panic.

"What's wrong?" Jen screeched and seized Shay by her shoulders. Her terror-stricken glare fixed on her. "We thought you were dead, lying in a gutter somewhere."

"Dead?" She locked eyes with Dean. "You knew where I was." She waved her hand. "We talked right over there on the stairs to the lower bungalows."

"Shay, that was nearly five hours ago."

"Five hours ago? No, no way." She shook her head. "It couldn't have been. It was just . . ." She scanned the oceanfront, looking for a glimmer of orange on the horizon, but was met with only a murky blackness. Spirit's eyes shimmered with the light of the porch lamp. She looked at Jen apologetically. "I am sorry you worried, but as you can see, everything is just fine." She scratched Spirit behind one of his perked ears, straightened, and looked curiously at Jen. "And why would you think I was lying in a gutter somewhere?"

"Because you're riding a ten-year-old's bike, and Clara Wylde, the owner of Wyldeflowers on High Street, told us when you passed her flower shop, you were swerving all over the road like—"

"Like you were drunk," Dean grunted. "Lillie Andrews of Lillie's by Design told us she saw you come out of Liam's pub just before you took off down the street—in her words—'wibbling and wobbling all over the place.'" He crossed his arms over his deputy sheriff's jacket-clad chest. "Was that why Hunter's bike went flying down the steps, you'd been drinking?"

"No!" Shay shot Dean a look of disbelief. "I was trying to keep my knees from whacking the bars, and the next time you see those two busybodies, you can set them straight on that."

"Then what were you doing in the pub?" Dean pushed his deputy's hat back on his head. "It's still closed off, as I recall."

"I was . . . I was only curious as to how someone got up on my greenhouse roof, that's all. Look, I'm tired. I think it's time for bed, don't you all?" She gazed from one blank face to the other.

"Weren't you sleeping when we pounded on your back door?" snapped Jen. "We came down the back way from Liam's when we stopped to ask him if he'd seen you. When you didn't answer the back door . . . well . . . if I hadn't checked around the front here and seen the bike on the porch . . . we'd still be"—Jen waved her arm frantically— "searching ditches right now." She grabbed Shay's arm. "So yes, you're right. Let's get you home to bed, and we can discuss this in the morning."

Shay pulled her arm free. "No, I'm not one of your kids, and if you remember correctly, I am home. I'm staying put tonight."

"That's silly, and you know it. You don't even have a toothbrush here with you. I'll get your purse." Jen moved to step past Shay in the doorway, but Shay remembered the bottle on the floor and thrust her arm up, resting her hand on the door frame to block her passage.

"Shay, this is ridiculous. Come home with me now," pleaded Jen.

"You don't understand. For the first time since I had to leave the home that Brad and I built, I finally feel like I am home again."

"Here, in this? You don't have your clothes or . . . or anything and I bet there's nothing to eat either. I'm pretty sure Julia didn't stock the pantry for you, did she?" Jen's frustrations were clear by the rise in the pitch of her voice.

"No, she didn't. That would have been too much to ask of her, but I'm fine really, and I'm not hungry, so I'll manage until morning. Now please, don't worry—"

"I could bring her bag back," said Dean, "if that makes everyone feel better."

"See, at least he understands. I'm fine here. Besides, I can't leave Spirit . . . he's finally home again."

"I'm not sure what's gotten into you, Shay Myers, but I don't like it," Jen huffed.

"Touched by the fairies if I'm not mistaken," whispered Liam from the shadows.

Shay shot him a glare, and he snapped his mouth closed, looking sheepishly down at his boots.

"Touched by something, that's for sure." Jen scoured her hands over her flushed cheeks. "Okay, I give up. Everything you've wanted to do today is beyond me. You keeping that white elephant of a tea store to moving in here tonight when we have a perfectly good guest room is beyond me, but go ahead and stay." She straightened her shoulders. "You were right when you said you weren't one of my kids, and I have to remember you're a grown woman now and capable of making your own decisions and *mistakes*." She pivoted and tramped down the steps and up the wooden sidewalk toward the terraced stairs.

"Don't mind her," said Dean, giving Shay's arm a reassuring pat. "She's been frantic trying to find you, and it will take a while for the adrenaline to wear off. Drop by tomorrow for coffee. You'll see, you two will be right as rain by then." Dean started down the steps after Jen and turned. "I'll be back soon with your bags. Are you sure you don't want something to eat? Jen kept your dinner warm in the oven."

Shay shook her head. "Please don't worry about the bags. I know you've had a long day, and they really can wait until tomorrow."

"It's fine, and I know it would make Jen feel better."

"No, there's nothing in there that can't wait until morning."

"Okay, if you insist. See you tomorrow then." Dean waved over his shoulder as he disappeared into the darkness.

From the shadows came a musical Irish voice. "Are you okay?"

"Oh, so you do speak something other than nonsense about fairies?"

"Aye, but it was a family thing, and I didn't want to get involved." He stepped forward into the brighter light of the porch. "If I can be so forward, you don't quite seem like the same woman I met earlier today."

"Yeah, it's just been a long day with lots of surprises, and I guess I must have dozed off. If you'll excuse me, I think I will head to bed." She backed through the door and raised her hand to close it.

Liam's hand pushed against the closing door. "I have a pot of stew simmering on the stove. It's my gran's recipe and the best in County Clare, they say."

"No, really, I'm not that hungry, but thanks anyway."

"Then, at least, let me collect your bags and bring them back."

"That's fine. Honestly, everyone's been put out enough by me tonight as it is. I'll go get my suitcases tomorrow."

"And how do ye think you'll be getting them here?" He waved at the bike. "On the handles? No, it's no trouble at all and won't take long."

From inside the cottage came a howl, and Shay peeked around the door frame. "What the . . . ?"

"What is it?" asked Liam, sliding in behind her and peering over her head.

Spirit sat, his tail wagging beside the bottle and pouch on the floor. After grasping the pouch in his jaws, he trotted over to Shay and laid it at her feet.

"What's that?" whispered Liam, his warm breath wafting across the top of Shay's head.

She looked up at him and shrugged, feigning naivety.

Liam picked up the pouch and turned it over in his hands. "It's roughly crafted, but by the appearance of the leather, I'd say it's a few hundred years old. Very nice. Did you find it here in the cottage?" He held it out to Shay.

Shay waved it off and walked around to the front

of the sofa, retrieved the note from where it had fallen, and held it out to Liam. "Since you seem to have experience with things like this . . . through your gran anyway . . . maybe you can tell me what you think this all means?"

Liam came to her side and, without questioning, slipped the note from her shaking fingers and read, *"Gaze upon this magic bottle to determine what healing methods to prescribe. Do not follow your ancestors and bury this bottle under a fireplace, floor, or inside a wall, but always wear this bit of fairy magic close to your heart as a protective charm against spells, evil spirits, and magical attacks from those who wish to do you harm. May the blessings and love of the old ones surround you—Bridget Early."*

Spirit let out another howl and pawed at the blue bottle still lying on the floor. Liam bent down to pick it up.

"No. Don't touch it," Shay cried and grabbed his hand, forcing it to the side.

"But the note says to keep it close to your heart. I just thought perhaps you'd want to put it in the amulet pouch."

"So that's what that is? Some of that *magic* Bridget was talking about in her note." She uncertainly scrutinized the bottle.

"I think you'd better sit down and tell me just what has you in this state." Liam grasped her shaking shoulders and steered her toward the sofa. He took a seat beside her and clasped her icy hands in his. "Now, tell me everything from the beginning."

Shay's heart raced at the welcoming warmth of his fingers.

From the beginning? Which beginning? The past

sixteen years leading up to this moment, or her blurry recollection of what happened after opening the package earlier this evening?

She glanced down at her hands in his. Why did this stranger render her senseless? Generally, she had a pretty good instinct about reading any given situation, but with him, she wasn't certain if his touch was more reassuring or disconcerting. If she dared to look up, she risked being captured by his electric-blue eyes, and she'd be rendered speechless. Either way, his closeness was too much for her, and she slid her hands from his and folded them in her lap. She sucked in a deep breath, locked her gaze on Spirit, whose eyes seemed to urge her on, and delved into the event that led up to the five hours she had no recollection of.

After she finished, Liam, without a word, picked up the bottle. She opened her mouth to protest, but when nothing happened, she snapped it shut and stared at it in disbelief as he slipped it into the pouch. Did this mean everything she'd seen or thought she'd seen earlier was only a dream?

Chapter 10

Shay ran her fingers over the long leather cord as Liam fastened the pouch around her neck. She didn't dare to touch the leather bag itself in case her earlier experience with the contents repeated itself. It was one thing to tell someone what she thought happened, it might be different to relive it, and she wasn't ready for that—not just yet.

As his hands dropped, they lingered on her shoulders, and he whispered, "Bridget was a wise woman, and if she told you to 'always wear this bit of fairy magic close to your heart as a protective charm,' then you'd better listen."

He gave her shoulders a light squeeze and took his place back on the sofa beside her.

Shay glanced down at the pouch resting over her heart. "Thank you. I just wish I knew what it all meant."

"I have no idea, but I'll ask my gran. Fairies are her specialty, and if anyone knows their magic, it will be her."

"You really think this has something to do with fairy magic? I mean, do you believe in all that?"

"I'm not sure." He shrugged. "But one thing I do know is that those"—he gestured to the pouch—"are what they call witch bottles and have been found in a lot of cultures as protective charms. According to Gran, our Irish ancestors brought the custom to America, where loads of bottles have been discovered in archaeological digs."

"Really?"

"Yeah, and as Bridget mentions in her note, they were found buried under the fireplace, floorboards, and some even hidden inside walls, exactly the places she told you *not* to keep it," he said with a wink.

Shay sighed. "Well, at the heart of every legend there is truth, so who am I to argue. But, please, let me know what your gran says about it."

"I will, and speaking of my gran, are you ready to try some of her famous stew?"

Shay's tummy took that opportunity to answer for her.

"That answers that question, doesn't it?" Liam chuckled and as he rose to his feet, his phone dinged out a text alert. "Sorry." He paused and dug his phone out of his back pocket. "Hmm, Dean just heard from Sheriff Burrows and needs to talk to me tonight. He also wants me to bring back Hunter's bike." He shoved his phone back into his pocket. "Since you won't even have that to balance your suitcases on tomorrow, will you let me retrieve your bags, now?"

"I guess since you're going there, sure. Everyone is more worried than I am about my meager belongings, so if it will make you all happy, yes, bring them back with you. Thank you." She smiled and avoided eye contact.

"Do I have something in my teeth?"

"Not that I've noticed. Why?" Heat crept up her neck, and she prayed it wouldn't leave a blotchy mess across her cheeks. Oh, why couldn't she be a pretty blusher like Jen?

"'Cause you seem to avoid looking me in the eye, and as a former police officer, I generally assume people are guilty of some crime, or that I have a chunk of spinach wrapped around my tooth."

She dropped her gaze to her damp hands folded in her lap and shook her head. "No, it's not the spinach."

"So, there is spinach?" He dashed over to a small mirror on the wall in the reading nook.

"I didn't mean there was spinach. I meant . . . oh, never mind. No, there's nothing wrong with the way you look—" *Understatement of the year.* "I'm just tired, I guess, and as you've reminded me with all your talk about stew, I realized I'm also starving. Not a good combination for me."

"As long as I don't have to tell Dean you would make a great suspect in the death of that man found on your rooftop this morning."

Shay stared at him in disbelief. "You can't be serious?"

"Ah, finally, eye contact. I knew that would get

ye." He winked impishly. "I'll be back soon," he said, his brogue deepening as he scooted through to the kitchen. The back door softly clicked closed after him.

Shay took one last wipe around the inside of her bowl, easing out just enough beefy sauce to cover the corner of her last morsel of bread, popped it into her mouth, and shoved the bowl aside. She sat back and patted her tummy. "I guess I was hungrier than I thought, or that was the best Irish stew I've ever had."

"Could it have been a little of both?" quipped Liam as he cleared the table and placed the bowls in the sink.

"Thank you again for picking up my bags. Are you sure Jen didn't say anything to you? Is she still mad at me?" Shay dug around the tall pantry cupboard beside the sink and searched for something to feed Spirit. She pulled a can of dog food from the back corner of the shelf, checked the expiration date, and smiled. She glanced at Liam wiping down the table. "Well, did she?"

"Like I said before, I never saw her. She packed the bags, and they were on the porch when I arrived. Dean came out, we talked for a minute, I got the stew, and came right here. Satisfied now?"

"I know you don't want to get involved in my family's tiffs, but it's just so weird that she can hold a grudge against me for this long."

"It has only been a few hours, and you're forgetting she was scared half to death about what happened to you. Remember, there's been far too many unexplained deaths in Bray Harbor recently, and people's imaginations tend to get the best of them in times like that."

"You are talking about the man on the roof, right?"

Liam paused and wrung out the dish cloth. "Yeah, and . . ."

"And Bridget." Shay scooped dog food into Spirit's bowl. "Tassi told me she suspected foul play there too. Do you?"

Liam hung the dish cloth over the sink divider and turned to her. "I don't know what to think about that one. I never saw the autopsy report, but something about Burrows's final report seemed off. He was pretty quick to close the case, stating it was an accidental drowning. Since she had no relatives that we knew of, there was no one to advocate for an investigation, so his ruling stood."

"But now there is."

Liam nodded.

"What about you?"

"Me advocating for Bridget? I hardly think Burrows would listen to me."

"But you'd think in some way he has to value all your years as a fellow police officer. You must be able to make a case for an investigation into her death. After all, you obviously convinced him of your innocence today or you'd still be sitting in a cell. Or are you out on bail?"

"No bail. Tea?" he asked, picking up the kettle.

"Sure, so you *did* convince him you were innocent, and that proves he will listen to you."

Liam tossed his head back, and a musical laugh escaped his chest. "If that were only the case. No, it took a photo of me appearing on this morning's front page of the *Monterey Times* to prove to him that I was nowhere near Bray Harbor last night. A photo that, by the way, was kindly provided to my *friend* Burrows by Duncan Bradley, the editor in chief of our local newspaper."

"You weren't at the pub at all last night?"

"No, and I was in Monterey attending a veterinarian convention with my good friend Doctor Laine, and we didn't get back until this morning. I told Burrows several times throughout the day to question Doctor Laine, but he chose not to listen to me until he couldn't ignore the proof Duncan slapped down on the desk in front of him."

As Shay poured the boiling water from the kettle into a teapot, she recalled the button she had discovered. "Tell me, did you wear a light blue dress shirt to this convention?"

"No, it was a black-tie event."

"Do you own a light blue dress shirt?"

"Not exactly my style," he scoffed. "Why do you ask?" Liam retrieved two cups from a cupboard and set them on the table.

"It's just that when I went up to the roof to see how someone could have ended up where the dead man did, I found a mother-of-pearl button off a man's dress shirt. I guess I'm just trying to figure out if it has anything to do with the murder."

"And you automatically thought of me?"

"No." She squirmed, now realizing how her words had come out. "It's just that it's next to your pub so . . . never mind. It could have been there for months for that matter. I guess I'm only trying to rule things out."

"Where's this button now?"

"I gave it to Dean . . . oh no . . ." She dug around in the front pocket of her jeans and tugged out the tissue. "I forgot to give it to him. This is it. Does it look familiar?"

Liam turned back the edges of the tissue and studied the button. "How do ye know it's from a man's shirt?"

"Because if it was from a woman's blouse, it would likely be rounder on the surface and probably larger. And look here"—she pointed to the short, frayed strings—"some of the threads are still attached in the buttonholes, and this teeny-tiny piece of material on the end of the thread appears to be some of the silk fabric."

"Which indicates the button was torn off and didn't fall off."

"That was my thinking."

"Dean needs to see this. You didn't touch it, did you?"

"No, I used tweezers to pick it out of the crevice I found it in, but like I said, I can't tell how long it's been there."

"Testing can give them an idea of that, but in any case, this might be the first real lead they have." He glanced down at the button. "And if it tests like we think it will, it's a good one. Now, we just have to figure out who was in the pub, wearing a dandy shirt."

"A dandy shirt?" she asked, digging around in a drawer for something to put the button and tissue into.

"Yeah, an expensive shirt worn by a man who dresses in expensive clothes to impress. A dandy.

We don't get many like that in the pub, so someone must remember seeing him."

"Carmen was with me when I found it, and she didn't recall anyone like that, but she also wasn't working last night. She was going to ask the bartender who was on shift."

"Leave that to me—and this, if you don't mind." He gestured with a wave of the small plastic bag she'd given him to store the button in. "I'll make sure Dean gets this."

Shay's tummy rolled over. If this button was as important to the case as Liam said it was, then leaving it in his hands might not be the best idea. After all, she didn't know him. He seemed like one of the good guys, and he was Dean's best friend, but he also had been at the top of the suspect list. He had barged in on her tour of the shop that morning, and the misgivings she had about all that bubbled back up.

Then she remembered Dean's reassurances about him; and Spirit, sound asleep under the table, eased her reservations. Spirit seemed to have a sixth sense about people, and he was relaxed around Liam—even though the mere closeness of *Mr. McHeart-Flutter* sent her usually spot-on radar all haywire. So, yes, maybe it would help get Liam out of Burrows's sights once and for all.

"What did Dean need to talk to you about tonight? Have they any more leads in the case, since you said you have a strong alibi?"

"They finally got identification on the dead man. His name was Grady Kennedy, and he was a private investigator from County Clare in Ireland."

"County Clare? Isn't that where your grand-mother lives?"

Liam nodded. "Dean figures that Burrows is going to try to draw a connection again between me and this fellow, and he warned me not to let my guard down because the sheriff's not done with me yet."

Shay studied the button that Liam still held. "Is there any chance that came off the victim's shirt?"

"Good question. I'll run this over to Dean first thing in the morning, and he can check Grady's shirt to see if it is a match. If it is, we're no further ahead because it doesn't give us a clue as to who attacked him."

"Unless, of course, there's some DNA they can pull off the button."

Liam chuckled. "Look at you going all Miss Marple on me."

Chapter 11

The next morning Shay couldn't shake the dream-invading thoughts that had kept her tossing and turning all night. However, the missing puzzle piece that really deprived her of sleep was the fact that she didn't know enough about Bridget Early's past; Liam wasn't the only person in town who had a connection to County Clare. Shay wondered if Bridget might have had a stronger connection to their ancestral home in Ireland than Liam, who just happened to have come from the same county when he was twelve years old. Meaning Bridget possibly could have had a more current connection to the victim, Grady Kennedy. After all, his body was discovered on her roof. In Shay's mind, that alone must mean something.

She locked the front door and glanced across her front garden to the cottage next door, belonging to Pearl Hammond—Bridget's only known friend. When she garnered no sense of morning stirrings, she mentally crossed her fingers that Pearl would be at Swirls Ice Cream Shop, preparing for the day's business. If anyone in town could give her some insight into her mysterious benefactor, it would be Pearl.

But it was far too early in the day to play—what had Liam called her—Miss Marple? Did that mean he thought of her as an amateur sleuth or an old spinster? She paused and laughed, shaking off his comment right along with all the other puzzle pieces floating aimlessly through her mind. Yes, it was far too early to figure it all out now, so she headed for the beach to survey her new surroundings.

As Shay approached the water's edge, the air crackled with static, sending prickles up her arms. The bright morning sunlight reflected off the churning waves, and she marveled at the clarity of every minute detail. Water droplets danced with rainbow swirls, and the rolling surf intensified. Today, it was as though she was experiencing the world with new eyes.

She stroked her hand over the long leather thong that hung from her neck. The pouch nestled under her muslin blouse and rested over her heart. Could the fairy magic Bridget had written about be the reason for her new sight? Or was it simply that for the first time in the past two years, she had a home and a sense of belonging again? She glanced back at Spirit sitting sentry on the beach. His ears perked, and his blue eyes glistened in the sunlight. There was a stirring within her, and her entire body pulsated. She felt a part of everything around her.

She scooped up a handful of water and let it run between her fingers, watching as the sun's light glistened off each droplet like a jewel before it fell back into the source from where it had come. The spray from the splashing waves against her shins washed the last sixteen years from her soul. She smiled as she stood and walked back onto the dry sand and slipped her sandals back on after brushing the wet sand from her feet. "Come on, Spirit. Since it seems I'm here to stay, let's go see if we can find some new wheels."

Shay paused at the small building on the beach that housed Swirls Ice Cream Shop and framed her hands around her eyes to shield them from the sun. She peered through the window but saw no sign of Pearl, but her heart did a little skip when she saw there were still the nineteen-fifties chrome and Formica stand-up tables inside the small ice cream parlor. Relief swept through her. Here was one more place that hadn't changed much over the years.

Shay hummed quietly as she passed the B&B set back from the beach in the trees and climbed the wooden stairs from the beach that led either out onto the long pier or straight ahead from the steps, south down the wide boardwalk. Not in a rush to get anywhere, she meandered along the boardwalk. It was clear by the activity up ahead that several merchants along the long wooden-planked walk were in the process of setting out their wares and sandwich boards. She smiled and waved as she passed, then stopped and said a quick hello to Larissa Laurence, the owner of the Beach Side Café, and someone she vaguely remembered from school.

Farther up she paused and studied the window display of a bay-windowed shop called Teresa's Treasures. It was clear that it was an antique, souvenir, and gift shop, and Shay wondered if the owner was Teresa Boyer, another old high school acquaintance, who, if she recalled correctly, always spent her weekends at estate and garage sales instead of partying on the beach with the rest of them.

She stopped and exchanged pleasantries with Beverly Lewis as she set up her sidewalk sign in front of Tasty Treats—a to-die-for chocolate, popcorn, and candy shop—which Beverly's parents used to run but, according to Beverly, they had since retired and moved to Florida.

Shay drew in a deep breath and hugged her arms around herself. The sights and smells along the boardwalk took her back to her youth . . . but her little walk down memory lane crashed and burned when she reached the south end and stared across the beach. Gone was the community bonfire-pit area that had been there for as long as she could remember. In its place towered a massive stone-and-log cabin structure adjacent to Bray Harbor Marina and Boat Rentals.

The WHARF HOTEL sign on the High Street entrance boasted four-star fine dining on the water's edge. Shay shook her head. This addition to the town would have most likely put a damper on the B&Bs in town, especially Faye Pemberton's, back on the north end of the boardwalk. Shay wondered if tourism had increased enough to warrant a large hotel or if this was one of Julia's husband's financial ventures that Jen had told her about. Karl's dabbling in murky finances seemed to be paying off—if the rumors were true.

With a sigh of relief, she spotted a quaint beach shack nestled up against the far side of the hotel's beach perimeter fence with a familiar sign: LAND AND SEA RENTALS, stating they specialized in bike, WaveRunner, and board rentals. Maybe there was still hope that not *everything* had changed.

"Come on, Spirit. Let's see if we can make a deal on something." Shay trotted across the pebbled beach path, her companion close on her heels.

Shay entered the shack, and after waiting for her eyes to adjust from the light change, spied a figure hunched over behind a refitted surfboard serving as a sales counter. "Hi, Mr. Ripley, it's been a long time, and I bet you never thought you'd see me again." She grinned, but when the figure stood and turned toward her, her grin melted into a look of bewilderment. "You're not Jonas Ripley."

"And you're not Larissa with my coffee order." The sun-bleached, blond-haired man gave his head a slight flip to clear his long bangs from his eyes. "Ah, but I do know you, don't I?" He rested his suntanned hands on the surfboard countertop.

Shay studied the aging surfer sporting a sleeveless T-shirt and board shorts. Then a glimmer behind the sea-blue eyes of the boy who had once been the captain of the high school beach volleyball team came into full view in her mind. "Oh my goodness! You're Mike Sturgis."

"Hi, Shay." He grinned sheepishly and tossed his long locks back with another flip of his head.

"When did you take over the rental company?"

"About five years ago." He gestured behind him with a tick of his head. "The conglomerate that owns the hotel was hounding Old Man Ripley to sell, and he was about to cave under their pressure when my brother, Jerry, and I stepped in and offered him a fair deal to keep the place running. Of course, he jumped at that." He glanced around the storefront and smiled. "This was his baby for over fifty years, and it broke his heart that they wanted to tear it down."

"Poor Mr. Ripley." Shay shook her head. "It would have been hard on him to even imagine his entire life's work was worth no more than a few moments under a bulldozer."

"Yup, but all's good now for him, and he's retired. Although that doesn't stop him from dropping by from time to time and giving me the benefit of his years of business expertise," Mike said with a light laugh. "But what brings you back to the Harbor and in here today?"

"Actually, I'm looking for some new wheels, and I hoped you might have an old bike you could rent me . . . cheap." She cast her gaze to the wooden-planked floorboards, hoping he wouldn't see her embarrassment and then press her for an answer about her current financial predicament.

He let out a hearty laugh, and she glanced up in time to see his hand waving toward the showroom behind him. "As it is the end of tourist season, I have nothing but bikes, some old, some new. What did you have in mind? Or perhaps a scooter? They were a big hit this summer with the tourists. Although if you want one for long-term, I'd suggest you go see my brother, Jerry, at Round Again Sports. He has a secondhand sporting goods store off High Street on Fifth Avenue, and I'm sure he would make you a good deal on a secondhand one if you decided to buy."

"No, no scooters. I don't trust myself with one of those. I was hoping you might have an old leg-powered bike, nothing fancy, no gears, just good old-fashioned pedal power."

He stared thoughtfully into the back room and then shook his head. "Nope, nothing comes to mind. The best I could do is an old three-speed, but I'm just in the process of rebuilding it and won't have it done for at least another week."

Spirit stood from where he'd been sitting at Shay's feet and loped over to a wooden door secured with a padlock, whined, and scratched on the door.

"Spirit, stop, you're going to make me have to pay for damages."

"Nah, he can't hurt that old door, don't worry."

But Spirit didn't stop and yelped louder this time, scratching frantically on the door.

"I'm sorry, Mike, I have no idea what's gotten into him this morning." Shay beelined to Spirit and gave his leather collar a tug. "No, stop. Sit and be a good boy."

Spirit whimpered, sat back on his haunches, and fixed his glacial blue gaze on the door.

"I have never seen him like this before—" She

paused and looked at Mike. "Unless he thinks there's food in there, but I fed him this morning, so I really don't understand his fixation on what's behind the door."

"No food." Mike retrieved a set of keys from the cash register and fit one in the padlock. "There's just some tools and old bikes that I use for parts when I'm doing repairs." He flung the door open. Spirit trotted into the dark room and barked.

Mike flipped on the wall switch and whistled. "Well, I'll be."

"What is it? What was he after?" Shay peered past his arm and gasped when Spirit pawed at a row of bike tires leaning up against the back wall, causing them to tumble with a crash to the floor. "Stop, no," she cried, bolting toward him.

She stopped short when she saw what was behind the tires. It was a beautifully restored red framed vintage ladies' bicycle.

"Wow," said Mike. "I completely forgot that was in here."

"It's perfect. It even has a wicker basket attached to the handlebars. How much?" She spun around to face Mike.

"I don't know. Like I said, I forgot that was even here, but—"

"Well, Spirit"—she gestured to her furry sleuthing partner lying on the floor with his head on his paws and his gaze fixed on the bike—"seems to think it's exactly what I need. Besides, if you forgot all about it that must mean you wouldn't miss it if you sold it, right?"

"It's not really mine to sell," Mike said, rubbing

the back of his neck. "Bridget Early brought it in a few months ago and asked me to hold it until someone picked it up for her. No one ever did, and that's why I kind of forgot about it."

"Did she say who was going to pick it up?"

"No, I asked her, and all she said was 'You'll know when the time comes.'"

Spirit raised his head and let out a deep howl. Shay's chest constricted as a cold shiver snaked its way up her back.

Chapter 12

"Hi, Tassi," said Shay as she coasted to a stop in front of CuriosiTEAS. "What brings you around so early?" She removed her helmet, shook out her long ponytail, dismounted her bike, and balanced it on the kickstand beside Tassi's ten-speed.

Tassi raised her head from her perch on the bench in front of the tea shop. Black lines of melted mascara streaked down her cheeks.

"Oh no." Shay scurried to her side and slid onto the bench beside her. "What's the matter?"

"Can I come and work for you?" Tassi sobbed, sniffled, and swiped the back of her hand across her nose.

"What? You already work for your aunt Joanne. How in the world would you manage two jobs?"

"No, I quit this morning."

"What do you mean, you quit? Why would you do that?"

"I want to work for you." Tassi wrung her hands as she shifted on the bench, and her red, puffy eyes locked on Shay's. "Please, I have to have a job, or she'll send me back home, and I never want to live in that house again."

Shay rubbed her temples and tried to block the intense energy that unexpectedly rushed through her. She glanced across the street and locked gazes with Joanne standing on the sidewalk in front of Cuppa-Jo. Her hands were planted on her rounded hips, and her eyes ablaze. Shay broke away from the torrent of anger emanating from her old friend and refocused on Tassi, whose tears had since renewed.

"Why don't you start from the beginning and tell me what happened." She removed a tissue from her satchel and handed it to Tassi.

"Thanks." She blotted her eyes and then blew her red nose and crumpled the tissue in her hand as though it were a lifeline. "It started this morn— Is that Bridget's bike?" Tassi rose to her feet and swung around, staring questioningly at Shay.

"Uh, yeah, Mike Sturgis had it down at his bike rental shop and—"

"That's so weird." Tassi dropped back down on the bench with a thud, but her gaze never wavered from the bike. "I always wondered what happened to it. Bridget rode it everywhere, and then just before she disappeared, she was walking. I asked her about the bike, and she said it belonged to someone else now."

Spirit lifted his head and let out a yowl that sent a shiver across Shay's shoulders.

Tassi's eyes widened when they came to rest on the neck of Shay's blouse. "Is that Bridget's amulet too?"

Shay's hand flew to her chest and poked the pouch back under her shirt. "Do you know anything about this?"

"Yes, that was something she also never was without." Tassi's sobs grew. "I thought it had been lost along with her."

Shay pulled out another tissue and placed it in Tassi's hand. "Do you know the significance of it?"

"Not really," Tassi said, blowing her nose. "But I do know there's a little blue bottle inside it, right?"

Shay nodded.

"She used it in all her readings. When I asked her about it one day, all she said was that it kept her safe and showed her things about people."

Shay stared thoughtfully at Tassi, whose gaze had since refocused on the bike. Perhaps having the girl come work for her wasn't a bad idea. After all, she did say she and Bridget were friends of sorts, and Tassi did seem to have some insight into the mysterious woman—at least, more than Shay had managed to garner from anyone else in town. She took a deep breath. *Count to ten before making a decision* . . . "Tell me what happened with your aunt this morning and why you quit."

Tassi's voice quivered with tears. "Okay," she said, gulping in a breath. "Well, it started before we even left the house to open at seven. Aunt Jo was in a state about something and wasn't giving me the time I needed to get ready. I didn't know what the big rush was, but she kept hollering at me to hurry up." She looked at Shay. "I mean, we weren't even late. It was only six thirty, but she acted like it was going on eight." She shrugged. "Anyway, we opened, and Auntie was in the kitchen prepping for the day. This guy came in and ordered a cappuccino. Since we started serving them, I've made a lot, but when I gave it to him he took one sip, pushed it away, and said it was awful and to bring him another one."

"Really?"

"Yeah, I was shocked because no one's ever complained about my cappuccinos before. I thought maybe I had misunderstood him. He had a really heavy accent, so I asked him again what it was he had ordered. He stood up, shook his finger in my face, and started shouting at me. At first, I didn't know what language he was ranting in, but Aunt Jo heard the commotion and came out, went right over, and started speaking to him in his language."

Shay recalled that after Joanne's graduation, she had gone to art school in Paris for a year, but something had happened. Shay never knew what it was because Jen and Jo wouldn't tell her, but it must have been big because Joanne dropped out of the school and came home before she finished her degree. "Could they have been speaking French? Your aunt is very fluent in it as I recall."

"That's the first I've heard her speak it, but what was really weird . . ." Tassi twisted her fingers together. "She seemed to know this guy."

"Is he a regular customer?"

Tassi shook her head. "I've never seen him before, so after he left, I asked her about him. You know, like where she knew him from. Then she got really mad, and I mean *mad*. She told me to mind my own business, and that I'd better learn how to make a better cup of cappuccino because if she started losing customers over my incompetency, my dad would be hearing about all the trouble I've gotten into since I came to live with her. Then she stormed back into the kitchen."

"That doesn't sound like the Joanne I know."

"I know, right? I mean, she's been tough on me, but I haven't been in any real trouble since I got here. She makes sure of that, but she was so mean in what and how she said it." Tassi straightened her shoulders and sat upright. "I couldn't believe what she just said to me and that she was taking Mr. Fancy-Pants's side over her own niece and—"

"Mr. Fancy-Pants?"

"Yeah." She motioned toward the harbor. "He looked like he just stepped off one of those big yachts out there."

Shay's mind conjured up an image of the button and the blue shirt it might have come off. "Was this guy someone who might wear, say . . . a blue silk shirt?"

"Oh yeah, for sure."

"And you've never seen him before this morning?"

"Nope, and I won't be again because Auntie and I really got into it after she insulted me and took his side without even hearing me out, and I told her I quit, and then I left."

Shay gazed across the street at Cuppa-Jo's storefront, and a shiver raced through her. What did

Joanne know about this guy and could Mr. Fancy-Pants have had anything to do with Grady Kennedy's body ending up on her greenhouse roof?

She took Tassi's hand in hers, and the girl's trembling subsided. "I would have to okay it with your aunt, of course, and I couldn't pay you much, at first, anyway. But I really could use help with clearing out the shop and selling some of the items I won't be using in my business . . ."

"I'll take anything, and because I spent so much time here with Bridget, I can help you sort through everything easier."

"You spent a lot of time here?"

"Yeah, and I got to know a lot about what Bridget did."

"But I thought you only came to live here six months ago, and Bridget's been gone at least two of those months, and with working for your aunt and going to school—?"

"True, but I'd been coming most weekends and holidays before that because my parents were fighting all the time." She hung her head. "I'd hang out with Bridget in the shop because I couldn't stand being back in Carmel or at home. Then after my dad left for good . . . I got into big trouble at school. My mom said maybe I could behave better if I was busier and shipped me here to work for Auntie when I wasn't in classes. Which at first was great because . . . well, I was across the street from Bridget and could still come by when my after-school shifts were over and on my days off." She added quickly, "Like I said before, she was my only friend, but then . . ."

The girl's heartbreak over the loss of her friend

was clear, but perhaps working for Shay here in Bridget's shop just might be a stepping stone to the healing and closure she needed. Shay knew it was exactly the kind of help she could benefit from—someone who had insight into Bridget's unknown and mysterious rituals and her curious collectables. "All right, let's give it a try. But only if your aunt agrees, okay?" she added hurriedly.

"Awesome, and the best thing is I can start right away."

Shay's brows rose.

"I know, I know, after Auntie says it's okay, of course."

"Yes, as long as you understand that, and the fact that there won't be much money or a regular paycheck until I can get the place in shape to open to customers."

Tassi nodded in agreement, and the smile on her face grew to an ear-to-ear grin.

"Let me speak with Joanne. You sit tight or maybe take Spirit for a run on the beach down by the cottages. He likes it there. When he's done playing, come check back with me."

Tassi hopped on her bike, called for Spirit, and the two headed off down the street toward the north end of the beach by Shay's cottage. She drew in a deep breath, expelling Tassi's emotions, untangling them from her own about the situation, and strolled across the road to Cuppa-Jo and took a seat at one of the patio tables.

She fought to focus on something other than what Tassi told her. It wouldn't go well for the girl if Shay and her aunt ended up in an argument about the situation. Although Shay was torn between giving Jo a piece of her mind about what she had said to the girl, she knew Jo well enough to not get emotionally involved. What had Liam said last night? Oh, yeah, it's a family thing so don't get involved.

"I suppose she told you she was innocent in the whole situation this morning, and I was the one being unreasonable?" A dour-faced Joanne, standing wide-legged and with her arms crossed over her heaving chest, peered down her nose at Shay.

"Uh, no. She said you two had a falling out this morning, and she asked me if I was hiring." Shay hated not being totally honest with her old friend, but sometimes spilling the whole truth led to bigger problems. For Tassi's sake, she knew she had to keep this amicable.

Joanne dropped into the chair beside Shay. "Honestly, I don't know what got into that girl this morning."

Shay bit her tongue.

"She made a customer some sort of slop and tried to pass it off as a cappuccino; then when I told her she'd better brush up on her technique, she up and quit."

Shay wasn't the only one not being forthright—that is, if Tassi was telling her the truth about what happened. "She said she had a customer with a heavy accent, and after he complained about his order, she wondered if she had misunderstood him, so she asked him again what he ordered, and he started yelling at her."

"That's not what he told me," Joanne huffed.

"Maybe that's the problem," said Shay, reaching

for Jo's hand. "You didn't hear both sides of the story, and that hurt Tassi."

"Nonsense, I've known Pierre for years—" Her hand flew to her mouth.

Shay squirmed in her seat. "Yes, Tassi said it appeared the two of you knew each other, but she also said she had never seen him before."

"I told the girl to mind her own business, which clearly she didn't listen to, and that same thing now goes for you too." Jo jumped to her feet and backed away. "Did you want to order something or ask my blessing about hiring that little . . ."

"I came to ask you if you would have a problem with her working for me."

"Not as long as she makes enough money to continue to pay the room and board she, her parents, and I decided she had to pay to learn that things don't come free in this life." Joanne swung around but stopped. "I guess it goes without saying that the whole incident with Pierre will never be mentioned to *anyone*, right?" She glared at Shay, and her tone and mannerisms strongly suggested she wanted an answer.

Shay nodded mutely.

"Good, let this be the end of it." Jo marched across the patio and inside the coffee shop, letting the door bang behind her.

Shay reeled when her old friend turned and glowered back at her through the glass. She blew out a breath, counted . . . eight . . . nine . . . ten to dispel the bristling trail Joanne left in her wake, and looked across the road at her tea shop. Images of all the work she had ahead of her to ready it for customers shot through her like darts of lightning. Yes, Tassi's help was exactly what she needed, and Jo, although not pleased, had more or less said it was okay with her. Paying the girl a decent wage was going to be the big obstacle now, though. But she hadn't said no, and the rest would work itself out.

Shay started to rise to her feet, but the fluttering yellow police tape around the entrances to CuriosiTEAS and the pub caught her eye. She paused mid-sit and glanced back at the coffee shop door. Joanne hadn't moved. Her hardened gaze was still fixed on Shay. A cold shiver raced across her shoulders. It made her wonder about her old friend's reaction to any mention of this Pierre. What was he to Jo, and why didn't she want anyone to know about him?

Chapter 13

Shay carefully set a black cast-iron gothic medieval cat statue on the sales counter, and she crossed her fingers that the weight she and Tassi were piling on the top wouldn't shatter the glass. Tassi's knowledge, which she had picked up in the short time she had known Bridget, astonished Shay. Tassi had informed Shay that Bridget told her a lot of cultures revered cats, including the Celts, like this little fellow with the hand-painted jade-green eyes. Shay judged by the growing collection on the counter of nearly another dozen similar cats, along with the assortment of gargoyles, that Bridget thought these would be a big seller. But based on the amount of dust they had to wipe off . . . Shay didn't think so.

"Bingo!" cried Tassi, darting over to Shay's side. She shook her phone in excitement. "There's a woman in Monterey that runs a place called Mystical Gardens, and she wants to come and see *every-thing* we're selling. She can be here in an hour and asked that we not sell to anyone else. She told me she's been dying to get her hands on Bridget's collection for years, and can't believe that now she finally can!"

"You're kidding, right?"

"No, I'm not. I just spoke to her."

"How did she know we were looking at selling all this?" She waved her hand over the counter filled with other odds and ends of mysterious mystical relics. "Plus most everything else in here that she might want to buy?"

"I remember her calling one day when I was in here, and Bridget told me later that the woman had no patience. She'd told her time and time again that when the time was *right*, she'd be able to buy most of the collection."

"What did she mean by that?"

Tassi's eyes sparkled mischievously. "I have no idea, except that Bridget was a *seer*, remember, and today seems to be that *right* time"—Tassi hooked her fingers in air quotes—"for Madam Malvina."

Shay surveyed the shop. The massive collection of various statues of cats, goddesses, crystal skulls, amulets, amulet boards, carved wooden boxes, wrapped taper candles, incense packages, dragon figures, and the various-sized cast-iron cauldrons she and Tassi had set aside on the long sales counter covered the entire surface. Bridget was known as a seer, but had she truly foreseen the future of her shop? Shivers raced through her. Had she predicted her own death? Was that why she had taken her bike to Mike's and mailed her amulet to the lawyer in New Mexico just before she disappeared? However, the bigger question was what did any of this have to do with Shay and why had she become the beneficiary of Bridget's life's work?

Exactly an hour later, Madam Malvina and a pale-faced young man sporting charcoal-blackened eyes bustled through the door like a whirlwind. The woman's braided hair, pulled up high on top of her head, gave the impression that she was wearing a black crown that matched her black below-the-knee-length dress and stockings. The only color the woman adorned herself with was a vibrant rose-colored scarf secured with a crystal skull brooch at her shoulder, allowing the ends to waft in the air behind her as she seemingly glided on air around the store.

For the next two hours, Tassi and the young man boxed items the woman pointed to, and Shay checked their prices on the crude inventory list she had found in the desk drawer in the small alcove-office upstairs. As the assortment of items on the counter—in addition to a wide range of wind chimes, brass bells, Tarot cards, cast-iron cauldrons, fairy figurines, and Celtic door knockers—were packed up, Shay ticked off a box noting the price Bridget had paid for them and discussed a mutually agreed-on purchase price with the woman. Orion, as Madam referred to her young helper, loaded the boxes in the large white cube van they had arrived in.

When Madam had made her last rounds and

the cargo area of the van was packed to the roof, Shay pulled up her bank information on her phone and studied the amount of money Madam Malvina had transferred to her bank account. Tassi could get paid, and for a few months after too, plus there would be plenty left over to get her through the first stage of renovations she wanted to do. Hopefully, she would have it all finished by the time the police barrier came down at the end of the week . . . *if* Sheriff Burrows stuck to his one-week threat and didn't find another excuse to further punish Liam and, inadvertently, her.

Shay tapped the screen closed in triumph, waved at Madam Malvina and Orion as they pulled away, and trotted back inside to find Tassi behind the sales counter, scrolling through her phone.

"I don't think there's much left to sell if you're looking for another buyer."

"No," said Tassi, shoving her phone in her jeans pocket. "It was just Auntie reminding me my rent is due the first of the month." She cast her gaze down, and Shay knew the threat of her aunt sending her back home to Carmel, because she broke the contract arranged by her parents in order for her to stay, was very real and weighed heavy on the young girl. She hadn't even flirted with Orion, which Shay found strange as they appeared to be close to the same age and seemed to have so much in common, but Tassi had been business focused, as though this was a make-it-or-break-it day for her.

"Don't worry. There's going to be enough money this month for you to pay your rent and for a few more months after that, as far as I can see."

A dewy sparkle replaced the haunted look in Tassi's eyes.

After swiping her finger across the now-barren countertop, Shay grinned. "We hit the jackpot with Madam Malvina today, and I have you to thank for that. By the time this money runs out—fingers crossed—we'll be up and running as a regular tea shop and bringing in a steady business."

The sparkle in Tassi's eyes faded. "You're not going to do readings like Bridget did but *only* sell tea?"

"I don't know anything about doing the kinds of readings she did. I thought you picked up on that today when you had to explain to me what everything was and what they were used for."

"But you have her amulet and the blue bottle. She must have left them to you for a reason."

Shay fingered the bulge of the leather pouch under her blouse. Was Tassi right? Had Bridget left this to her so she could carry on her work? "I don't know. There's so much to learn and—"

The door flew open, sending the overhead bells into a frenzied jangle. "What's wrong?" demanded Liam, his eyes filled with panic. He came to a stuttering stop in the doorway and glanced around the shop. "Were ye robbed?"

"What?"

"Spirit showed up at my cottage door, pacing back and forth like he wanted me to follow him, and . . ." Liam's look of panic turned to confusion. "This is where he led me. I thought something happened."

"Something did happen, but it's all good. Tassi

found a buyer for most of the trinkets that were here and—"

"Trinkets? Is that what ye saw them as?" He clucked his tongue. "Don't be letting me gran hear ye talk like that, especially when ye look like an incarnation of the Fae Queen yerself."

"Coincidence, that's all."

Liam ambled to a bookcase, retrieved a book, and handed it to Shay. "Here's a good one to start with."

Shay read the title. "*Ancient Legends, Mystic Charms, and Superstitions of Ireland*, volume one by Lady Wilde. You can't be serious?"

"Aye, but I am," he said with a mischievous wink that set the electric blue of his eyes sparkling. "If you look at the date, you'll see it was published in 1887, and Lady Wilde was a renowned Irish nationalist at the time. Plus, she used her husband's research on mythology and legend extensively in her books."

Shay tossed the book on the sales counter. "Well, I think the more urgent reading for me is all the books about herbal teas and brews, since"—she gazed around the nearly empty storefront—"I am supposed to be running a tea shop now."

"Don't forget about these." Tassi scrambled down the length of the bookshelves, grabbing one book after the other and plopping a stack on the counter. "Bridget would have wanted you to read these too," she said with a saucy grin before grabbing a broom and sweeping.

Shay scanned the assortment of books on palm reading, crystal balls, and developing your own psychic powers. She shook her head and glanced over at Spirit, sitting by Liam's feet. "What do you think? Would Bridget approve of me learning some new skills?"

He raised his head and barked loudly.

"That answers that, doesn't it?" Liam's soft laugh soothed her frayed nerves. "Now, the question is what are you going to do with what's left over?"

"Phew, good question. I guess I could post them online and hope someone wants all these shelving units, or maybe have a sidewalk sale for the left-over *trinkets*." Shay glanced at Tassi pushing the broom up and down the empty aisles. "Tassi, I think we've put in a full day, and we haven't eaten anything except those muffins you picked up from the Muffin Top Bakery on your way back this morning. What do you say, should we call it a day?"

Tassi looked up. "I'm fine. Don't worry about me, but if you want to leave, I can move some of this in the back room so we can start on the painting first thing tomorrow."

"I can pitch in, too, since I'm locked out of the pub for at least a week." Liam pushed up his sleeves and surveyed the shelves. "If ye aren't going to be holding readings—"

Tassi coughed and cleared her throat.

"At least not for a while." He grinned knowingly at the young girl. "Then we should store all these in the back room and set ye up a bit of a library. That way ye can study some of these books. What do you think?"

Shay's tummy picked that exact moment to rebel over its lack of food, and she rubbed it when the gurgling increased in volume. "I think that if we're going to carry on, we'll need some fortification. Why don't I run out and grab some burgers or something?"

"Perfect! The best burgers in town, aside from mine at the pub"—he winked—"are at Brew n' Chew."

"What is a Brew n' Chew?"

"It's the diner and microbrewery down at the far end of High Street around the corner toward the beach, between High Street and the Boardwalk."

Shay looked questioningly at him.

"It's in the old cannery warehouse."

"Huh, really? I never knew it had been renovated, but I'll take your word for it because I'm starving, and I'll take your orders too, please." Shay grabbed a sheet of paper off the counter and propped a pen in her hand. "Shoot."

Shay scribbled down Tassi's and Liam's dinner orders and glanced at Spirit lying prone by the door with his head resting on his front paws. "And you, mister, what are you in the mood for?"

Spirit yawned and flopped onto his side.

"All right then, I'll surprise you," she said with a laugh, gathered up her satchel, stepped around the seemingly sleeping dog, and opened the door. Spirit leapt to his feet and followed her out onto the street. "Oh, now you're awake," she mocked and reached for her helmet in the basket but stopped when she spotted Jen and Joanne with their heads huddled close as they chatted at a table on the coffee shop patio.

"Hmm, funny, Jen's right across the street but didn't stop into the tea shop." She glanced down at Spirit and shrugged. "I guess if peace is going to be made between us, she's sending a loud and clear message that I'm the one to do the grovelling and beg for forgiveness, right?"

Spirit barked.

"I know, I know, I guess I do owe it to her since she was just scared, which shows she cares, right?"

Spirit barked again and wagged his tail.

She yanked the helmet on her head, slipped her arms through her satchel, backpack-style, released the kickstand, and froze. A distinguished silver-haired gentleman wearing a dark blue blazer and buff-colored trousers set three cups on the table, took a seat beside Joanne, and casually slung his arm over the back of her wicker chair.

Mr. Fancy-Pants? Shay was tempted to run back into her shop and have Tassi identify the man, but her tummy wrestled with her brain and won. She needed food, and since it appeared that Jen knew the stranger too, she could confirm his identity later.

Shay hopped on her bike, crouched low over the handlebars, and pumped like mad toward Brew n' Chew. If she could get back to the tea shop quick enough, maybe they would still be outside, and Tassi could tell her if that was the man from this morning. If not, well, then that meant swallowing her pride and apologizing to her sister for *unknowingly* scaring the bejesus out of her last night.

Then she'd be free to pump her for information about the stranger. She coasted to a stop in front of the restaurant, hopped off, and dropped the kickstand. Although, if he was the man at the pub wearing the blue silk shirt the night Grady was killed, it also meant Jen and Joanne were unwittingly friends with a possible murderer.

Chapter 14

Shay popped the last piece of her burger into her mouth, tossed the wrappings into a trash can, dropped onto a chair, and eyed Liam as she sucked up the last of her chocolate shake. "So, you're saying that the button was sent to the Monterey crime lab, and it could be weeks until they have the DNA results?"

"Yup," he said, tossing his milkshake cup into the garbage can beside Shay. "But the good news is Dean said it should be a lot sooner when they have the analysis back on the shirt material."

"What good is that?" asked Tassi, dusting crumbs into her hand from her place at the table.

"If it's a high-end material like Shay thinks, it might tell us where the shirt was made."

"Oh, you mean like Paris or Milan?" Tassi swooned. "My money is on Mr. Fancy-Pants, and he's French . . . so yeah . . . I bet it comes from Paris."

"It's too bad the man I saw at Jo's when I left to get dinner was gone by the time I got back. You could have had a peek, and then we'd know for sure if he's your Mr. Fancy-Pants."

"But that also means your sister knows who he is, right?" Tassi dumped her handful of crumbs into the garbage can.

"Yeah, I might be able to get his name out of Jen . . . if she ever speaks to me again," Shay murmured to herself and then glanced at Liam. "But I've been thinking. Is identifying the material or finding out where it was purchased enough evidence for a murder charge or conviction?"

He shook his head. "At best it would make the owner of the shirt a person of interest in the case. Then the real investigating would begin. Like finding out the motive, being able to place the shirt-guy at the scene, giving him opportunity and hopefully leading to a murder weapon that could be connected back to the suspect. Without any of that"—he shrugged—"there isn't enough to bring about a murder charge, let alone a conviction."

"Yeah, the motive is something I'd be interested in hearing. I find it all too coincidental that the body was discovered the day I took possession of the shop. It might be a warning or something."

"I think *coincidental* is the key word there. No one knew who the new owner was, so why would they want to send you a message?"

"Maybe it was a warning to the owner in general and not directed personally at me."

"Sadly, until a real person of interest crops up—"

"And not one of Sheriff Burrows's making," added Shay. "My money is still on the fact that Burrows could be behind all this and is setting you up."

"Yeah, that's always a possibility, but, unfortunately, until more information comes to light, we have no way of knowing what any of the who, what, when, where, why, or how of this case involves."

"I just know that I'll sleep better when we find out this was all a coincidence and not targeted at me or the shop or some vendetta against you."

"Dean also told me that they found out Grady Kennedy was staying at a little B&B in Carmel, but when they went through his belongings, there weren't any clues as to why he was in the area. They still suspect that since he was a PI he had a client here, but"—Liam shrugged and wiped a kitchen cloth over the table—"there was no communication trail, so it's a dead end for now unless they can decipher some encrypted text in his emails or find a burner cell phone. He must have had some communication with someone here. It's a long trip from County Clare for there to be no mention of it anywhere in his electronic devices or papers."

Shay paused fastening the garbage bag. "Could Mr. Fancy-Pants and Grady have been working together?"

"Like a partnership gone bad and Fancy-Pants killed Grady because he double-crossed him?"

"You have to admit," said Tassi, "that it is kind of strange that both men showed up in town around the same time."

"Yes, yes, it is." Shay tied a knot in the garbage

bag and tossed it toward the back door by the kitchen. "Yeah, I gotta talk to Jen. Maybe she can fill in some of the details about Fancy-Pants."

Spirit's ears perked, and he let out a yip.

"What's that noise coming from the front of the store?" asked Liam, his hand automatically going to his hip.

Shay assumed that after years on the force, the reaction to reach for his police-issue gun was instinctive. She didn't miss the shoulder slump when his hand only touched air.

"You did put up the closed sign and lock the front door when you came back, didn't you?" he whispered.

At Shay's nod, he slowly opened the back-room door and peered out onto the salesroom floor. Spirit shot past him and scampered to the front door, his feathery tail wagging as the tapping sound persisted.

"It's Jen," said Liam, "and she looks upset. Should I let her in or should we just close the door and pretend we didn't hear her?"

Shay peered around his arm. "Yikes, she does look mad, doesn't she? I hope it's still not about last night." She waved her hand. "You might as well let her in, and we can get this over with once and for all. Besides, I need to know if I can rest easy or if her fancy friend might have another surprise waiting for me soon."

Liam nodded and crossed the room to the door.

"What happened last night?" whispered Tassi.

"I . . ." Shay's fingers stroked the pouch around her neck. "I lost track of time, and Jen got worried about me, and she was—"

"Sorry to interrupt." Jen strutted into the shop and cast her gaze on Liam and then on Tassi, hidden halfway behind Shay. "But when I saw the bikes out front, I knew you had to be in here. I just didn't expect to find a party." She fixed her piercing sapphire-blue gaze on Shay's. "We need to talk . . . *privately*."

Spirit let out a yowl, and a cold shiver quivered across Shay's shoulders.

Liam glanced at Shay and gestured with a very slight uptick of his head. She softly smiled and clutched the pouch tighter to her chest. It was as if they were of one mind in that moment. "We can go upstairs if it's that urgent, because Liam and Tassi have graciously offered to help me organize this space tonight so I can start painting."

Jen fixed her gaze on Liam. "Don't you have a standing Sunday night date with Dr. Laine tonight?"

Shay's brow rose. Had she misread Liam's energy so badly? Jen told her he did his best Colin Farrell impression when he was trying to impress the ladies; and the way he turned his brogue on and off, she thought that's exactly what he was doing with her. "Wait, so your airtight alibi, this . . . this veterinarian friend you were in Monterey with Friday is someone you're dating?"

"He didn't tell you?" asked Jen innocently. "That's odd, since one of the photos in the *Monterey Times* was of them having a cozy brunch together Saturday morning in the hotel dining room, which is why Burrows had to let him go."

Shay shook her head and glanced sheepishly away, fighting to steady her breath. Who knew the friend who provided him with an alibi Friday night was a she, and by what Jen just said they'd spent the entire night together at the conference's hotel venue. Oh well, she wasn't looking for a relationship now anyway, but nevertheless, another fantasy bubble burst into tiny fragments of could-have-beens.

"Yes, he and Zoey Laine have become quite an item around town lately, haven't you, Liam?" said Jen, appearing rather smug as she folded her arms across her chest and eyed Liam. "I'm guessing then he also didn't mention the shiny new gemstone she's wearing on her hand today, either?"

Liam glowered at Jen. "My *friendship* with Zoey has nothing to do with you or anyone else in this town."

"Friendship?" Jen softly chuckled. "I wonder if Zoey knows that's all she is to you, with the way she was showing off that ring today."

"If you must know, it was a gift to celebrate her receiving an award for her animal rescue work at the conference Friday night." Liam shoved an empty shelving unit to the side.

Shay glanced apologetically at Liam even though she felt like she had just been kicked in the gut. "Jen, I think you and I better go upstairs and talk." She took Jen's arm and steered her into the back room, allowing Liam to cool off and Tassi to put her bugged-out eyes back in her head.

Jen was out of character, and Shay had to get to the bottom of this sudden lashing out at everyone and anyone. Surely, it couldn't all be related to what happened last night and her time warp. She closed the back-room door and swung Jen around so they were face-to-face. "Hey, if you're still upset with me that's fine, but you don't take it out on anyone else, got it?"

"I'm not lashing out. I'm protecting you."

"How is being rude to Liam protecting me?"

"Come on, Shay, I can see it in your eyes every time you look at him, and I did tell you that half the women in town felt the same as you. When I met Jo for coffee today, Zoey came in on her way to the animal shelter where she does volunteer vet checks a couple of times a week, and, well . . . she couldn't wait to show us the ring Liam gave her Friday."

Shay choked back a response, recalling the dinner she and Liam had shared last night and how he gave no indication he was a recently engaged man.

"When I saw him here, I assumed—"

"You assumed wrong. He asked to help because he's bored, and the pub's shut down just like my shop, remember. He was doing something nice for a neighbor."

"Okay, okay." Jen raised her hands in surrender. "Just don't come running to me when he breaks your heart."

"Why do you think every time a man talks to a woman, he wants more than friendship or that the woman does too?"

"I just know Liam better than you, that's all."

"Speaking of knowing people." Shay leaned back against the table. "Who was that guy you and Jo were having coffee with?"

"What guy?"

"The older, well-dressed guy in the blue blazer and beige pants?"

Jen's gaze dropped. "I . . . I . . ."

"Come on, Jen, what do you know about him?"

"I . . . I can't say."

"Can't or won't?"

She shook her head. "Please, just let it go."

"No. That's the guy who got Tassi in trouble with Jo this morning, isn't it?"

"That was just a misunderstanding."

"Some misunderstanding."

"He is French, and sometimes his use of English is a bit off and—"

"Okay, so you know he's French. What else do you know about him?"

"Why does it matter?"

"It just does."

"Shay, leave it be. You have no idea what you'd be opening if I told you."

Shay's heart dropped to her toes. "Jen, what are you involved in?"

"Me? No." Jen averted her gaze. "Not me. Jo."

Shay's hand went to her chest. "What has Jo done?"

"Let it go. Please, for everyone's sake."

"I can't let it go. That man might well be the prime suspect in a murder case."

"Pierre Champlain? No way." Jen shook her head. "That's impossible. I just met him recently, but Jo has a history with him and—"

"What kind of history?"

"Nothing, forget I said anything." Her fingers bit into Shay's shoulders. "Please, just let it go. You have no idea what trouble even talking about him could bring about."

Shay jerked away from her sister. "Is he threatening Jo?"

"No, it's nothing like that."

"Then tell me what's going on and who he is to her."

"Shay, please." She glanced at the closed door and then tugged Shay toward the circular staircase at the back of the room. "You have to forget we had this conversation and just let it go. It could lead to trouble, big trouble for Jo. Do you hear me?" she whispered harshly.

Shay planted her feet and stared at her sister. "No, if Jo's gotten herself involved with a potential murderer, this won't protect her, and she could end up being a victim too."

"He's not a murderer," Jen hissed. "He's her son's father."

"But that's impossible because Gary's Caden's father."

Jen shook her head.

Shay's eyes widened. She sensed something was off with the whole Pierre thing from the beginning, but this . . . it wasn't even on her radar.

"Look, what I'm about to tell you has to stay between us. Promise?"

Shay nodded.

"Say that you promise me?"

"Yes, I promise, but how? I mean, when? She

and Gary dated all the way through middle school and high school, then she went to Paris for a year, but as soon as she came back, they were engaged and got married right away. How could this man be Caden's fath—" Shay placed her hand over her pounding chest. "Ooh, she was pregnant with Pierre's baby when she married Gary!"

Chapter 15

"Come on, it's more private up here," Shay said, steering her sister up the stairs to the greenhouse toward the bench beside the potting table. "How long have you known about Caden's paternity?" she leaned in and whispered.

"From the beginning," said Jen, perching on the edge of the wooden bench. Her knuckles whitened as she clasped her hands in her lap.

"And all these years, you never told anyone?"

"No, she's my best friend. I couldn't betray her." Jen puffed out a deep breath. "At least, until now it seems, and it's all because Jo was afraid of what Tassi might have seen or heard."

"What do you mean?"

"When Pierre complained about his cappuccino this morning and was trying to explain to Tassi what the issue was with the drink, Jo heard

Tassi raise her voice and came out of the kitchen to see what the problem was."

"I guess he was being rude to Tassi, and from what she told me, she had a right to be upset with him."

"Yeah, maybe, but then Jo sent Tassi back into the kitchen to finish prepping, and she tried to settle Pierre down. Jo said he speaks very animatedly when he becomes excited, and some people take him wrong and think he's angry. It was clear that Tassi had mistaken his passionate way of speaking as anger and that it was directed at her."

"She is only sixteen, so I doubt she has much experience with international tourists or their cultures."

"I know, and Pierre is probably the first Frenchman she's ever encountered, so I'm sure she really didn't know what to make of his animated manner."

"And that was it? That's the reason Jo turned on her?"

"No." Jen buried her face in her hands. "I guess when Jo was talking to him, he told her he couldn't stand being away from her all these years and kissed her. She said she could never resist the entrancing charm he seemed to hold over her, and she was putty in his hands, so she let him. When she turned around, Tassi was standing in the doorway. Jo didn't know what she saw or heard and panicked, which ended up in her lashing out at Tassi because she's scared to death the truth is going to come out."

"Phew. Does Gary know about Caden not being his son?"

"I think he's always suspected. But he never wanted to talk about it. There were a few times Jo tried, but he'd cut her off and just say, 'You came back to me, and we're raising our baby boy together. That's all that's important,' and he wouldn't talk about the subject anymore. But now she's scared the truth might come out and everyone in town, including Caden, will know and . . ."

"Has she thought of something to say if other people besides Tassi put two and two together and figure out they didn't just meet but are old *friends* and that Caden looks more like Pierre than Gary?" Shay nearly choked on her last words because now that she thought about the boy's slight build and features, he didn't look at all like the taller, robust, dark-haired Gary.

"Yeah, because several people have asked her about him since he's been spending so much time at the café lately. Even Caden asked her if she knew him from when she went to art school in Paris."

"Yikes, what did she say?"

"Only that he was someone she'd met in France, and he happened to come to Bray Harbor looking for investment property, and they accidentally ran into each other after all these years. And . . . well, it's close to the truth."

"How so?"

"Because I found out today that he's Julia's mystery buyer."

"Really? He wants to buy a tea shop?"

"Apparently, he wants this place desperately. He told Jo it's because it's across the street from her café, and the location is perfect for an art gallery.

He ran a couple in France, and that's where she first met him."

"He looks about fifteen or twenty years older than her though."

"So?" Jen shrugged. "You remember how easy it was for an older dashing guy to make you go weak in the knees, don't you?"

"Yeah." Shay thought of Brad being ten years her senior.

"Anyway, she was young and in Paris, and he was debonair and handsome and said all the right things and swept her off her feet and then . . . Well, he told her he was sorry about how badly he had reacted to the news about the baby and wanted to make it up to her now. He thought if he opened a gallery right across the street from her café, it would allow him to be close to her and Caden without arousing any suspicions."

"But clearly that's not going to happen now."

"Especially if other people besides you notice Caden's similarities to Pierre and how little he looks like Gary."

"Then I guess for everyone's sake it's a good thing that I'm not selling the tea shop. Now maybe he'll move to Carmel or farther up the coast and won't be constantly around for people to be able to make the comparisons."

"That's what Jo's hoping. She doesn't want him to never spend time with Caden, but she also doesn't want the truth to come out. If he lived farther away and they just ran into each other occasionally, it would arouse less suspicion than if he was working across the street or lived in the same town." She looked at Shay and bit her lip. "He wants the cottage too, you know."

"Yeah, that's what Julia said." Shay scanned the greenhouse. "Do you know if he ever toured this building?"

"I'm not certain if Julia ever took him through, although I guess she did meet him through her husband, Karl, because he was looking for an investor and needed property for his art gallery."

"I wonder if he ever went up to the roof from Liam's pub to have a look at the greenhouse. Which," Shay murmured more to herself, "could explain why one of his buttons was found there."

"What button?"

"The day we discovered the body, I went up to Liam's patio to see how easy it would have been for someone to get onto my roof, and I found a button from a man's shirt wedged between the metal tracks securing the sheets of tempered glass."

"How do you know it came off of Pierre's shirt?"

"We don't. It might not have anything to do with him. He was just a good candidate because, as Tassi called him, he is a Mr. Fancy-Pants and he was the only one around town lately who might wear a shirt like the one the button came from." Shay reached over to Jen's damp hands intertwined in her lap. "Look, I'm sorry I pushed you into telling me about this. I know it must have been hard to break your friend's confidence after all these years, but I really did think it was a matter of life and death because the only lead there is that button."

"It is a matter of life and death. For Jo, at least.

Don't you see?" Jen raised her eyes, meeting Shay's gaze. "If this ever got out, it would destroy her reputation in town, not to mention what the revelation might do to Caden."

"I get that, and now I know Pierre has a good motive for being in town, which doesn't seem to have anything to do with me or my shop except for the perfect location to give him an opportunity to see his son when Caden picks up shifts during the holidays and after school. It looks like it takes him off the suspect list."

Shay walked Jen downstairs and when they got to the front door, Jen hesitated. She embraced Shay, and whispered, "Promise you won't tell anyone?"

Shay nodded and hung tightly onto her sister. It was as though she could feel Jen's heart breaking for Jo inside of her chest.

"Thank you." Jen gave her a weak smile. "And by the way, I had Dean bring down that trunk of Mom and Dad's from the attic, so you can drop by anytime, and we can take a look through it."

"Sounds good, thanks." Shay smiled in appreciation and closed the door behind her sister.

She turned to find Liam's and Tassi's curious gazes fixed on her. "What?"

Liam leaned back against the counter, crossed his ankles, and folded his muscular arms across his chest. "When you two were clearing the air, you missed an interesting visitor."

"Here, tonight?"

"Mr. Fancy-Pants came in," squealed Tassi. "And we got his name." She beamed proudly.

"Yeah, I know, Pierre Champlain. Apparently, he likes the location and wants to turn it into an art gallery. But why would he come in here to-night? The police tape is still up and the closed sign is on the door."

"He said . . ." Tassi cleared her throat and added in a French accent, "Zee lights were on, and I wanted one last chance to make a sales pitch to zee owner since my estate agent failed mizerably."

"But," Liam added, "when he told us about his idea to turn the shop into an art gallery, it got re-ally weird when he realized that you'd already sold off most of the store inventory."

"Yeah," piped in Tassi, "since he would have had to sell it all anyway to run it as a gallery, right?"

Shay glanced around the nearly empty shop and looked at them thoughtfully. "Maybe he was hop-ing to sell the stock himself and make some extra money. After all, Madam Malvina did pay well for what she purchased."

"Maybe," Liam slowly said, eyeing her.

"Regardless," Shay said, waving off his look of skepticism, "I think he's a dead end and not a mur-der suspect." She cast her gaze around the shop and faintly smiled. "But I see you guys made great progress, which means I can start painting tomor-row."

Liam kept his gaze on her. If he was taken aback by her sudden change of topic and her noncha-lance about Mr. Fancy-Pants, he gave no indication except by the questioning look in his eyes.

Tassi looked at Liam and then at Shay in bewilderment. "Just like that we don't think that guy had anything to do with the murder?"

"That's right." Shay focused her gaze on Tassi, hoping she could get through her explanation without breaching any confidences. "Jen told me Pierre Champlain is, in fact, from Paris and is an old friend of Jo's from when she went to art school there. It's just a coincidence he's in town. He was scoping out towns to open his gallery and liked Bray Harbor and just happened to run into Jo one day, that's all."

"That kiss I saw him give her told me they were more than just friends," said Tassi with a smirk.

"He's French, and the French are very affectionate, and they often greet someone with a kiss. That's just part of their culture." Shay averted her eyes.

If she had a solid sixth sense when something didn't ring true to her, Liam, with his law enforcement background, had it too and wouldn't easily be fooled. Her skin tingled, and she risked a glance in his direction. Sure enough, his eyes searched her face. Probably looking for her tells—just waiting for her to slip up like some criminal during one of his past police interrogations. But that wasn't going to happen. Jo's secret was not hers to disclose, no matter what.

Chapter 16

Shay laid the roller in the paint tray, peeled off her rubber gloves, and eyed their day's work. "What do you think?"

"I think," said Tassi, resting her brush on the rim of the paint can situated on the painter's tarp covering a table, "that we're finally done. I don't see any missed spots, and if you ask me, it looks pretty awesome."

"Yeah, it's amazing what a fresh coat of paint can do to a room, isn't it?"

"Do you think it's dry enough to put the new curtains up?"

"Let's not chance it. Besides, it's almost dinnertime, and your aunt will be expecting you. I don't want to hear her complaining that I'm working you to death or filing a child labor charge against me." Shay laughed and gave the paint can lid a good, sealing thwack.

"I'm hardly a child," Tassi grunted.

"I know, but you've also put in over ten hours today, and you are still considered a minor." She met Tassi's defiant gaze. "Let's not push it. I'd hate for Joanne to say she won't let you work here anymore."

"You're right." Tassi relaxed her stance. "Even though the work has been completely different than what I expected, it's still way better than working for that old shrew."

"Tassi, she's not much older than me, and she definitely is not a shrew."

"You don't live with her. I mean, wow. You should see the way she treats Uncle Gary lately. It's like he's invisible or something, and don't get me started on how she's been spending so much time in her bedroom on the phone, whispering to whoever she's talking to and ignoring Caden and me."

Shay glanced out the window and spotted Pierre across the street, sitting alone on the patio, seemingly staring off into the distance until a half smile crossed his lips, and he raised his cup to her in a salute. The look in his eyes sent a ripple of uneasiness through her, and it was clear that he had been watching her and Tassi through the windows. She danced a step back, but when Caden came out of the café, carrying a steamy cup and headed toward Pierre's table, she lingered and peeked around the window casing. When the young man leaned over, removed Pierre's cup, and replaced it with the new mug, Pierre's attention was solely diverted to Caden.

A soft gasp escaped Shay's throat.

"What's the matter?" asked Tassi, coming to her

side and gazing out the window just as Caden headed back inside the café. "Yikes, it looks like my cousin's already started his evening shift, which means Auntie's gone home to fix dinner. I'd better go, or she'll be on another rampage about me taking their hospitality for granted."

"Um . . . yeah . . ." Although the young man hadn't lingered at Pierre's table long, it was enough for Shay to compare their profiles. The strong resemblance was clear, and she mentally crossed her fingers that Tassi would never see the two of them together and notice the similarities between them. She was a smart girl, and if she did and started putting two and two together, especially after witnessing the kiss between Pierre and Jo, it would spell trouble for the family. "You're right. You'd better hurry straight home."

"I think I'll go and talk to Caden for a minute first, though. He gets home late, and I'm usually in bed, but I want to find out what Auntie said to him about me not working there anymore."

"That's probably not a good idea right now." Shay cringed inside. "Mr. Fancy-Pants is there, and you'd hate to get into another altercation with him. Also, you're on your bike, and it'll be dark soon," she added quickly.

Shay stood sentry at the window, and when Tassi hopped on her bike and pedaled off down the street without stopping at the café, she exhaled a sigh of relief. She knew if Jo's secret was going to be kept, it was up to her. She was the one holding all the cards. Somehow, Shay was going to have to make it clear to Pierre that her shop was not now nor would ever be for sale. Hopefully, that would make him move on to Carmel or Monterey to open his gallery. She needed to make certain that he would be far enough away and someplace that he and Caden couldn't be observed together by people who knew the young man or recalled that Jo had lived in Paris for a year, leading them to suspect the truth.

Perhaps now was the perfect time to have that talk. She shook out her ponytail and finger-fluffed her hair, untied the painter's apron she'd been wearing, tossed it on the side table, and shored herself up. Yes, this was as good a time as any. If she saw the family resemblance, it was only a matter of time until others did too. She had to get Pierre out of town for her old friend's sake.

Shay paused with her hand on the door handle. On the other hand, was it really her place to get involved? Didn't she have enough drama happening in her own life right now? Discouraging Pierre from setting up shop in Bray Harbor was Jo's job. She was the one who would suffer the consequences, even though she might not see it at the moment. If anything, Jo was the one she needed to talk to . . . not Pierre.

Then again, if the truth came out, it could hurt Caden and Gary deeply, and that was something Shay just couldn't stand back and watch unfold when she had it in her power to stop it. No, she'd have to put an end to Pierre eyeing her shop as a potential location once and for all.

She flung the door open and stopped. A black Range Rover pulled up across the street. Although she hadn't seen Karl Fisher, Julia's husband, since high school, there was no mistaking the once burly star football player as the man sitting in the driver's seat. Pierre hopped into the front passenger's side, and the SUV pulled away and turned left off High Street.

"Well, dilemma solved for tonight anyway," Shay muttered, stepping back inside her tea shop.

At that moment, her tummy let out a mournful growl. She glanced around for Spirit, as it sounded exactly like the sounds he often made. But seeing no sight of the white shepherd inside or out, she rubbed her tummy. It had been a long time since she and Tassi had taken their lunch break. She tugged her phone out of her back jeans pocket, glanced at the time, and smiled. Knowing her sister and the stickler she was for routine, this would be the perfect time to stop in and look through that old trunk of her parents'.

Her thumbs flew across the small keypad. She waited for a thumbs-up reply, hopped on her bike, and hoped Jen had something yummy planned for dinner with enough leftovers to also feed her starving little sister.

Shay pushed away her plate, now cleared of the last dregs of chicken piccata and lemon sauce. "Thank you. You have no idea how much I needed that, Jen." She grinned over the top of her water glass.

"Anytime. You know we're here for you, and I said I'd support you even if it's only through making sure you don't starve to death while you're pursuing . . . whatever it is you are doing right now." Jen waved off her sister's remarks and rose to rinse Shay's plate. "Maddie," she called, "could you please come and load the dishwasher. Your aunt and I have something we need to do now."

A tousle-headed blond girl, the spitting image of her lanky mother, trotted into the kitchen. "Why can't Hunter clean up tonight? Why is it always me who has to do the dishes?" She groaned as she dropped silverware into the dishwasher's utensil holder with a clatter.

Jen glanced at Shay and rolled her eyes. "He did the dishes last night, so it's your turn tonight. Stop whining. Sheesh." Jen jerked her head, gesturing that Shay should follow her into the living room. "I tell you, the closer she gets to thirteen and being a full-fledged teenager, the more tempted I am to send her off to live with Great-Aunt Elsie. She'd whip her into shape in no time," Jen snarled, clearly frustrated as she flopped down on the sofa.

Shay recalled when their aunt Elsie had come to stay with Jen and Shay after their parents' boating accident and shivered at the thought of sending her niece to live with the personification of a Viking warrior queen. Family resemblances were an odd thing. Great-Aunt Elsie was the epitome of her Norwegian heritage. Much like Jen. Shay watched her sister's graceful movements as she dug out a large photo album from the trunk and placed it on the floor. Maddie and Hunter had also inherited those qualities from their northern European ancestors.

Shay stroked her cheek and remembered what Liam had said about her delicate features. Glancing at her own locks of dark red hair hanging freely, she wondered what dormant gene in their family tree had swum to the surface with her conception.

"I took a look through this after Dean brought it downstairs, but I really didn't find anything that's going to help you sort out the Bridget mystery." She fixed her blue eyes on Shay. "Also, I'm not sure what you feared was in here all these years, because it's just some old photo albums, some notebooks from their early research, a few love letters Mom had kept from when they were first dating. Nothing of earth-shattering importance. Their lawyer gave us all their legal documents after they"— she swallowed hard—"were killed," she whispered.

Jen's words held no comfort for Shay as she scrutinized the trunk. That same feeling of panic and inability to breathe she always felt when she was near it rushed through her. "Are you sure?" She pushed her breaths back into her lungs where they belonged. "They were both marine geologists. I can't believe there're no journals pertaining to the research they were working on at the time of the . . . when it happened, or . . . anything . . ." Her voice dropped. "Is there at least something about Bridget? Anything that can give us a clue about who she was to our family and how well Mom and Dad knew her? Otherwise, none of my mysterious inheritance makes sense."

"No, there's nothing. I'm sorry. I know how much you need the answers about why she left you the tea shop and the cottage, but . . ." Jen shrugged helplessly. "At any rate, I think it's time you accept the fact that Mom and Dad's deaths were exactly what the Coast Guard said they were. A freak non-weather-related maritime accident and not related to their work off the coast of Mexico."

None of this made sense to Shay. All these years she was afraid the edgy feeling she got when in the presence of the trunk was because it contained something she didn't want to know about her parents or their deaths. Then when she got the inheritance, she hoped there might be something in it that would explain who Bridget Early was to her family. However, according to Jen, there was nothing. Had she been wrong all these years about the trunk and the fact was, deep down, the feelings she got when around it were simply because she didn't want to face the truth that her parents were never coming home, and going through their locked trunk would make her face it once and for all? After all, she wasn't even eighteen when her parents were suddenly taken, and she had so much confusion, anger, and resentment building up inside her then. But—she glanced at the trunk—that still left the matter of the Bridget mystery to figure out. There were secrets somewhere. If not in there, then where?

Chapter 17

"Look at Mom. She looks so young in this one." Shay sighed and pointed to a photo in the album.

"That was the day I was born," said Jen, her voice catching in her throat. "And here's some"—she flipped to the next page—"of Dad holding me in the hospital."

"Aw, you looked so sweet and innocent. I guess they had no idea what a hellion you'd grow up to be." Shay giggled and leaned over Jen's arm, snuggling closer to her sister for a better look.

"Me?" Jen bonked Shay on the head with the photo album teasingly. "You were the one who kept them on their toes. You and Adam Ward, your little playmate who you'd disappear with for hours without a word. Your shenanigans sent them into a state of panic nearly every day." She glanced at Shay thoughtfully. "Then again, I guess with your disappearing act the other night, you really haven't changed much, have you, except now it's me worrying about what trouble you got yourself into instead of them."

"I said I was sorry."

"I know, but to be honest, I almost went to Adam's house to see if you were there," she said with a chuckle as she flipped to another page. "Oh look, here's one of me holding you the day they brought you home from the hospital. I don't remember much of what happened then because I was only two, but I do remember Aunt Elsie dressing me in that frilly dress and using a curling iron to make those ringlets because she got so mad when I wouldn't sit still for her." She laughed and curled a strand of her hair around her finger.

Shay peered at the photo. "I don't remember ever seeing any of these pictures before."

"No, me neither, there were lots of albums around of when we were a little older, but these ones are new to me too. Look, here's one of you and me in front of the tree on your first Christmas, and you're standing up by yourself. Isn't that just precious." Jen sighed wistfully.

Shay studied the photo, and a surge of uneasiness rippled through her. She flipped back a page and looked at the photos of her sister holding her, then more closely at the ones of her mom and dad cradling her in their arms. "These are the first pictures of me, and you say you recall this was the day I came home?"

"Yeah," said Jen, shifting the album on her lap. "I remember it clearly. Trust me, I will never forget Aunt Elsie and her need for perfection; and my burning scalp because I wiggled around too much can attest to that."

Shay narrowed her gaze as she examined the images. "How old would you say I look in those pictures?"

"Since you were just born, I assume a few days old. I never got to go to the hospital because Mom said the nurses wouldn't let a toddler visit, so Auntie came to stay with me when Dad went to get her and bring you home."

"But look. Compare my newborn picture to yours." Shay flipped back to the first page. "You look like a red, tiny, plucked chicken, and then compare it to mine." She flipped to the first picture of Jen holding her. "My complexion isn't mottled, my face is fuller and rounder, my hands are chubbier . . . not that I have any experience, but that's not usual for a newborn, is it?"

"Hmm." Jen brought the album closer. "I never thought of that." She flipped to the Christmas photo. "Then this means you were standing by yourself at five months old? I always knew you were precocious, but . . ."

"It doesn't make sense," said Shay, examining the photos. The ripples within her swelled to a tsunami. "My birthday is in July, but clearly in this first picture of you with me, I'm about . . . what?"

"Based on my own kids, I'd say . . . um, about two months old?" Jen closed the album with a thud. "But I remember that day so clearly. Maybe my mind's playing tricks on me, and I'm confusing it with another life-altering event brought on by the hands of Aunt Elsie. I was only two," she said, sheepishly glancing sideways at Shay.

"But then why aren't there any pictures of Mom and Dad with me in the hospital like there are of you?"

Jen chuckled. "I can tell you by experience that second babies, and any after, never get the same doting attention that the firstborn receives. Everyone is too busy, because when you were born, I was a toddler and keeping them busy on my own. It's just something that happens. It's not personal. My friend Amy has four kids and hardly has any pictures of her middle two and even less of her fourth. She feels guilty about it, but it's just something that happens when you're busy with so many other responsibilities that come with raising a busy family."

Shay reached over and slipped the album from her sister's lap and turned to the Christmas picture. "I get that, but could either of your children stand by themselves at five months old?"

Jen paled and shook her head. "Maddie was close, though. Even though it was only for a few seconds when she was seven months old she could, and she was sort of walking around furniture by nine months, but at five months?" Jen fleetingly cast her gaze down at the photo and then back at Shay and whispered, "Most babies are just starting to sit by themselves."

Shay pursed her lips and flicked through the rest of the album, but when she got to the last page, she hesitated. It was a picture of Mom, Dad, a four-year-old Jen, and most likely two-year-old Shay, standing on the bow of a boat watching what appeared to be an orca off the starboard side of the boat. The profiles of the four of them sent her internal tsunami crashing into the shoreline.

Her mind reeled as she recalled Pierre and Caden's profiles. Just as Maddie was the spitting image of her mother, Jen was a younger version of their mother. She studied her father's profile and saw the same squared Scandinavian jawline and noticeable family resemblance to Jen's, something she didn't see when she compared her heart-shaped profile to theirs.

The album's images haunted Shay as Jen drove her home to Crystal Beach Cottages. The evening must have stirred up something in Jen too, since neither of them uttered a word until Shay unloaded her bike from the back of the Explorer.

"I'll drop by the tea shop tomorrow and give you a hand with some decorating ideas if you like," said Jen tentatively. Her face glowed from the reflection of the moonlight, a perfect resemblance to their mother's.

Shay bit back unexpected tears and smiled. "Sure, that would be great. Thanks again for dinner. See you tomorrow." She trekked down the stairs to the wooden sidewalk below. When she got to the bottom, she glanced back up just as the Explorer's taillights disappeared out of sight. An overwhelming sense of sadness engulfed her. She wasn't certain where the feeling came from, but she knew she had to find out the truth no matter what. Too many things weren't adding up. She paused at the bottom of Pearl Hammond's garden gate when a movement on the front porch caught her eye.

"Spirit?"

He trotted down the stairs, barked, raced back up, stood on his hind legs, and pawed at the doorbell.

The front porch light flicked on, bathing the porch in luminescent light, starkly contrasting to the blackness surrounding Shay standing on the sidewalk. The door opened and a small silverhaired woman cautiously peered out. "Spirit, what in the world are you doing ringing my doorbell, silly dog," she muttered. "Have you finally decided to come in and have some dinner?" She stood back, holding the door open.

Spirit barked again, paced back to the top of the stairs, yipped, and then returned to the open door.

Pearl shielded her eyes with her hand and squinted into the blackness. "Is someone there?"

Shay stepped into the light cast by the porch light. "Hi, Miss Hammond, it's me, Shayleigh Myers."

The woman's hand went to her throat, and she let out a soft gasp.

"I'm sorry about Spirit. I really don't know what's gotten into him tonight."

Pearl glanced at Spirit, and the open door wobbled under her hand. "I should have known," she said, locking her gaze on Shay. "He's been here all evening as though he were waiting for something." She sucked in a deep breath. "I guess this was it. Come in, please." She pushed the door open and stepped back as Spirit brushed past her.

When Shay entered, she could see the woman

was shaken by her appearance. Not that she could blame her, though. It was getting late, and it was clear by the dressing gown she wore that Pearl was ready to retire for the night.

"I really do apologize for the intrusion. I have no idea why he's so insistent that we come in." Shay scanned the small living room for her furry friend, who had seemed to do what he did best and disappeared. "Where is he now?"

A yip came from the back of the cottage, and Shay locked her confused gaze on Pearl's. "I really don't know what he's doing."

"It's okay. I think I know, and I knew when I heard you were back in town that this time would come, even though I was trying to avoid it. I think he's making sure I follow through on a promise I made . . ." Her voice wavered as her body did. "Wait here, I'll be right back." Her open-backed slippers softly smacked her feet with each step as she trudged down the short hallway to what Shay suspected was the bedroom.

Shay blew out a breath. Pearl's living room was similar to hers except much smaller and didn't have the reading alcove at the back. The fireplace was also stone, but instead of a wood-burning hearth, it had a cast-iron stove inserted in the wide opening. The furnishings were comfortable, but it didn't give her the homey feeling Bridget had created in her cottage. No, it reflected its owner. When Shay was a child, all the kids had called Pearl "the Grinch That Sold Ice Cream." Like her tasty treats, she was cold, and Shay had the feeling not much had changed.

"Here." Pearl thrust out an ornate wooden chest about the size of a breadbox into Shay's hands.

"For me?"

"Yes, Bridget told me one day you would come for it."

Spirit let out a mournful howl as he sat at Pearl's feet.

Shay took the box from the woman's trembling hands and staggered under its weight. "When did she give this to you?"

"The day before she disappeared."

The day before she disappeared? That matched what Mike had said about Bridget's bike and probably was when she sent the amulet to the lawyer. Tassi had mentioned seeing her wearing it before she disappeared. The chest clutched in her hands grew heavier. This too had eventually made its way to her. That meant Bridget *must* have seen her own fate, or . . . she had planned it.

"Since you and Bridget were close friends, can you tell me something?" At the woman's nod, she continued. "Was she . . . was she sick?"

Pearl's eyes widened, and she let out a chesty laugh. "Not one day in the thirty years I knew her did that woman suffer from any of the ailments that living and aging bring. She was as fit as a fiddle, that one was." Pearl quirked a brow. "But it's clear you have a lot to learn about her, so maybe what's in there will help."

"Can you give me a hint as to what's inside?"

Pearl shrugged. "She never told me exactly."

"That's it?" The lid was carved with Celtic symbols. Shay placed her finger over the small antique key latch on the front. "Do you have the key for it?"

"She said you would have it."

"Me?" Then Shay remembered the small antique key on the ring Julia gave her. "Yes, at least, I think I do."

"Good, now that I've fulfilled my promise to my dearest friend, maybe I can get some sleep again."

Shay looked curiously at her.

"Ever since the day she gave it to me, it's been sitting on my dresser, haunting me. That had been my last conversation with her before she disappeared, and I knew then something was wrong, but she wouldn't say."

"That must be a raw memory for you since the two of you were so close."

"You have no idea." Pearl dropped her gaze and kneaded her time-worn, blue-veined hands together. "I knew if I gave it to you, then you would come back with questions, and she made me promise to tell you everything I knew, and that is a conversation I have been dreading."

"So, my hunch was right, you have been avoiding me."

"Yes, until Spirit seemingly made that impossible any longer," the petite woman snapped, and pushed past Shay to the door, flinging it open. "But it's late and past an old woman's bedtime. Take it and come back if you need to. We can talk more then."

Overcome with breathlessness at being so abruptly

ushered out with no answers but only more questions, Shay stared in disbelief at the closed door. Spirit barked. She glanced down at him. "Just great," she said, leaning over and threading her fingers through his soft fur. "Now what can of worms have you opened up for me, my friend?"

Chapter 18

With one hand balancing the wooden chest in the handlebar basket, Shay steered her bicycle with her other hand through the side gate of the white picket fence surrounding her cottage. She didn't dare take a breath until the bike, and its cargo, were tucked safely inside the storage shed beside her back stairs. With shaking hands, she removed the chest Pearl had charged her with. Questions zinged through her mind as she struggled to balance it and fish her keys from her front jeans pocket.

White light illuminated the lane behind her cottage, and at the sound of crunching gravel, Spirit yipped, shot across her back garden, and leapt the fence in one surreal motion as a car pulled into Liam's parking spot in front of his cottage.

"Traitor," she grumbled. "You brought me to it, and now you can't even see me through it?" She cursed her four-legged friend, nudged the door open with her hip, and deposited the wooden box on the kitchen table. "Phew, what in the world is in that thing?" But the bigger question racing through her mind was, did she really want to know?

Small pearls of perspiration from her brow cooled her flushed cheeks, and she closed her eyes and slowly exhaled. Her hands rapidly opened and closed at the battle raging between her mind and her heart. Open it or stuff it away somewhere and forget she ever received it? If only the key ring Julia had given her didn't lie on the table beside it, seemingly taunting her.

Her head won out, and she filled the kettle with water to distract herself, but no matter how hard she tried to ignore its presence, the ornately carved box called out to her. She knew if she opened it, there would be no denying what she found inside. Was this her very own Pandora's box?

She toyed with the pouch's cord around her neck, not certain if this box coming into her life was fate or destiny, but she couldn't shake the sensation that an unseen hand had been guiding her every movement lately. It was eerily like the whispered message she'd received when holding the blue bottle. *Look beyond the amber veil.*

She turned away, placed the kettle on the stove top, and switched on the gas burner. "Can I do this?" she whispered and risked another peek at the box.

Decision made, Shay shored herself up and took a step toward the table.

The door beside her flew open. An involuntary shriek escaped her lips.

"What's wrong?" Liam demanded as he burst into the kitchen, Spirit on his heels.

"What's wrong?" Shay grabbed a chair back to support her wobbly knees. "You just scared the be-jesus out of me, storming through the door like a SWAT team!"

He halted, gave her a quick once-over, and then glanced around the kitchen. "But . . . but Spirit was doing his barking-pacing thing again, like he wanted me to follow him, and this is where he led. I assumed—"

She fanned her blazing face and tried to stuff her heart back in her chest from where it had landed in the pit of her stomach. "Well, obviously you assumed wrong, *again*!" Then she glared down at Spirit. "And you, *mister*, I think I've had about enough shocks for one night, don't you?" She scolded him with a wagging finger.

Spirit let out a groaning whine, lay down, and covered his eyes with a paw.

"That's right, you'd better hide." She puffed out a breath and spun toward Liam. "And you! Do you think I'm a damsel in distress who you always have to rescue?"

He shook his head, backing away until the door that had swung closed behind him blocked his escape. His Adam's apple quivered, and he whispered, "No."

She growled and stomped over to the counter, grabbed the antique teapot off the floating shelf above the stove, and banged it down with a thud. "Do you want some tea? I found a tin of chamo-mile in the pantry cupboard."

"I thought ye didn't like tea?" he murmured.

"I don't! I loathe it, but it seems it's my fate, so I've decided that I'd better learn to like it. Besides, I read in one of those books that chamomile is good for calming the nerves, and I *need* that right now."

"Tell me, *a chara*, what's got you so frazzled tonight? Surely, it can't be just my bursting in, thinking ye were in trouble?"

The Irish lilt to his voice calmed and soothed her. Her stiffened spine relaxed, and she replayed his words in her head—wait a second—she glared at him in disbelief. "Did you just call me a chair?"

Liam coughed out a strangled laugh. "No, it's pronounced uh-KHAR-uh, and it means *my friend* in Gaelic."

"Ah . . . okay." She dropped the tea strainer into the pot and poured the boiling water over it. "The instructions said to let it steep for about five minutes. Are you hungry? I think I have some cookies."

"No. I'm not. I just ate, but . . ." He spun her around until they were eye to eye, or in this case, more like his eyes to her forehead. "Ye didn't answer my question, though. What's got ye so on edge tonight?"

"It's a long story."

"I have all evening."

"No date with your fiancée?"

His brow crinkled. "My fiancée? And who do ye think that is?"

"That veterinarian . . . what's her name." Shay pulled away and took two cups down from the shelf.

"Zoey? She's not my fiancée. It sounds like someone's been spreading rumors."

"But Jen said you gave her a ring."

"Aye, I did, but you were there when I made it clear that it was a gift of friendship commemorating her achievement award."

"Yes, but . . ." Shay hadn't really listened to what he had to say after Jen made the disclosure about the ring Zoey had shown off at the café. She had been too busy trying to suck air back in her lungs when she thought *Mr. McHeart-Flutter* would only have those electric-blue eyes set on someone else for the rest of his life. Not that she cared or anything. She still had her ex to deal with, legally, of course, but still . . . "I guess I misunderstood." She cast her gaze to the floor, berating herself for her silly, schoolgirl-like overreaction.

"But, ye still didn't answer my question."

"Right . . . what's got me on edge." She balked, struggling to find the words that would explain to this virtual stranger what she'd been dealing with tonight.

He must have seen her trepidation because he gently took her hand in his and led her to the table. "Take a deep breath and start from the beginning," he said, taking the chair beside hers.

She wiped her cheek with the back of her trembling hand. After averting her gaze from the carved chest on the table, she told Liam about going to Jen's and sorting through their parents' trunk. She explained that since her parents' accident, she had avoided having anything to do with it, and for the first time, she shared with someone other than her sister the strange feeling that overcame her when she was in its presence. Shay caught herself. What was it about this man that made her let her guard down and tell him her deepest secrets?

She regrouped and told him how she'd always justified her apprehension about its contents, thinking it would confirm what she had always suspected but was never proved—that her parents were killed because of the research they were working on. Through all this, Liam sat quietly, intently listening. His facial expression never changed and not once did he interrupt with his opinion. A far cry from how Brad had listened to anything she had to say. Liam actually appeared to listen to her. He must have been a great police detective.

She drew in a shaky breath and explained how when she got there, Jen had gone through the trunk earlier, and informed her there was nothing inside it that pointed to their parents' deaths as being anything more than an accident, just as discovered in the inquest. But what was just as important, given Shay's recent turn of fortune, there was also nothing that linked her parents to Bridget Early or any hints as to why the woman might have bequeathed her estate to Shay.

She went on to tell him how all this forced her to put her fears aside and how she and Jen had spent the evening looking through a photo album that was in the trunk, one that neither of them had ever seen before. Except that it didn't take her long to notice something odd about all the photos.

For the first time through her monologue, Liam appeared confused. "What's that?" he asked.

"The pictures of when Jen and I were very young . . . there was something off, you know?" At his puzzled expression, she explained, "You see, most of my life, I always looked at my family and could never see the resemblance to any of them. Jen had the perfect hair, smooth and shiny, just the right volume to curl it any way she wished, a flawless complexion, and then there's me . . . little ol' Mottle Monster"—she tapped her cheeks and glanced down at her unmanageable thick red hair—"with hair the color of Raggedy Ann's."

Before he could pipe in with what would probably be consolatory comments out of pity, she babbled on. "It's just that lately I've been thinking a lot about family likenesses because of the strong resemblance that"—she caught herself—"that a father and son in town have to each other. The photos made me realize that I don't look like anyone else in my family. You know how most children look like their parents, and even though it might not be exact, there are the eyes or the turn of the nose or the jawline, something that says yes, you are your mother's son or daughter."

"Okay." He sat back and folded his arms across his chest. His gaze settled on her face.

"Well, anyway, Jen is the spitting image of my mother, but she has my father's Nordic square jaw, a lot like my Aunt Elsie's side of the family. Don't you see? They look like family but I don't look like anyone else in my family. I never felt like I belonged and always wondered what ancestral genetic mutation entered the gene pool when I was conceived."

"Oh no, *a chara*." He held her cold clammy hand in his warm one. "Instead of thinking you are the spawn of some ancestral mutation, believe in your heart that over a thousand years ago one of those Norse kings in your bloodline fell in love with a fair Irish maiden, and you're a descendant of their union. Remember, we all come from love no matter what we look like."

"Look at you going all William Butler Yeats on me," she said with a sniffled laugh.

"Aye, now he was one of the Irish greats. Of course, he has some stiff competition with the likes of James Joyce, Samuel Beckett, and Oscar Wilde rounding out the Irish writers' top ten list, but he didn't do too badly in his own right."

"Next you're going to tell me you've been so inspired by his work that you write poetry and novels in your free time at the pub?" she said with a teasing grin.

"You're insufferable." He dropped her hand and feigned rebuke. "Here I was trying to cheer ye up and off you go and mock my new career."

Her face fell.

"'Twas a joke, *a chara.*" A laugh rumbled in his chest as he rose to his feet. After fetching the teapot from the counter, he returned and filled their two cups. "I am very happy running the pub. Come by it naturally, as me gran says." He pointed to the box. "Was this a treasure ye found in this trunk of your parents'?"

"Um, no." She paused her sip from the teacup and set it down. "That was another weird occurrence from tonight."

"How so?" he asked, taking his seat and scooping sugar from the bowl on the table into his cup.

"Jen dropped me off, and I was wheeling my bike along the main sidewalk when I heard Spirit bark. He was on Pearl Hammond's porch and then he started doing—what did you call it? Ah, yeah, his barking-pacing thing and led me to her door. She thrust this into my hands and really only said Bridget Early made her promise to give it to me, so she has. Then she showed me out. I have no idea what's inside it, but the thought of opening it scares the heck out of me."

"So, it's Bridget's?"

"That's what she said, and she also said Bridget wanted me to have it when I arrived."

Liam stared at the box—for what to Shay felt like an eternity—pushed it closer to her, and rested his hand on the top. "Bridget was a very wise woman, and if there is something in there that ye need to have, then you should have it, like her amulet. She never did anything without purpose, and by opening it, you might find some answers to all those unanswered questions ye have."

Shay wasn't exactly certain if opening it would verify what she suspected already tonight. It could send her whole world reeling sideways or lead to more unanswered questions. She only knew that she'd had enough of those lately and didn't need any more.

Her fingers played over the leather tie around her neck. The pouch warmed her skin under her blouse. Hands shaking, she reached for the box and then dropped them on the table. "I can't. I don't know if I'm ready to know what's inside."

"I'm here if ye can't cope." He glanced down at

Spirit curled up by the door. "Besides, I don't think I'm the only one looking out for ye." Liam pushed the box in front of her. "You can do this. Bridget had faith in ye."

Shay took a deep breath and then another. Although her fingers itched to open the lid, she knew once she did, there would be no turning back.

Chapter 19

With each second the clock on the wall ticked off, the warmth from the amulet grew and beads of perspiration trickled down Shay's chest as her trembling hands struggled to fit the small key into the lock. When it finally clicked, she glanced at Liam.

He encouraged her with a nod. "You got this," he said softly.

She looked over at Spirit, who sat beside the table. His blue eyes sparkled with the reflection of the overhead kitchen light. He let out a short woof.

If she was right about what would be revealed, nothing in her world would ever be the same. Pins and needles electrified her fingers. But it was now or never, and she needed some answers. She squeezed her eyes closed and flipped up the lid, not daring to look at what lay inside.

"Ye can open your eyes, *a chara*, it is only a photo of a wee babe and a beautiful young woman."

She peeked out from under her thick lashes and tried to focus on the image. Her breath caught in her chest. Tears seeped down her hot cheeks, and she gently removed the photo from the box, mesmerized by the similarities she saw between herself now and the young woman cradling a newborn baby. It was the missing link between her birth and the first photos Jen had shown her.

"There are more photos. Here." Liam handed her a stack of Polaroids.

Shay patted her thudding chest and shuffled through the images of a beaming young woman bathing, playing with, and rocking the small baby in a wooden cradle, but she paused when she came to the last picture. The baby appeared to be around the same age as the one in the photo of her and Jen, but the woman was no longer smiling and happy. Her eyes glistened with tears, and her face reflected her internal agony.

"They looked so happy. I wonder what happened to change that?" She softly laid the photos on the table and wiped the tears from her eyes.

"There's more in here." He thumbed through the box contents. "It looks like some journals. Maybe they can tell ye." He removed six thick leather-bound notebooks and set them on the table.

Shay flipped back the cover of the top one and scanned the handwritten page. She pushed it aside and glanced through the next and then quickly the next. "These are all recipes for her tea potions, and the other is notations she made about her readings. There's a whole section in the last one on palmistry and another on crystal balls and the like. I guess Julia was wrong."

"What do ye mean?"

"She said what Bridget did was all hooey, and she faked it, but this tells us that she really was trained in herbology and natural healing practices and knew what she was doing, at least, with her teas and potions."

Liam picked up the top book and flipped it open.

"What's that?" Shay pointed to the corner of papers that slipped out between the last page and the back cover.

Liam took out the papers and unfolded them, scanned over the first page, and then handed it to her. "This looks like the adoption certificate and this one . . ." He quickly scanned the second paper. "Well, you'd better read it yourself. It looks personal." His face flushed as his shaking hand put it in hers.

Shay clasped the paper and began reading.

My darling daughter, Shayleigh:

I know you have many questions, and I've tried to collect as many of the answers as I can and secure them in this chest for your arrival, but my time is limited so forgive me if you still do not find all the answers you desperately need. Please feel free to seek out my good friend, Pearl Hammond. She will tell you everything she knows. Additionally, a man from your ancestral home in County Clare will be arriving in Bray Harbor. Do not fear him. He brings you a message of the utmost importance to your fu-

ture happiness, and please heed his warnings for there are those who desperately seek to possess what you hold most dear to your heart.

Love you forever and beyond, your Mam

Hot tears pooled in Shay's eyes. "Phew . . . I . . . I don't know what to say. This means that—I don't know what it means." Her tears turned to sobs, and Spirit let out a mournful howl.

"First off"—Liam cradled her trembling hand in his—"it means that Grady Kennedy was most likely the man who was supposed to bring you the message."

"Yes," she said, between biting sobs, "and now he's dead. So, I won't ever know what he was supposed to tell me. It also means there is no question about it. Bridget Early was my mother, but"—she flipped through the photos—"who was my father? Or was my father really my father and had an affair with her? Is that why my mother—my other mother—and my father adopted me?" She thumped her fists on the table and jumped to her feet. "I don't think any of this helps." She slid to the floor in a crumpled heap, her sobs wracking her body.

"Ah, *a chara.*" Liam scooped her into his arms. "Ye've had a bad shock," he softly whispered as he picked her up and carried her into the living room and laid her on the sofa. "Ye rest now. In the morning all will become clearer." He covered her with a throw from the back of the sofa.

*   *   *

The light flooding the room stung Shay's eyes, and she groaned, flipped onto her side, and pulled the cover over her head. Then she sat straight up. Liam, his long legs stretched out in front of him, reclined in the chair in front of the fireplace and quietly snored. Spirit was curled up in his bed at Liam's feet. The dog's ears twitched, and he cast his gaze to hers, groaned, and closed his eyes.

Liam stirred, opening one eye at a time. "Good morning," he said, yawning and stretching his long arms out over his head while righting himself in the chair. "I trust ye slept well?"

"Did you sleep there all night?"

He pressed his hands into the arch of his back. "I did that, and I must say, did you know ye snore?"

"I do not." She huffed, tossed off the blanket, and sat on the edge of the sofa, trying to focus her foggy morning brain on her surroundings.

"Okay." He laughed, folded his blanket, and set it on the chair. "If ye say so."

"I wonder what time it is. It seems awfully bright out there." She squinted out the window.

He glanced at his wristwatch. "It's almost half past nine."

"Oh no! That means Tassi's sitting out in front of the tea shop waiting for me, and Jen said she'd drop by this morning," Shay cried, and dashed down the hall to her bedroom.

She rifled through her dresser drawer, plucked out a T-shirt, ran a brush through her unruly hair, secured it in a high topknot, splashed cold water over her face, did a quick once-over with the tooth-brush, and raced back into the living room. "Can you drive me to CuriosiTEAS? It'll take too long on the bike, and I don't think I can waste any more time getting there."

"Well, aren't ye a little whirlwind this morning?"

"What?"

"Never mind. Yes, we can put the bike in the back. Just let me use the facilities first. That is if ye think we can spare the minute I'll need?" An impish glint twinkled in his eyes.

"Um . . . yes, sorry. I'm just a stickler for punctuality, that's all. While you go . . . in there"—she gestured down the hall—"I'll call Tassi and tell her I overslept and will be there shortly."

"Good plan." He grinned and made his way to the bathroom.

"Tassi, I told Bill Fry I'd drop by sometime today and look at the tables and chairs he has." Shay glanced at the time on her phone. "And since you're due for a *very* late lunch break, maybe it's a good time for me to go see him."

"Bill Fry? Is he the guy that runs the second-hand furniture place up on Fifth? Wooden Relics, right?"

"Yes, but it's more of a furniture restoration shop. He's a carpenter by trade, and an old friend of my father's—" That word caught in Shay's throat like a wad of cotton. "And he takes something old and makes it look new again or repurposes it into something different."

"Does he have . . . what do you think? Five or six tables and"—Tassi ticked her fingers in calculation—"at least twenty-four to thirty chairs that would match?"

"That's the best part. He bought all the tables and chairs that were in Molly's Tavern and has sanded them all down, repaired them, and will paint them any color I'd like."

"Score!"

"That's what I thought. So, I was thinking maybe a darker shade than the new pear-green curtains. With cream-colored tablecloths matching the walls, this room will look sharp. What do you think?"

"What color did you say the roll-up blinds are going to be?"

"I ordered them in cream to match the walls. Are you thinking that's too much cream color? If we break it up with lots of leafy dark green plants around the room, it might work."

"No, I think it will all go great together. At least it'll be better than the grungy whitewashed walls and sun-yellowed lacy curtain thingies Bridget had up for years."

"Yeah, that's what I thought." Shay gazed around the double-bay-window storefront, a soft smile on her lips. "Yes, I think it'll make it look quaint and cozy while still being fresh and contemporary enough to draw in some new customers."

"I think it will too." Tassi pushed the floor mop and bucket into the back room that temporarily served as the storeroom for leftover knickknacks and shelving units. "When I'm out do you want me to pick something up for your lunch and bring it back with me?" she called back. When she returned, she was scrolling through her phone. "It's

Aunt Jo. She says if I haven't eaten yet to come by and have a late lunch with her."

"Maybe she's finally ready to hear your side of the disagreement with Mr. Fancy-Pants?"

"Pfft, that would be the day. No, it's more like she has a list of chores she wants me to do when I get home."

"Sheesh. Think positively, please. She just might surprise you." Shay grabbed her bag and locked the door. "Here's the key in case you're back before I am." She slipped it off the ring. "If not, I'll just sit out front in the sun until you're finished, so don't panic about time."

"Thanks," said Tassi, shoving it into her front jeans pocket.

"Now, promise me that you'll hear your aunt out and *try* to enjoy your lunch, okay?"

Tassi weakly nodded and, head down, moseyed across the street, looking more like she was going to a funeral than to lunch.

Hopefully Tassi's nod of agreement didn't signal that she only intended to humor Shay instead of actually going through with her promise. Jo had hurt Tassi's feelings, and Shay suspected since Jo was the closest thing the girl had to a mother figure, the hurt probably sliced deep.

Shay had the same foreboding about Jen, her current mother figure, and what might happen the next time they met. This life-changing burden that Shay carried with her since last night haunted her thoughts as she pedaled the block up the hill to meet with Bill Fry to discuss something as insignificant to the larger picture as tables and chairs.

However, during her half hour with Bill, Shay

learned an important lesson. Don't discount the small things. They may not be earth-shattering or life-changing, but they make the bigger events much easier to manage simply with the joy they bring into a chaotic life.

She breathed deeply as she stepped back outside the front door of Wooden Relics—Furniture Restorations with one more item checked off her growing to-do list. It was a small victory for the day, but one she would gladly accept. Now if everything else in her life was so easily resolved as ordering tables and chairs and selecting a paint color, the day would be near perfect. What still gnawed in her gut though was a different matter. How would she ever find the words to tell Jen that everything they thought about their lives was a lie?

Shay pushed the thought away. It was something best left locked up in a box in the corner of her mind to deal with later. She closed her eyes, tilted her face to the sun, and drew in a deep breath of briny sea air to clear her head. A cooling shade cast over her, and she opened her eyes. "Liam?"

"Sorry to startle ye, but it is important. I saw Tassi at Jo's, and she told me where ye were headed."

"You look flushed."

"I jogged up here."

"Why? What's so urgent?"

"I was at the police station and—"

"Were you taken into custody again?"

"No, Burrows is out on a call up the coast, and Dean is re-interviewing some of the witnesses today and can't get away, but there's something he thought you should know as soon as possible."

"Have they found something out about Grady?"

"No, nothing like that," he said, running his hand through his thick black hair. "He wanted you to know right away because something happened, and there's going to be some fallout, and he wanted you to be prepared."

"You're scaring me."

"It's just that it involves something that happened in New Mexico."

"Yeah, a lot happened, but the investigation and final forensic audit of the business is in the hands of my lawyers now. They're looking for evidence to prove Brad was the guilty partner, not me."

"It seems Brad has now implicated you in something else."

"Like what?"

"Like breaking into your old shop and stealing some pretty pricey gemstones."

Chapter 20

Shay staggered back a step and grabbed the window frame of the furniture shop to help steady her crumpling knees.

"It seems Dean got a call from the Santa Fe police department wanting him to check into your whereabouts last night."

"Last night?" She stared at him. "I was with you, and we were going through Bridget's chest and . . . Oh no, you didn't tell Dean why you were at my cottage and what we found, did you?"

"No, of course not. I didn't even mention I was there, but you're going to have to tell him and Jen soon. Because, well . . . I'm your alibi since I did spend the night with ye."

"Yeah, in my chair!"

"That's the thing. Given my reputation in town, it might reflect badly on you if the word got around that I stayed the night. You know, us just having met and all that. What would ye sister think if she didn't know *why* I stayed?"

"Oh," Shay said. "I never thought about that. Which means, in order for you to be my alibi, I'll have to admit to being a mental basket-case, and that you needed to be my guardian and protector, right?"

"No. You were in shock, and after what ye discovered that's understandable, but ye do have to tell Dean and Jen why I was there, and soon."

"I will, but maybe I don't have to right away. I'm pretty sure between Jen confirming I was at their place for dinner and throughout the early evening, and then Pearl Hammond being able to verify I was at her cottage later, we can keep your name out of it." She grabbed her bike from where it leaned against the shop wall.

"That's the thing. They've narrowed down the time of the burglary to between three and five a.m., which they said would have given ye plenty of time to fly there, commit the robbery, and get back this morning. Remember, you were late meeting Tassi, and she might mention that if they question her. It sounds like Brad is trying to build a pretty good case for them to look at you."

Shay hesitated as she mounted her bicycle and glanced back at him. "Of course, he has. He knows the forensic audit my lawyer and the courts are now conducting will show him to be the slime ball I always said he was."

She climbed on the bike, retrieved the helmet from the basket, and tugged the chin strap tight. "I'd say they'd better look a little closer to home and look at Brad. He was going to lose everything if they found he did commit the fraud and blamed me for it. He thought after he framed me for his crimes, the shop and inventory would be all his. Now he's probably worried it might not go his way after all and committed the gem theft last night as an insurance policy." She pushed down on the pedal and bounced off the curb onto the road.

Fueled by rage of yet another dark shadow over her head, it only took her moments to fly down the slight hill of First Street toward the harbor, skid around the corner, and come to a screeching stop in front of Crystals & CuriosiTEAS. Liam sat, panting, on one of the storefront benches.

He wiped beads of perspiration from his forehead with the back of his hand and met her stunned gaze. "Trained police officer," he gasped, "took short cuts."

Still eyeing his unexpected appearance in front of the tea shop with disbelief, she slipped off the helmet, tossed it in the basket, and took a seat on the bench beside him. "Here's a riddle for you, *Detective*. The gem store has a state-of-the-art security system, and when everything went sideways, any access to the codes that I had previously were frozen. I couldn't get inside that shop now for anything. When my lawyers mounted the investigation into Brad and got a court order to seize the property and contents, he lost all access to it too. So, explain to me how in the world did someone break into a court-seized property with a state-of-the-art security system?"

He shrugged. "But it's clear someone did."

"Well, it wasn't me, and you know it."

"I know it wasn't and never said I suspected any

different. I only said you were going to have to tell Dean why I was at your cottage last night and spent the night. Then they won't continue to investigate your involvement any further."

"You're right. I do have to tell Dean and . . . Jen what I found out. The thing is, I'm—"

"Scared?"

"Terrified. Because once I do, there will never be any going back to the way things were. All of our lives will be changed forever." She rose to her feet and spied Tassi through the tea shop's window. "When I can come to terms with all this and can wrap my head around it all, I know one person who will be thrilled to hear I'm Bridget Early's . . . *daughter*." She puffed out a hesitant breath as the word stuck like a piece of fluff to the roof of her mouth.

"Who's that—Tassi?"

"Yes, she adored the woman and keeps pushing me to be like her. When I work up the courage to tell her, there'll be no letting it go after that."

"She might already have figured it out or at least has a hunch."

"Do you think?"

"She's smart." Liam shrugged. "My guess is yes. She's been putting the pieces together and that's why she's so set on you learning Bridget's ways."

"Phew." Shay blew out a breath. "That's all I need is for her to say something to Jen before I tell her everything I know. Okay, I'll go see Jen and Dean this evening, and we can get this all straightened out."

He gave her hands a light squeeze. "Okay, but

don't leave it too late, or you'll have the FBI at your door before you can explain it all."

"Great, how much *better* can things get?"

"I do have some good news though." His blue eyes sparkled mischievously as they held her gaze.

"Good news? I wish you would have led off with that."

"Maybe not *good* news, but it's interesting, nonetheless. While I was at the station, I also discovered that apparently Burrows was in the pub Friday night."

"What?"

"Yes, it was his wife's birthday, and they and some friends had been over at the hotel for dinner, indulged in a few cocktails. When they left, his wife was so taken by the laughter and music coming out of the pub, she convinced them to stop in for a drink."

"You're kidding? After all his efforts to shut you down, he had the nerve to go in?"

"Yeah, and according to Kenny, the bartender on shift, their group got quite rowdy, but as Burrows was part of the posse, he was afraid to ask them to leave. He suggested they take their celebrating upstairs to the patio."

"Where Grady was?"

He nodded. "Yes, and it gets better. It seems that later most of Burrows's party came downstairs, including his wife, and joined in the dancing."

"Burrows didn't though?"

"No."

"Was anyone else upstairs that he might have hung back to visit with?"

He shook his head. "Everyone else wanted to dance. Penny, the server for the patio, said it looked like when they got there, all Burrows wanted to do was drink. When they came down, she went up to see if he wanted another one and found Burrows sitting alone at their table. The only other person up there was the guy who had been there all evening drinking coffee alone at the corner table by the ladder. She said she'd tried to encourage him a few times to join the fun downstairs, but the guy didn't seem to be very sociable. She thought maybe he was waiting for someone."

"You mean Grady, not Burrows, right?"

He nodded. "Then, she said, eventually Burrows came downstairs and danced—as best as he could in his state—with his wife. Then they all left. Penny recalls it was just before closing because she had to call a taxi for them because none of them were in a condition to drive. She then went upstairs, remembering that the coffee-drinking man was still up there, and she thought she'd better let him know they were closing, but he'd already gone. So, she cleaned up the patio, ushered all the lingerers out, closed up, and left with the rest of the staff."

"And what did Burrows have to say about his time alone with the man upstairs when he questioned Penny right after we found the body and she told him what she saw?"

"That's the thing. He never questioned her, Kenny, or any of the other staff on shift that night."

"What? That sure doesn't sound like police procedure, does it?"

"No, it's not. The only person he questioned was Carmen."

"But she wasn't even working Friday night."

"I know, and when she told him that, he left and never called in anyone else."

"Something seems fishy about that, doesn't it?"

"It sure does, and I'm going to get to the bottom of it because now I'm thinking . . ."

"What?"

"That Burrows was angry with his wife and friends because they wanted to party and dance, and he was already three sheets to the wind and didn't want anything to interrupt his drinking. I think when they all went downstairs, he was in one of his foul moods. The other guy, who we're assuming was Grady, might have said something to him. Burrows took offense in his drunken state and . . . well . . . we have a body."

"You don't think Burrows knew Grady?"

"It's hard to say without a background check on the sheriff, but I'm leaning toward the fact that Burrows has a vile temperament at the best of times, which sounds like it gets worse with the drink, so maybe—"

"Grady was just in the wrong place at the wrong time," Shay said thoughtfully. "That means we don't even have to tell Dean about Grady being here to see me. They've been working on the assumption he was here to meet someone or working for someone in Bray Harbor, and that's what led to his murder. But if Burrows killed him in a drunken rage that makes his murder one of opportunity, then—"

"No, Dean still needs to know everything."

"That means I have to tell Jen the truth too." Her bottom lip quivered with her words, and she whispered, "It's going to tear my family apart."

Liam raised her downcast chin with his finger and fixed his gaze on hers. "But family isn't always what ye were born into. Sometimes it's where ye end up. All that matters is ye were wanted, and loved, and surely you can see that you were, and that's what's important and makes a family. Knowing her, you're not going to lose your sister. She'll be by your side through this and for the rest of your life because she truly loves you."

"I hope you're right." Shay swiped at the hot tears spilling down her cheeks.

"But that's not the most interesting news I found out."

"There's more?" She sniffled.

"Aye. Witnesses said Burrows was wearing a navy-blue blazer and—"

"A light blue shirt?"

He nodded. "And when he came downstairs later in the evening, the jacket was flung over his shoulder and his shirtsleeves were rolled up."

"Like he was trying to hide a missing button maybe?"

Liam shrugged but the twinkle in his eye told Shay that's what he suspected too. "But the problem is that when Dean mentioned something about the shirt and tried to make light of Burrows dressing so fancy for a night in the pub, you know, not to arouse any suspicion in Burrows's mind,

Burrows reminded him they had been to the hotel earlier for dinner and the pub was a last-minute decision."

"But Dean's going to get a warrant for it, right?"

"Nooo, not just yet. Given the dynamics of the situation, something like that could be a career-ending move for him. So until he gets more evidence"—Liam raised his shoulders in a helpless shrug—"he's going to have to investigate on the down-low."

"How's he going to do that?"

"It seems Dean overheard Burrows talking on the phone to his wife and asked her if she had picked up the dry cleaning yet, and wanted to know if they got the stains out of his dress shirt."

"Really," Shay said thoughtfully.

"Yeah, so Dean's going to stop in at the four dry cleaners in town to find out if any of them cleaned the shirt and if perhaps it had a missing button."

"And if one of them did—"

"Then Burrows can be nailed with no threat to Dean's career."

He placed his hands supportively on her shoulders. "But before we get too excited about all this, I suggest you go and talk to Pearl. Find out the whole story about your adoption and anything she can tell you about Bridget because you know Jen will have questions later, and you'll be able to answer them better. What do you say?"

She nodded. "Then I can tell her and Dean about the letter and why you were at my cottage all night."

"Exactly, and then you have an alibi that Dean

can confirm for the break-in at your gem store, taking you off the suspect list."

"What about the whole Burrows thing?"

"Hopefully, it will lead to a *real* police investigation, and they'll figure out exactly what went down."

"Which might lead them to Grady being here to see me?"

"Yes, but maybe they can find out what it was he was supposed to tell you, especially since Bridget's letter hinted that you might be in danger too."

"Yeah, it did, didn't it?" There was something about the combination of his words and the tone of his voice that squeezed at her heart, sending it into a hammering rhythm in her chest wall. "It appears I have a lot to discuss with Dean and Jen tonight, don't I?"

Chapter 21

"Tassi, where are you?" Shay scanned the shop from the doorway.

"Back here!"

Shay headed toward the voice coming from the back room just as a breathless Tassi scampered into view.

"I was just cleaning and organizing all the stuff you still want to sell." Tassi grinned, and dropped a rag on the sales counter. "Auntie told me today that the High Street and Fifth Avenue merchants are planning a huge end-of-summer sidewalk sale in a couple of weeks. Both streets will be blocked to traffic, and there's going to be food, and games, and music too." Her eyes lit up. "It will be the perfect time to get rid of some of these things that Madam Malvina didn't want."

"Yes, yes, it would be." Shay peered into the

back room. A side table covered with knickknacks displayed just how many items she still needed to purge. "Actually, it will be perfect, won't it? Plus," she said, turning to Tassi, "by then the tea room should be finished, and we can start showing it off and hopefully building a customer base."

"I also set up a bookcase back there and arranged all the books you'll need to learn Bridget's trade, so they'll be easier for you to find." A hopeful lilt brightened her voice.

"Thank you, and I found a few more at the cottage." An image of the wooden chest and the leather journals flashed in her mind. "But you do realize that it's going to take time for me to learn it all, right?"

"Yeah, yeah, I know, but I can help you with that. I was here a lot with Bridget and learned a bit from her myself."

"I know." Shay smiled. "You're a valuable resource, and I'm so glad you're here."

Tassi's face lit up in a grin that had nothing to do with the sunlight streaming through the windows. It came from the girl's heart as she beamed back at Shay from across the room.

"I don't want to take advantage of you so that you regret working here, so I have decided that since I have a few errands to run"—she took a quick glance over her shoulder out the front window and then looked back at Tassi—"why don't you take the rest of the afternoon off and go enjoy yourself. Take Spirit for a run or something, whatever. The rest of the day is yours. Paid, of course." Even though she had turned her back on the glaring yellow police tape, she could feel its presence. "Besides, it appears we're in no rush to open."

"Wow! Thank you, but I haven't seen Spirit since this morning. I thought maybe he went off with you to the furniture store?"

"No, I haven't seen him all day either." Shay shrugged. "I guess he's a free spirit. Your aunt told me my first day that he comes and goes as he pleases."

"Yup, he always has. I just thought he was attached to you like he was with Bridget and would always be within earshot." Tassi looked out the front glass door, giggled, and pointed. "Like I said, always within earshot."

Shay laughed and opened the door. "Did you hear your name? Well, don't just stand there, come in."

Spirit sat back on his haunches and barked.

"What?" She glanced up and down the street.

He trod over to her bike and pawed at the tire.

"What, you want *me* to take you for a run?"

Woof.

"What if Tassi takes you to the beach?"

He lay down and let out a soft groan.

Tassi poked her head out the door. "What? I thought you loved our run on the beach the other day."

He leapt to his feet, stood erect on his hind legs, tugged Shay's helmet out of the basket, and dropped it at her feet.

She rolled her eyes. "I guess now I have a dog that thinks he's the boss of me, and it appears I'm the one taking him for a run today." Spirit let out a short yip. "Okay, mister, you win, but first I have a few stops to make."

Spirit yipped again, lay down, and set his gaze on her.

Tassi's bottom lip puckered in a pout. "Should I be hurt that he doesn't want me to take him?"

"Not in the least," said Shay. "He loves spending time with you, don't you, boy?"

He rose to his feet, wagged his tail, let out another sharp yip, and set his blue eyes on Tassi.

"See? If dogs can smile, I'm pretty sure he is. I think it's just that he senses where one of my errands is, and if I'm right, he's attracted to the treats she always seems to have for him. So, you go have some fun with your friends this afternoon and enjoy the rest of your afternoon."

Tassi's eyes darkened, as did her previous glow.

"What's wrong?"

She shrugged. "Like I said before, Bridget was my only friend in town."

"You didn't make any friends at school before the summer break?"

She shook her head.

Shay's chest tightened. "Hmm, what about your cousin Caden? He works evenings. Maybe you can hang out with him this afternoon?"

"Nah." Tassi waved her off. "He has his own friends, and they all think I'm a weirdo."

"Well, they're wrong, and I hope you know that."

"Yeah, I think *they're* the weirdos. I can't stand how childish and silly they are. They're into the stupidest things. So, if you don't mind, I'll just stay and finish up in the back room, instead."

How could she say no? Spirit had already rejected the poor girl, and if she insisted, Tassi might take that as another slight. Shay recalled too well the emotional drama and oversensitivity the teen years had held for her, and she smiled approvingly.

She slipped the front door key off the ring and handed it to Tassi with strict instructions not to lose it or forget it in the morning, or they wouldn't be able to get back in. She really was going to have to pop out tomorrow and get a copy cut for Tassi. It only made sense since she'd be heading back to school soon and would only be able to come in after classes. Fingers crossed, Tassi would be the one closing at eight when the other shops on the street closed. At least, that's what Shay hoped. It would be nice to put in a regular eight-hour day and have someone else pick up a few hours in the evening, allowing her some down time to enjoy her beachside cottage.

Her fingers fondled the leather pouch hanging around her neck, and a soft smile crossed her lips as the eager girl snagged her cleaning rag and headed back into the storage room. Boy, she was going to miss having Tassi around full-time. It was funny to her how everything had worked out. It was equally hard for her not to wonder if this was all Bridget's doing.

Shay pushed the front door open, expecting to see Spirit doing his dancing-pacing thing as he wasn't the most patient when he had his mind set on something. Instead, he was sitting sentry-like at the curbside, staring across the street. Shay ruffled the soft fur behind his ear.

"What is it, boy, what do you see over there?"

She scanned Jo's patio, and a low growl emanated from Spirit when her gaze settled on Julia and Karl seated at a table. "Oh, I see. You really don't like her, do you?" His growl grew louder when Pierre came out of the café, carrying a small tray with three cups, and took a seat at their table.

"I wonder what's up with that? We can only hope, for Caden and Gary's sake, that Julia found him another property far, far away from here." She patted Spirit's head. "Should we be off? I still have to get to Jen's sometime this evening or . . ." she added, muttering, "or do all my explaining about what I discovered, from a jail cell."

She slipped her helmet on, clipped the chin strap, and pushed down hard on the pedal, launching the bike down the street. Spirit led their way up High Street, setting a brisk pace as she swerved around open car doors and wove in and out of traffic to keep up. Not once did he slow his stride, and it was clear that her canine friend was on a mission of his own. In no time, she was at her cottage, collected the photos and letter from the trunk, tucked them securely in her bag, and with Spirit leading the way once again, headed back toward Swirls Ice Cream Shop.

She inwardly cringed at the take-out window line. Pearl wouldn't be able to talk to her now. They were far too busy. When Spirit came to a panting halt and yipped outside the Staff Only entrance, she powered on. Clearly, he knew best. She needed some answers before she spoke with Jen and Dean, and only Pearl could give them to her because it seemed—she shuddered—everyone else who knew Bridget's secrets was, well . . . dead.

After taking a deep breath, she knocked, then knocked again and again. The door swung open and a ginger-haired, freckle-faced boy around Tassi's age stared questioningly at her.

"You got a late delivery?"

"No, I was hoping to speak to Pearl Hammond, if she's not too busy."

"She's not hiring now. The season's over soon." He started to close the door.

Shay thrust her hand against it to keep it from closing. "No, I'm not here about a job. It's . . . it's personal."

He grunted and called out, "Pearl, there's someone here who wants to talk to you." He disappeared, leaving the door open a crack.

Pearl flung the door open, but when she saw Shay, she glowered. "Look, I know I said I'd talk to you, but that didn't mean during the day when I'm working. Come by my cottage tonight," she said, starting to close the door.

Shay thrust her hand up again, not allowing the door to close in her face. "But it's important. I'm in trouble, and I need to ask you some things."

Pearl's eyes narrowed. "What kind of trouble?"

"It's a police matter, and I have to tell . . . well . . . I have to explain to someone very dear to me where I was last night and why, or—"

Her hand went to her throat and she gasped. "Bridget's vision."

"What vision?"

"Harold, Katy, Michelle, I'll be back in a few minutes. Oh, and give Spirit a small vanilla ice cone, he likes those," she called over her shoulder and stepped out, eyeing Shay. "We'd better go out on the beach. It's more private." She didn't wait for Shay to respond as she thumped down the steps, bustled across the rocky beach to the shore, and stood, staring off into the distance as the waves crashed around her shoed feet.

The sensation of a slow-burning fire spread through Shay. At any moment that fire was going to backdraft on her. What could this woman have to tell her now that was any less life-changing than what she had already learned? Her nerve endings sparked as she hustled behind Pearl to catch up.

Chapter 22

"What can you tell me about my adoption?" Shay wheezed as she finally caught up to Pearl. "Did Bridget have an affair with my father? Is that why they adopted me? Did my mother find out and agree, or didn't she know?" Shay's nerve endings blazed as she waited for what seemed like an eternity for Pearl to answer the questions, even though she wasn't certain she was prepared to hear what she would have to say.

However, Pearl let out a soft chuckle and turned toward her with a faint smile on her craggy face. Shay backed away slightly, taken off guard by this unexpected reaction.

"No, child, that was just lucky happenstance for all involved," she said. "Although to hear it from Bridget, you'd think it was fate or destiny that you should find two such lovely people to raise you and protect you when she couldn't. So, don't worry. The man you know as your father was not a philanderer but a good-hearted man who loved his wife dearly."

A tidal wave of relief surged through Shay. "Then tell me who my father was." She clasped Pearl's hands. "I need to know. Did he reject me and her, is that why she gave me up for adoption?"

Pearl glanced nervously up and down the beach and stepped in closer. She lowered her voice just enough to be heard above the waves breaking at their feet. "Bridget would never really say who he was. All she said was it happened on her sixteenth birthday. Your grandmother had given her that pouch"—she pointed to the leather strings around Shay's neck—"and told her it was time she learned of its magic."

The woman sucked in a deep breath and glanced over her shoulder. "Bridget said that she was thrilled with the gift. You see, it had been her great-grandmother's, later it was passed down to her grandmother, then her mother, and now it seemed it was hers. She scampered off into the woods to try to figure out what it did and what the secret behind it was. She'd only heard stories, so she wasn't sure what was real or—"

"Folklore?"

"Yes, that's it." Pearl dropped her gaze. "She said she was pretty giddy about it all. She was feeling all grown-up because her mother had passed the family torch, so to speak. But before she had time to inspect the blue bottle inside the pouch, she came across a handsome stranger." A wistful smile crossed Pearl's weathered face. "He turned her head. You know how fanciful a young girl can be. She was young and excited about her gift, and it was her birthday, and she was feeling like the Faerie Queen herself. He was a little older and very handsome and said all the right words to turn her pretty young head, and when he proclaimed his love for her, she couldn't resist him."

"She loved him then and there, a stranger?"

"Yes, she said he held a magical charm about him. She said it was as though he'd bewitched her, and she fell into his arms." Pearl's eyes darkened. "But after was when his true spirit came out. She said . . ." Pearl wrung her hands and sniffled. "After, his hands, which not long before held so much tenderness for her, squeezed her throat as he tried to remove the pouch from her neck. She fought him off, grabbed her clothes and ran back to her family cottage, where she found her mother severely injured. All her mother could manage to say was that a wicked fairy man came to take what was theirs and told Bridget to flee and go far away so he couldn't find her, ever."

"A fairy man?"

"Well, of course, I didn't believe a word of it. Far too fanciful for me, but I do remember that fantasies like that do go on in the heads of young girls, especially ones who live in a family where tales of fairies and potions and such are a part of it. I figured it was Bridget's way of saying she had a liaison, shall we say, with one of her father's farmhands, and when she discovered she was going to have a baby, she had to leave town. Her family was very set in the old ways, I gather, and wouldn't have put up with it."

"What happened to my grandmother after the man hurt her?"

"Bridget never spoke to her mother again, from what I gathered. I guess she was too afraid the man would track her down."

"Is that when she came to the States?"

"I suppose. She said she went to San Francisco, and because she was so young and inexperienced and only knew the trade her mother had taught her, she got a job working in a tea shop, reading palms."

"I recall my mother mentioning that when Jen was a baby, they went to live in the Bay Area for a year while my father did a short contract teaching at Berkeley when a colleague of his went on a sabbatical. Is that where they met?"

"That's right. You see, your mother was stuck in the apartment with a baby, and your dad was at the university all day. She got lonely and would wheel your sister around in her stroller, exploring San Francisco. One day, she dropped into the tea shop, and Bridget did a reading for her. I guess your mother was so taken with the accuracy of what Bridget told her, she became a regular customer. When your mother discovered Bridget's secret, that you were on the way, and that she was so young and all alone in the city, your mom became a mother-figure to Bridget and a close bond was formed between the two of them."

"So Bridget just gave me to her?"

"No, it wasn't that simple. Bridget also told me once that your mother confided in her that her delivery of your sister was very difficult, and there were complications making it impossible for her to ever have any more children. Your mother envied Bridget that she was going to have a baby and vowed to help her any way she could."

"I didn't know Jen's delivery was hard. Mom never talked about either of our births."

"Now you know why," Pearl said, pinning Shay with a kindly look. "Your mother was a good woman, and even though she helped Bridget with what she could, after you came along, Bridget found it difficult to work and make enough money just reading tea leaves to pay for a babysitter—there was still rent to pay and food to buy and Bridget became more and more despondent about her situation."

An image of the last few Polaroids reflecting the sadness in the young mother's eyes formed in Shay's mind.

"But everything changed for all of them the day a man came into the tea shop when Bridget was in the back room getting ready to start her shift. She heard a familiar voice asking about her and when she peeked through the curtains separating the back room from the shop, she saw him. The man from the woodland in Ireland, the same man she had . . ." Pearl wrung her hands so tight her fingers whitened. "Well, you know, and here he was in San Francisco and clearly still after the secret to the Early magic. Bridget ran, and never went back to the tea shop again."

"So, the man who was my father—" The word caught in Shay's throat. "He had followed her?"

Pearl nodded. "So it seems, and Bridget was convinced, given her destitute situation and the man showing up when he did, that it was fate taking over your lives. She begged your mother to take you, and to protect you at all costs because she couldn't anymore, and, well . . . that's it. Your parents adopted you, and here we are today."

Shay thought about the times she'd encountered Bridget when she was young, and the odd things she'd said to her. "Were my parents okay with Bridget following them here? You'd think they'd be afraid she would change her mind and decide she wanted me back. I mean she was only what, sixteen or seventeen when she gave me up."

"Oh, she wanted you back all right, always did. She was sick about having to give you up. But she was wise enough to know that she had to keep you and the Early legacy safe from the man, and the only way she could do that was by staying away from you."

Shay's heart pounded wildly in her chest as images of this man's fingers around Bridget's throat raced through her mind. "But wasn't she afraid her attacker would follow her to Bray Harbor, putting us both at risk again?"

"No, she stayed away until she knew it was safe. She had an old family friend keeping an eye on the man's whereabouts. When he told her the man had returned to Europe, she waited a few years longer to be sure he didn't come back to the States and by that time, she'd saved enough money to start the tea shop and set down roots. I'm sure she did think about taking you back then, but when she saw you and your family together—well, she could see that you were a part of something she knew she could never give you, so she let it be."

"That means this friend of the family knew the identity of the man from the woodland. Did Bridget ever tell you her friend's name? Maybe I could contact him, and he could tell me this fairy man's name, and we could find out if he did come to Bray Harbor and had something to do with Bridget's death."

"Let me think . . . she told me the family friend was from County Clare and had gone to work for Scotland Yard in London, and had since become a private investi—"

"Grady Kennedy?" As soon as Shay blurted out the name, she had second thoughts and hoped that wasn't something the sheriff's department wanted to keep close to their chest right now. However, it couldn't be just a coincidence that the man on her rooftop and Bridget's old family friend were both PI's, could it?

"Yes! That was the name she called him."

Shay staggered back a step. "Then you haven't heard?"

"What?" Pearl grabbed Shay's hand. "Don't tell me he was the man I heard about who had died?"

Shay nodded. "He was murdered and his body was discovered on the tea shop roof."

"Oh dear." Pearl frantically fanned her face with her hand. "I had no idea. I don't pay much attention to the goings-on in town lately, been keeping pretty much to myself since . . . Bridget died. Oh dear. Oh dear." She puffed out a shaky breath. "It's all worse than I thought, and to think he got in touch with her just a few months ago and whatever he told her sent everything else into motion, and for the first time in the thirty years I'd known her, she seemed scared."

"Did she tell you what he said that scared her?"

"No, she wouldn't tell me that. She said the less I knew the safer I'd be, and only said she'd leave it to this Grady fellow to explain it all to you when he got here. But I always suspected it had something to do with the man from Ireland, since he'd been keeping tabs on him all these years."

"And now Grady's dead too, so I'll never know." Shay fought the tears burning behind her eyes and stared out to the open sea past the breaking surf. She recalled all the years she felt like she didn't fit into her family but had brushed it off as a genetic mutation.

"Are you going to be okay, dear?" Pearl placed a warm hand on her arm.

Shay sniffled and nodded her head as a breakaway tear rolled down her cheek. "It's just all been so much to take in. I can't believe that I'm thirty-five years old and no one ever told me *any* of this before."

"I know it must come as a shock now." Pearl hung her head. "But if it helps any, after Bridget moved here, she and your parents came to an understanding of sorts."

"What kind of understanding?"

"So there weren't any more secrets, they all decided that on your eighteenth birthday, the three of them would sit you down and tell you about the adoption and Bridget would explain what happened and why it was necessary."

"But . . ." Shay said, her voice a faded whisper, "my parents were killed just before my birthday and I'm still left with all these secrets and few answers."

"Yes, it didn't quite turn out as they hoped, but after your parents' accident, Bridget never felt it was her place to tell you the truth. She wasn't sure you'd believe her. You were so young yourself and in so much pain after they died." Pearl shored herself up and drew in a deep breath. "Instead she made an effort to keep an eye on you from a distance. The reason she made all those trips over the years to Santa Fe."

"Phew," was all Shay could manage to force out of her lungs.

"I really have to get back." Pearl gave Shay's arm a reassuring squeeze. "Even though those kids have been good this summer, they tend to slough off when not supervised. It's so hard to find good help these days," she muttered, glancing nervously at the shop.

Shay's chest constricted, and the sense of suffocation spread through her. To ground herself, she fixed her gaze on Spirit, sitting guard by her bike beside the ice cream shop door.

"Wait!" She gasped and forced her trembling legs to keep up with Pearl as she headed back. "You've been most helpful, but tell me what happened the day Bridget disappeared. Anything else you can tell me would help me put all these jigsaw pieces together. Please."

Pearl stopped in her tracks, folded her arms across her ample chest, lifted her chin, and stared down her snub nose at her. "Bridget didn't just disappear and go missing for a month before her body was discovered, like everyone thinks."

"She didn't?"

"No, but when she left town, she swore me to secrecy about where she was going. Of course, I had no idea how it would turn out in the end, but at the time her going to Santa Fe to check on you didn't seem unusual." She shrugged. "She said she had some loose ends to wrap up and that her life and"—Pearl swallowed hard—"maybe yours depended on it."

"Writing up a *will* kind of loose ends?"

"No, she'd taken care of all that years ago. Bridget was determined the Early family legacy would be passed on to you when the time was right. But after that last trip she showed up at my cottage. She was in a real state that night, I tell you." Pearl shook her head. "I'd never seen her like that before. She told me now she'd be able to rest in peace, and thrust the chest and a small package, addressed to you through the lawyer's office, into my hands. She asked me to mail the parcel for her on my buying trip to Monterey the next day."

"Why Monterey?"

"She said when she went into town earlier, she felt like she was being watched and didn't want to chance someone seeing her mail a package. She also said it was only a matter of time until she was tracked to the cottage, so she'd have to go away again. She said if she didn't come back I was to give you the chest when you came, but to never tell anyone I had it, or that I had mailed a package for her." She gestured to Shay's neck. "That's also when she made me promise to tell you everything I know, and that's the last time I saw her."

"And then she left again? Where did she go that time?"

Pearl shrugged her shoulders. "I have no idea. When she didn't come back after a few weeks, I got worried so I reported her missing to the sheriff's office, hoping she was hiding out in the woods or something, but . . . a couple of weeks later, her body washed up." She pointed to the pier. "Under there against the pilings. There were no signs of foul play, so it was ruled an accidental drowning. But I knew it wasn't, because before she left that last time, she told me the wheels of what was going to happen were already in motion, and she couldn't stop any of it, and that she tried to warn you the only way she could."

"Grady coming and the letter in the chest," Shay said thoughtfully and sucked in another deep breath for courage. "How did this death vision come to her?"

"The blue bottle. It showed her all the secrets, but according to her, it doesn't reveal the whys or hows. That is for the living to discover." Pearl pivoted and walked back to the ice cream shop.

Julia was wrong. It wasn't hooey. Bridget was a seer after all, which meant whatever she saw she tried to warn Shay about. Shay replayed all the recent events over in her mind: Bridget's death, Grady Kennedy's body on her greenhouse roof, the break-in at her shop in Santa Fe. Was there a connection to them all? Did it have something to do with this Early family legacy? Shay's fingers played over the leather pouch as it warmed against her skin.

Chapter 23

If people thought Shay was drunk a few evenings before, because of her wobbling and bobbing bike ride, what in the world would they say after watching her try to steer straight as her mind reeled with everything Pearl had revealed? Focusing her willpower on her jellylike legs and encouraging them to not give up the fight like the rest of her body, she urged them to keep pedaling up the hill to the main residential area of Bray Harbor.

"Shay!" cried Jen. "I'm surprised to see you. Come in. I thought after the day I heard you had with redecorating the tea shop that you'd be in bed by now."

Shay whispered, "Not quite yet."

"I'm surprised. I ran into Tassi at Jo's this afternoon, and she took me across and showed me what you have done with the place. I must say, little sister, I'm impressed. I think that the interior design gene must run in the family," Jen said with a short laugh and stepped back so Shay could get into the small foyer of her sister's mock-Tudor-style home.

Tears pooled in the corners of Shay's eyes.

"What did I say? I mean you do have an eye for design, which shows in your jewelry-making, and what you've done at the tea shop is—"

Shay's tears grew to a stifled sob.

"But that's not what's bothering you, is it?"

Shay shook her head, and her tears ran freely down her hot cheeks.

"Come on. Dean and I just opened a bottle of wine. It's the first evening he's been home in a week. Come, sit, and tell us what's going on."

Shay looked at Dean, who avoided making eye contact with her as he got up from the sofa, poured her a glass, and handed it to her, whispering, "I haven't told her yet."

Shay reeled. What hadn't he told her? That she was suspected in a jewelry-store heist, or did Liam, despite his denials, tell him about the contents of the chest?

Dean took his seat on the sofa beside Jen and swirled the dark red liquid in his glass before taking a big gulp. "Jen, there was an issue last night that seems to involve Shay, and I asked her to come by this evening so we can try and get to the bottom of it." He swilled back another mouthful and let the glass linger in his hands.

Jen gasped. "A police issue?"

"I'm afraid so," he said, calmly placing his glass on the coffee table.

Jen stared at Shay. "What in the world happened that has the police involved?"

Shay cast her gaze down and studied the red liquid in her glass. How was she going to explain everything to her sister?

"It seems there was a break-in at the jewelry store Shay and Brad owned in Santa Fe. The issue is Brad has strongly suggested to the police that given Shay's recent acquittal based on making restitutions to their clients for embezzlement and fraud . . . she is the most likely culprit. Since she knew the security system and—"

"You . . . can't be serious?" sputtered a wide-eyed Jen. "He really thinks she broke into a business that has been seized by the courts?" She leapt to her feet and spun around facing Dean, her once forget-me-not-blue eyes blazing to sapphire. "I hope you told them she was here last night. Your own daughter can attest to that."

"Yes, and I also spoke with Pearl Hammond, who also swears Shay was at her place last night for a short time, but the thing is . . ." He glanced apologetically at Shay. "The FBI says that only gives you an alibi for the early part of the evening, and there was plenty of time for you to get to Santa Fe and be back by morning since the time of the robbery is thought to be between three and five a.m."

Shay's tummy did a hard drop. "But it's over a sixteen-hour drive, one way. How in the world do they think I managed that?"

"They're checking all the flights in and out of the Monterey area. It seems they think you flew there."

"But they only have to check ticket purchases to see that she didn't, right?" cried Jen, rubbing her forehead. "This is ridiculous and can't be happening. If they want to investigate anyone, it should be Brad. He lost nothing in his swindle of the business. Shay lost *everything*!"

Dean nodded. "Unfortunately, that's the argument that Brad used for Shay's involvement. So now that the FBI are involved, they're also looking at who Shay might have hired to execute the robbery if she didn't. They contacted me today to find out if you"—he pinned his gaze on Shay—"have ever gone by any aliases, one you might have purchased a ticket under."

Jen let out an exasperated huff. "You've gotta be kidding." She perched on the arm of Shay's chair and placed her hand on Shay's shoulder. "It sounds to me like they're grasping at straws, and I'm sure that once they do a more thorough investigation, they'll discover that they have nothing, sweetie." She rubbed Shay's shoulder reassuringly. "After all, you do have us and Pearl as alibis."

"That's the problem," said Dean, glancing uncomfortably at Shay. "You only have an alibi until about nine p.m. They're working on the assumption that you had plenty of time to fly to Santa Fe and get back before you came into the shop"—he rubbed his chin—"late, according to your assistant. Then there's still the matter of tracing all your contacts and going through your phone and computer for any associates you might have hired to execute the actual robbery, and the FBI have asked me to confiscate those." He held out his hand. "I'm sorry, Shay, I'll need your phone now.

I'll call a deputy to take you home and collect your laptop, and we'll have to seize the shop computer also. I'll also need the tea shop keys. If you don't agree willingly, the FBI are prepared to issue a warrant and that won't work to your benefit in the long run." He waggled his fingers, waiting for her to comply to handing over her phone.

Shay's chest tightened, and she couldn't catch her breath. She was going to have to tell them everything, no matter the fallout or how it would destroy the only family she'd ever known.

"I spent the night with Liam," Shay blurted out.

Jen's chin dropped. "Is that what's got you so upset? What did he do to you? I warned you to stay away from him. He's too much a ladies' man and will only break your heart."

"No, it's nothing like that. He was a perfect gentleman. He even slept on the chair in the living room."

"Why?"

"Because I was upset about something, and he didn't want to leave me alone."

"I talked to him today." Dean rose to his feet. "He never said a word about being with you last night."

"Because . . . I asked him not to." Shay knew then that Liam had kept her secret, and her heart swelled. If only she had met him, or at least a man like him, before Brad . . . before Zoey. How different her life might have been.

"Why?" snapped Jen, glaring down at Shay. "Were you afraid of what I'd say?"

"No, I was afraid of what I'd have to say to you."

"What do you mean?"

Shay took a deep breath and braced herself. "When we were going through the photo album you found in the trunk, I got an edgy feeling that something was off, but I couldn't put my finger on it. I thought about it all the way back to the cottage, but whatever brought on the feeling was like trying to hold on to fog, and it kept slipping through my fingers."

"Yeah," said Jen. "I knew something was bothering you. I thought it was because there weren't that many baby pictures of you, that's why I tried to explain about second and third babies."

"I know, and I get that, but no. It was something else. Something was missing."

Jen's brow creased and she stared questioningly at Shay.

"Anyway . . ."

Shay went on to explain how Spirit had behaved and drawn her to Pearl's cottage. Then how Pearl had handed her the carved chest with instructions to go through it, and if she had any questions for Shay to come back, and she'd tell her what she could. Shay explained how Spirit then summoned Liam, who thankfully had been with her when she finally worked up the courage to look inside the chest. "Because that's when I found these."

From her handbag, Shay pulled out an envelope with the Polaroids tucked inside and laid them side by side across the coffee table. "It wasn't until I saw these photos that I could put my finger on what was missing. It wasn't fewer pictures of me, but the pictures of me as a newborn, with someone who looked like me."

Jen stared mutely at the photos.

"There were also these . . ." Shay's fingers trembled as she drew two more papers from her bag and handed Bridget's letter and the adoption certificate to Jen. "If Liam hadn't been there when I found all this . . ." She swiped at a tear that slid down her hot cheek. "I also talked to Pearl today, and she confirmed all of it." Shay waved her hand over the photos and gestured toward the papers Jen held, then sat back in her chair and waited for the fallout of what she'd revealed.

Jen dropped down hard on the sofa, reading over the papers, and then handed them to Dean without a word. Silence reigned for what seemed an eternity to Shay, who suspected the worst outcome to her babbling. Instead, her sister reached for the wine bottle on the table, refilled her and Shay's wineglasses, and gestured a toast. "To family!" she said and downed almost her entire glass in one gulp.

The tears Shay had been fighting rolled freely down her cheeks. Jen welcomed her into her outstretched arms and held Shay tightly, just like their mother used to when they were in pain. "We *are* and always have been sisters," Jen whispered. "No piece of paper will ever change that." She held Shay out at arm's length and forced Shay to look into her eyes. "Do you hear me? All this changes *nothing* between us. Our bond is stronger than blood."

Shay's tears turned to sobs as she clung onto Jen and openly wept on her shoulder. When her sobs subsided, she blew her nose on the tissue Dean handed to her.

"It changes nothing for me either, and I'm glad

you finally got the answers you needed," Dean huskily whispered, his voice filled with emotion as he patted her shoulder.

"Not quite all of them," sniffled Shay, "but it does answer the most important one, like why Bridget left me the shop and her cottage. Now I just have to figure out what her warning meant, and if that was the message Grady was supposed to give me, or if there was something else I had to know."

Dean took her hands in his. "I promise you we'll get to the bottom of it, and slowly but surely, we're putting the pieces together to figure out what happened last Friday night. Who knows, perhaps we'll find out it was the same person who committed the break-in last night. Someone who has it in for you."

"That would be Brad." Jen's upper lip curled back in a mother-bear snarl as she refilled her glass.

"Speaking of last night." Shay fished her phone out of her bag and held it out to Dean. "Here, I guess you need this."

He waved it off. "No, the FBI will want to question Liam, of course, but given his credentials, I'm sure they'll find him a more than competent witness to your whereabouts. I'm pretty sure they'll start looking at other suspects now. Given this new information and the fact that your ex might have gotten wind of your inheritance, I'm going to point them in Brad's direction for sure. However, we do have a few other suspects we're looking at in the case of Grady Kennedy's murder."

Shay perched on the edge of her chair. "I had heard that you found out Burrows was at the pub last Friday. It's funny how he never mentioned that to anyone, isn't it?"

"It sure is, and then today when I was re-interviewing witnesses because it seems Burrows missed a lot in his initial inquiries, I discovered that Carmen, one of the day bartenders, also happened to be there."

"You're kidding." Shay looked at Dean in disbelief. "I talked to her the day we discovered the body, and she told me she wasn't working."

"Working, no, but I have two other witnesses that place her in the pub as a customer that night."

"But why make a point of telling me that she wasn't there?"

"What exactly did she say to you?"

"She said she didn't know anything because Kenny was working. When we found the button, I asked her if she'd seen anyone wearing the kind of shirt it might have come off, and she said no."

"She went up on the greenhouse roof with you?"

Shay nodded.

"How did she react?"

"Fine, I guess."

"And that's it? When you discovered thc button, did she seem shocked or anything unusual?"

"No, she went and got the tweezers and helped me pry it out."

"What about after? Did she say anything that might have been related to Grady's murder?"

"No. Why, did she know him?"

"We're trying to find a link now," said Dean. "The day she was interviewed, she had told Burrows pretty much the same story as she told you.

She wasn't working, wasn't there, and to talk to Kenny, the evening bartender. At least, that's what he had in his notes."

"But if she was seen there and Burrows was there, they both lied."

"Exactly, because none of that was in Burrows's initial report—nada, nothing."

"That means if your investigator instincts hadn't kicked in, and you felt something was off in the sheriff's report—"

"Yeah, and that was only because the clues weren't adding up, but I still had a gut feeling there was something else going on. If I hadn't pursued it any further we wouldn't have discovered that not only Burrows was in the pub Friday, but also that two witnesses swore they saw Carmen go upstairs when the dancing started."

"Interesting that both she and Burrows lied," Jen said, staring into the distance, deep in thought, and then snapped her fingers. "That means Carmen must have seen Burrows upstairs, right? And he would have seen her?"

"It's hard to say. Neither of them is being very forthcoming right now. When I questioned Burrows about his oversight in the report, how he failed to mention he was in the bar, he said he was so drunk that night he had forgotten completely that they were in the pub until this morning at breakfast when his wife brought it up."

"What about Carmen?" asked Shay. "What was her excuse for not disclosing the fact that she *was* there when she said she wasn't?"

"She said Liam had asked her to go through a file of new hires to see what she thought about them. She'd forgotten to take it home, so she popped back in to get it. She said she was only there a few minutes, so she didn't think mentioning it was important."

"Did you ask Liam about it today?" asked Jen.

"Yeah, he said he had asked her, but when a deputy took him through the building on Saturday to make sure he hadn't been robbed too, the file folder was still exactly where he'd left it, and appeared untouched."

"Which means Carmen lied about more than one thing," said Shay thoughtfully.

"It appears so." Dean ran his hand through his hair. "The witnesses today are pretty reliable, and they swear Burrows hadn't come downstairs yet to join his party when Carmen was seen going up."

"Then he must have seen Carmen," piped in Jen.

"He denies it," said Dean. "But given his state, verified by everyone there, that might be the truth."

"Did Burrows talk to these two witnesses when he initially investigated?"

"Nope, and I only heard about them seeing Carmen go upstairs from someone else I talked to who said these two witnesses had mentioned it later that night. I guess they were offended when she rushed by their table, he grabbed her shirt sleeve, which, he swears, was a blue color, but she completely ignored them when he asked her to join them for a drink."

"She was wearing a blue blouse? Now that *is* interesting too, isn't it?"

Dean nodded. "But it's not against the law to wear blue, so I'd need more evidence for a warrant to examine it, but what I don't get is: If she knew someone had seen her, why not mention that she just dropped by for a file?"

"Especially since the waitress serving upstairs must have seen her too, right?"

"No," said Dean. "She swears when she went up to check on Burrows and the other guy, Grady, they were the only two upstairs."

"Then clearly Carmen was in the office as she said she was."

"Or," added Dean, "hiding in the office because she was there for another reason, right?"

"And then that Irish guy was killed," whispered Jen.

"Yeah, and they were both up there," said Shay. "Did anyone see Carmen come down or leave?"

"Nope." Dean shook his head. "Kenny said it was crazy by then, and people were out of their seats and dancing. When she did leave, Carmen must have slipped out unnoticed." He took a sip of wine, steadying his thoughtful gaze on Shay. "When you talked to her on Saturday, what exactly did she say about the murder?"

Shay racked her memory files. "There was one thing I thought odd."

"What's that?"

"She was referring to Burrows and how he had been harassing Liam and always closing down the pub, which affected all the staff, and she said, 'Someone needs to stop that man,' and then later said something like 'I hope that the discovery of a stranger's body on the roof was only a dress re-hearsal for the real intended victim, Frank Burrows.' But it was the way she said it that really creeped me out." Shay shivered as she recalled the dark energy that had pulsated off Carmen. "Oh, and then she said something about Burrows having broken a lot of laws, and she hoped he'd get locked up himself."

Jen's eyes widened. "Do you think she killed Grady Kennedy and tried to frame Burrows for it?"

"I guess that's one possibility," said Dean, staring at the table. "Before hearing Carmen's veiled threats, I was thinking that given how nasty Burrows can be normally—and it only gets worse when he's drinking—that maybe Grady said or did something to set him off, and Burrows killed him in a drunken rage, but now . . ."

Shay could almost see the wheels in Dean's mind working overtime with all this new information. She blew out a deep breath, deciding Liam was right. It was going to take Miss Marple to sort through this whole mess as there were just too many pieces that didn't add up.

Chapter 24

Although it was a great relief to Shay that her sister's feelings about them and the bond they had as family hadn't changed, Shay's mind still couldn't shut off all night. Haunted visions had her tossing and turning so much that she awoke in the morning tangled in her bedsheets.

Even now in the light of the day, there were so many questions that still niggled at her. She'd hoped her excursion to the storage locker this morning would bring a few more answers to the mystery that was her biological mother, Bridget Early. But in the end, it had accomplished nothing that would ease her uncertainties. If anything, her search of the locker only intensified them, making her think that what she had learned about her past was only the tip of a very large iceberg—one that she was going to run into head-on, and soon.

She powered down on the bike pedals and sailed around the corner onto High Street. Her only recourse now, it seemed, was to find the answer to the warning Bridget had left her. It seemed to also be the key to who killed Grady Kennedy, the man who was to explain whatever it was Bridget feared. Then, of course, there was the matter of deciphering Bridget's puzzling whispered words. *Look beyond the amber veil.* She shivered. She hoped they were Bridget's, and she wondered if that was the clue she should focus on instead.

Certain that her head was about to explode, she yanked off her helmet and tossed it on the bench beside her bike. After retrieving the contents of the basket, and tucking them securely under her arm, she trudged into her tea shop.

"Good morning, Tassi," she called, dropping an armload of leather-bound photo albums on the counter. She chuckled. "I guess I should say good afternoon, though, shouldn't I? You did get my message saying I'd be in later than I thought, didn't you?"

"Yeah, thanks," said Tassi, appearing in the back-room doorway. She glanced curiously at the book deposit Shay had just made. "More tea recipe books?"

"No, just a few photo albums. The only stuff of Bridget's that Julia put into the storage unit were her personal belongings like clothes and these, which I haven't had time to go through." She patted the stack of five albums she had arranged by size and shape to make transporting them in her bike basket easier. "The woman really didn't have that many personal possessions, which I found interesting, considering she lived in Bray Harbor for over thirty years."

"That was the kind of person she was, though, even though you'd never have known it by everything she had in the shop." Tassi flipped open the cover of the top album and then closed it. "Sorry, I was just curious, but it's not my place."

"Nonsense, you knew the woman better than I did, and I'm sure you're just as interested in seeing her photos as I am. Any glimpse into her life beyond this shop would help me put a lot of the puzzle pieces in place, because the only other thing I found in one of her dress pockets was this." Shay fished a small key out of her front jeans pocket. "Do you have any idea what this might fit?"

Tassi took the ornate silver key from Shay's fingers and turned it over. "No, I don't think it fits anything in the shop. The key for the file cabinets upstairs are just gold-colored, normal keys, and not detailed like this."

"Okay, thanks." Shay crammed the key back into her pocket. "It must be for something at the cottage. I was just hoping that since Bridget's life seemed to be all about the tea shop that it was something you'd seen her use here. I still can't believe that the woman had very few possessions given she was what, about fifty-one years old?"

Tassi's gaze flitted to the door and then back at Shay. "Didn't Spirit come with you? I was hoping he'd go for a run with me on the beach at lunchtime."

Shay shook her head and clucked her tongue.

"No, it seems our elusive friend has had enough today. He got up, ate his breakfast, did his business outside, and went directly to his bed, refusing to budge when I left." She shrugged. "I guess he needed a day off."

"I hope he's not sick."

"No, I don't think so. I checked his nose, and it's wet, and his ears didn't feel hot. Plus, he did eat and drink. I think he's just tired from keeping constant vigilance over me lately," Shay said with a laugh and then frowned at the shelves behind the counter. "What happened to all the glass jars that were up there?"

"Ooh-ooh," cried Tassi, clapping her hands excitedly. "That's what I've been working on all morning. Come see." She grinned and darted off to the back room.

Shay followed and stuck her head around the door. "What the . . ." A line of glass jars stood like sentinels along the long kitchen counter. A book and a marble pestle and mortar brought up the rear. "What's all this?"

"I figured that after we open, people will see what a great little tea shop you have now that all the other stuff is gone. The prepared tea pouches that Bridget made up before she . . . well . . . died . . . will be flying off the shelves, and we're going to have to learn to make our own tea blends." She stood back proudly and beamed. "So, I've been practicing."

Shay poked at a recipe. "Do you think we can do it? I mean, there seems so much to learn. Like,

look here, what exactly is *6 tsp. dried Melissa,* or"—
she stabbed her finger on another line—"*4 tsp.
lady's mantle?* These sound like something from
Middle Earth."

"That's the best part," said Tassi, pointing to the
yellow-highlighted *Woodland Meadow Tea* at the top
of the page. "Bridget marked all the teas she grows
upstairs in the greenhouse. Everything we need
for the ones she highlighted we have the ingredients for."

Shay scanned the page.

Woodland Meadow Tea

*This herbal tea works well as a stress reliever and will
help the consumer's system find balance in times of dis-
array.*

Ingredients
- 12 tsp. dried peppermint
- 6 tsp. dried Melissa (lemon balm)
- 6 tsp. dried verbena (vervain)
- 4 tsp. lady's mantle (Alchemilla)
- 4 tsp. chamomile
- 2.5 tsp. dried sage
- 1.5 tsp. dried thyme
- 4 tsp. dried nettles

Instructions
*In the pestle and mortar grind all the ingredients and
mix together well. You want the leaves roughly uniform,
not too small or powdery. They must be large enough to
settle on the bottom of the cup if they are to be used for
readings. For general use, fill required amount in a tea*

strainer. However, when using for a tea-leaf reading, discard the strainer.

Store the mixture in an airtight container and use as needed.

Combine 2–3 teaspoons of the dried tea mixture for every pot of boiling water or 1 teaspoon of tea for an individual cup. Allow the tea to steep for 3–5 minutes.

"A stress reliever. Now this blend sounds like something I need, and you say all of these grow upstairs?"

Tassi grinned. "I already have some prepared from the herbs Bridget harvested and dried before. Should we give it a try and see if it's something we want to sell?"

Shay pursed her lips. "I guess. I can't ask our customers to drink something I haven't taste-tested myself, can I? Okay, let's get the water on."

The doorbells jangled with a chaotic clanging, and Shay swiveled around to see who burst through the door. She let out a short laugh and eased into the storefront. "If Spirit brought you to rescue me *again*, please let him know there is a little thing called a telephone, and I'll call for help if I—" She halted at the haunted look in Liam's eyes. "What's wrong?"

"Dean asked me to come and collect you."

"To the police station? But he told me last night that you being a witness—"

"It's not that." Liam puffed, clearly trying to catch his breath. "He's at your cottage now, and he needs you to . . . well . . . just come. I'll explain on the way. And don't worry, Zoey is there, too, and Spirit's fine."

Shay's heart dropped to the pit of her stomach. "What happened to Spirit?"

"Nothing, it looks like it's the other guy who got the worst of it. Come on, we have to go."

"Liam, you're not making sense. What are you babbling about?"

"Your cottage," he said, opening the door. "I'll explain on the way."

Shay glanced at an equally mystified Tassi and shrugged. "Lock up when you're done, I guess."

"Lock the door behind us now, Tassi," ordered Liam, "and don't let *anyone* in. Do you hear me?"

"Liam, you're scaring me," said Shay, sliding past him out the door. "What's going on?"

"Just get in."

Tassi hustled to the door as it closed behind them. Shay turned and mouthed "I'll call you" through the glass. Tassi flipped the dead bolt, and her pale, worried face set Shay's nerves firing on all cylinders.

Liam settled Shay's bike in the back of his older-model Jeep Wrangler. "Hop in."

Shay scrambled in, and Liam sped off before she could fasten her seat belt. "Are you sure Spirit is okay? If you had to call the vet, something must be wrong." She struggled to latch her seat belt.

"He's fine. She's checked him, so don't let the blood on his fur scare you as much as it did me."

"Liam, what happened? This is really freaking me out."

"It appears someone tried to break into your cottage this morning. There's blood, lots of blood around the door, but Zoey said it's not Spirit's, so don't worry. He's fine. It's the other guy we have to watch out for because Spirit must have taken a good chunk out of his hand or arm."

Shay's heart flipped, or so it seemed because she couldn't get a breath. That's why he didn't want to leave the house. He knew something was going to happen. "But . . . but . . ." She wheezed when air rushed back into her lungs. "You're sure Spirit is okay?" She flung the door open when Liam parked in front of his cottage.

"As far as we can tell, but be prepared . . ."

Shay bolted across the lane and raced around to her front door, where the police presence caused her to come to a skidding stop.

"Shay, over here," called Dean.

Shay wove past the deputies swarming the small yard. "Dean, what's going on?"

"I thought Liam filled you in on the way here," he said, giving a head gesture of confirmation toward Liam when he came around the side of the cottage.

Liam stepped past a young deputy taking a swab of dark matter on her door frame and disappeared inside. Shay swallowed around the lump stuck in her throat. "Yes and no. He said Spirit was covered in blood, and it looked like someone tried to break in, is that right?"

"That's what it looks like," Dean said and nodded to an exotic-looking, dark-haired woman in a silk bathrobe, sashaying down the porch steps and gliding toward them. "Shay, this is Doctor Zoey Laine. She's been examining Spirit for injuries that he may have suffered during the assault."

"Assault!" Shay pinned her anxious gaze on Zoey's contrastingly calming one. "This intruder attacked him?"

Zoey took Shay's trembling hand in her cool, slender one, and gave it a light squeeze. "I've given him a quick once-over, and he seems fine. If you don't mind, I'd like to take him to the clinic so we can bathe him and get a better look to make sure there are no injuries under the bloodied, matted fur. That is, if that's okay with you?"

Shay's knees wobbled with the words *bloodied, matted fur.*

A young woman wearing medical scrubs led Spirit down the stairs. Shay's hand went to her throat, and she gasped. His muzzle and normally snow-white chest fur were dark red. "Are you sure it's not his?"

"Pretty sure, but I can't be positive until we get him cleaned up."

"Oh, of course, yes. Take him. Do whatever you have to." Tears welled up in Shay's eyes as Spirit trotted toward her. He lay down at her feet and moaned softly. She crouched down and stroked the fine hair behind his ears. "Oh, boy, what have you done for me now?"

Zoey tugged her robe belt tighter. "Speaking of getting cleaned up, I had just gotten out of the shower when Spirit showed up at Liam's door, so I'd better go get dressed." She turned to the clinic employee. "Sheila, you can take him back in the van. I'll be along shortly."

"Yes, Doctor." The woman nodded and tugged at the leash. Spirit fixed his gaze on Shay, let out a deep woof, wagged his tail, and trotted along beside the woman.

"Thank you," Shay said and met Zoey's stunning forest-green eyes, which gave her a very wood-nymph aura. "Please, do whatever you have to. The money isn't important. Make sure he has the best of care."

"Don't worry." Zoey's eyes sparkled in the afternoon sun. "I'm sure he's just fine." She turned and glided around the side of the cottage.

"She's right, Shay," said Dean. "Besides, Zoey is one of the best vets in the area. She'll make sure Spirit's okay."

The woman did have a calming aura about her, and Shay knew Spirit was in good hands. She could see why Liam was drawn to her, though it was like a punch in the stomach when Zoey had revealed her whereabouts when Spirit had his altercation with . . . She glanced back at the officers coming and going from inside her cottage. "What do you think happened here this morning?"

"It appears that someone jimmied the door lock, and when they opened the door, your guardian took it upon himself to fend them off." Dean pointed to the porch. "Judging by all the blood around the door frame, on the porch, and the blood splatter down the stairs and up the sidewalk, I'd say we're looking for someone with a pretty nasty bite or multiple bite wounds on his arm or hand."

Liam trotted out the front door and down the steps, shoving a pair of blue rubber gloves into his back jeans pocket. "There's no sign the intruder got inside, so it looks like a botched robbery attempt, thanks to Spirit."

"I hope you don't mind, Shay"—Dean glanced questioningly at her—"but I asked Liam to take a quick look inside with the deputies. I thought since he was just here the other night, he'd be able to see if anything was out of place."

"No, that's fine."

"Good, now do you feel like taking a walk-through with me just to double-check? Then we can wrap it up here and let you get on with your day."

"Sure." Shay sucked in an unsteady breath and tentatively made her way up the steps, pausing only long enough to eye the pool of blood by the door—an image she hoped she'd be able to erase from her mind later. "I saw an officer swabbing the door when I arrived. Does that mean you're going to test the DNA?"

"Yes," said Dean, "and it will also help us figure out if it's all human or . . ."

Shay shivered as she crossed the threshold into her small foyer.

Chapter 25

Shay cracked up when Spirit leapt out of the back of Liam's Jeep and raced across the alley, taking her short fence in one flying leap. "I can't believe he has the energy he's got given the day he's had."

Liam's grin was as wide as hers. "I'm just glad he's okay. From what I saw when he howled at my door earlier, I will admit I suspected the worst."

"Yeah, me too. There was so much blood it was hard to believe none of it was his. Well, thank you again for taking me to pick him up, and please tell Zoey I'm grateful for all her help too. Well, I'd better get inside and feed him some dinner."

"I think he deserves a nice juicy steak. What do ye say I throw a couple on the grill, and we join him?"

"Um, that's really nice of you, but . . ." She dropped her gaze. There was no way she could look into those blue eyes of his and not blush, or worse, have an attack of the mottles. Looking splotchy and diseased was not the best way to make an impression on anyone. "Look, you and Zoey seem to have a . . . special . . . relationship, and I doubt she'd be happy about you spending so much time with me."

There, she said it. Words she might regret because she really did enjoy his company and he— she nervously glanced up and then just as quickly away again—was *so* easy on the eyes, but clearly given his commitments and her situation, it was bad timing for both of them. Something it seemed that had become her life's new mantra.

"Pfft, I told you Zoey and I are just friends."

Shay wanted to scream, *Yeah, friends with benefits! She showered in your house this morning!* Instead, she bit the inside of her cheek to keep her words in check and forced a smile. "I know, but I really don't ever want to be accused of being like my ex's girlfriend. It's probably best we just remain neighbors . . . here and at work."

"Nope." He shook his head. "That won't do. Can't you see we're bound to each other now?"

"What do you mean?"

"Now ye know you're full-blooded Irish and from the same county as my clan. We have to look out for each other."

Shay stared off across the alley to her cottage. The proximity of his to hers felt comforting and not threatening, and she only meant threatening because she knew she couldn't trust her porcelain complexion to behave whenever she saw him. Knowing what she knew of Irish clans and how they looked out for each other and the tight bonds they had even for a stranger within their county, Liam *was* like family. Her mind flashed to Bridget's family photos she'd discovered, and she smiled. Yes, a whole new world had been opened to her. She had another family she never knew existed. "I guess I never thought about that. Okay, *cousin*, let's cook up some steaks."

"Cousin? Ye did mean like a third or fourth one, didn't ye?" he said, jumping in front of her, hope reflecting back at her in his questioning eyes.

"What else should I call you?" She laughed softly. "Certainly not *brother*." A familiar sensation of hot prickling needles spread across her cheeks. *Darn it, why now?*

If Liam noticed her blotchy, flaming cheeks, he gave no indication. He waved his hands in a time-out motion. "No, no, no, definitely not a brother. I've spent the night with ye, remember?" He flashed her a teasing wink. "Okay, cousin it is, as long as it's a distant, distant, distant one."

"Oh, all right, *cousin*." She grinned and opened the side door to her cottage. Spirit darted up the stairs behind them and scrambled around their legs, heading directly to his food dish. He flipped it over with one slap of his paw and then sat back. Shay could have sworn he had an ear-to-ear grin across his doggy face.

"Okay, okay." Liam laughed and held his hands up. "I'll get the steaks. Be back soon." His chuckle could still be heard as he trotted down the stairs and back across Shay's lawn to his cottage.

"You are something else, my friend." Shay bent down and ruffled the fur on the back of Spirit's head. "I really don't know how to thank you for everything you do for me."

Spirit pawed at his dish, flipped it upright, and barked.

"All you want for my gratitude is food?"

He barked again.

"You sell yourself short, my friend," she said with a short laugh and foraged through the fridge for something to serve along with Liam's steaks. "You're worth a lot more to me than the cost of feeding you, that's for sure." She grinned tenderly at him. "Thank you," she whispered.

He lay down beside his dish, and let out a soft groan, his tail thumping on the floor.

Liam pushed his plate away, sat back in his chair, and patted his stomach. "I must say, *a chara*, for someone who said they didn't have much food in the house, you outdid yourself with that salad and garlic bread."

"It only seemed like that because the steak was"—she kissed her fingers—"*perfecto*! Thank you, but I could have brought all this to your cottage. You didn't have to drag your barbeque all the way over here," she said, rinsing the plates in the sink.

"No trouble. Besides, I think our sleeping friend is glad to be home after what he went through today." He gestured to Spirit, asleep on the mat by the door.

"You're probably right." She smiled at her softly snoring guardian.

"Besides, I wanted to be here to get first dibs on the sofa tonight."

"What are you talking about?"

"As lovely as that chair is, I have no intention of waking up like a pretzel tomorrow, so I call sofa!"

"What's wrong with your bed?"

He shrugged. "I guess we could go over there. I just thought that Spirit would be more comfortable here."

"I mean, why are you even suggesting you stay for the night?"

"Like I told you on the drive from the clinic, the locksmith can't get here till tomorrow. I think it's for the best. Don't you want me to stay?"

"I just don't understand all the fuss. I guess my thinking is that whoever tried to break in knows Spirit is here and won't try it again."

"Ah-ha, but that's the thing. If there is something in here they want badly enough, they'll be prepared this time for a dog attack, and"—he glanced at Spirit—"it might not go as well for our four-legged friend here this time."

"Okay, maybe you're right, but I do have a bed, you know?"

"Are you suggesting that you and I—"

"No! I'm not suggesting anything. I'm stating a fact. I'll be sleeping in my bed. So, if you feel you must stay, the sofa is all yours."

"Hear that, Spirit, she said the sofa is mine, so don't let all this hero stuff go to your head. I draw the line with the steak."

Spirit let out a groan that sounded a lot like *whatever* and flopped onto his side.

"I still don't understand why someone wanted to get in here in the first place. It's not like I have anything of value." She waved her hand around the room and then paused. "Could it have been kids on a lark or a dare? You know, break into the *witch's cottage* and gain brownie points with their friends?"

Liam pursed his lips tight but remained mute. His eyes darkened.

"Do you think that's what it was?" She held out a pillow and blanket for him. "Could it have been kids playing around?"

"That's always a possibility, I guess, but combined with the break-in at your shop in Santa Fe, my gut tells me that someone is looking for something." He tossed the linens on the sofa. "Don't forget Bridget's warning." He gestured to the leather ties strung around her neck.

"What?" Her hand flew to the pouch under her blouse. "Do you think someone is looking for this? Do you think this is what she was talking about?"

"Well, ye do wear it close to your heart."

"Yes, but I thought she meant like my family or Spirit or you-ooweee."

"Youooweee?"

"Um . . . yes, a friend of mine back in Santa Fe." Flames of heat rushed up from under her collar right to her hairline, and she knew it wasn't going to be pretty.

"Oh." He eyed her skeptically, and the slight tug at the corners of his mouth told her he was fighting a laugh, but when it didn't come, she breathed a sigh of relief.

Phew, that was a close one, dummy. How could she tell him that from the first moment she met him she had felt a connection she couldn't understand? A vision of Zoey's radiant smile and her forest-green eyes popped into her mind . . . No, she couldn't even go there. Liam was with Zoey, and she was . . . well, she was moving on to her new future, whatever that was—

Spirit sprang to his feet and raced to the kitchen door, getting there at the same time as there was a loud knock. Shay shot Liam a stunned glance.

"Are ye expecting anyone this evening?"

She shook her head. Spirit let out a woof, sat back on his haunches, and swooshed his tail across the floor. "It must be a friend, though." She shrugged and started for the door.

"Let me, just in case," said Liam, side-stepping around her and turning the dead bolt to open it.

"My house, my door, my risk." She elbowed her way in front of him and swung the door open.

"And ye wonder why I worry," Liam muttered over her shoulder.

"Tassi?"

"Hi, I hope it's not too late?"

"No, not at all, come in," said Shay, stepping back.

Tassi nodded shyly at Liam, and Spirit immediately nudged her hand. When she held it out to him, he gave it a cursory lick, let out a short woof, and trotted back into the living room.

"Hello and goodbye to you too." Tassi chuckled. "I saw the board over the front door so just came around to the side. I hope that was right? I didn't know you had company though. It can wait until tomorrow if you're busy."

"You're not interrupting anything. We just finished dinner, and Liam was about to do the dishes, right?"

He rolled his eyes and nodded.

"So, what's up? Want some tea, lemonade, water?"

"No, I'm fine, thanks. It's just that I wanted to make sure Spirit was okay. Your text—well, you never know what someone really means in a text message—so I wanted to see him with my own eyes. You don't mind, do you?"

"Yeah, meaning is sometimes lost in text, but as you can see, he's just fine. But thank you for caring so much." Shay patted the girl's hand. "Wanna go in the other room and visit with him for a while?"

She grinned and nodded.

"Okay, you go ahead, and I'll be along in a minute. Let me just get this guy set up." Shay jerked her head toward Liam at the sink.

"There was one other thing, though." Tassi paused at the doorway. "Liam might have told you already since he used to be a policeman."

"What's that?" With a laugh, he swiped Shay's hand away from the bottle of dish soap. "I already put some in. See the bubbles?"

"It's about Madam Malvina."

"Is she having buyer's remorse?" asked Shay.

"Not exactly, but she did call and ask me about some of the things she bought."

"Why? Does she want to return or exchange them?"

"No, it seems her store was broken into last night, and someone smashed a few of the gargoyles and the cat statues and stole some of the necklaces and amulets. I just thought maybe Liam might have heard a police bulletin about it or something." She shrugged. "With everything that happened to you today it all seems kind of weird, don't you think?"

"Weird is right." Liam tossed the dishcloth into the sink and swiveled toward Tassi. "You say this happened last night?"

"Yeah, the alarm didn't go off or anything, and when she went in this morning . . . that's what she found."

Liam pinned Shay with an I-told-you-so look. "And ye wonder why I want the sofa tonight." He shook his head. "Now will you believe that someone is after something they think you know or you have?"

Shay stroked the bottle through its leather casing. The warmth emanating from it radiated through her fingers and across her chest. *What have you given me, Bridget? A blessing or a curse?*

Chapter 26

Shay stood back and nodded her approval. "I believe this has been a morning well spent. Don't you think?" She glanced over at Tassi pricing the last of the Celtic cat statues. "I only hope that marking all this stuff down seventy percent from what Bridget paid for it helps get the last of it sold at the end-of-summer sidewalk sale."

"What surprises me is how much of this, especially these statues, Madam Malvina didn't want," said Tassi, slapping a red sale sticker on the bottom of a bronze winged gargoyle cat. "I mean everyone who knows anything about them knows how important cats are to the Celts. You'd have thought she'd be all over these."

"Maybe she knows her market pretty well and knows that what she did take would sell and all this"—Shay waved her hand over the table—"would sit and collect dust like it did here."

"Let's just hope that there are some shoppers at the sidewalk sale who do know what they mean and buy up the whole lot, or better yet, a whole lot of cat lovers who want to put them in their gardens or something." Her gaze wandered over the back room. "It would be nice to start organizing this room for your readings," she said with an optimistic quirk of a brow.

Tassi was right. As much as Shay balked at becoming a tea-leaf reader and doing whatever it was Bridget had done with crystal balls and the blue bottle, she knew in her heart that this was part of her birthright. She was going to have to learn everything she could if she was going to make a go of carrying on her *mother's*—the word caught in her chest—legacy. A legacy she quickly learned she was closer to than she thought on her first day in the shop.

That day, Julia had welcomed Shay to her new future, and perhaps that future started with having more of an appreciation for the dozen or so various cat statues on the sale table. She skeptically eyed the display on the table. On the other hand, if what Tassi had read in one of the books that she'd found in the shop was correct . . . and the Celts associated cats with magic, and the druidic priests used cat magic so that they would be able to cross between the spiritual and physical worlds, who knew what power was hidden within these bronze and clay figurines? But who was she kidding? Tea-leaf reading was one thing, but magic and tea potions? She'd have to draw the line there. She tossed a dust cloth over the table. Cleaning in and around all the ornately carved crevices once was bad enough, and she didn't want to waste another morning cleaning all of these again along with all the other little doodads, whatever they were.

As the sheet fluttered in the air before enveloping the table, she hoped that there might be a buyer out there interested in all the bits and pieces they were selling at the sidewalk sale because she had no intention of going down a rabbit hole with them by getting into a world she didn't want to enter. Besides, her plan to take Bridget's tea shop into a new and more contemporary direction was solid. No more *woo-woo* or whatever it was Liam had called it the first day she met him. But when the amulet she wore around her neck grew warm against her skin, she conceded that, like it or not, she was going to have to at least learn the art of blending, brewing, and reading tea leaves.

"Okay, Tassi, you win," she called.

Tassi popped her head through the door from the front of the shop, confusion clear in her eyes.

"Let's take a lunch break. When you come back, we can start going through those notebooks of Bridget's and see if we can figure out the tea business."

"And readings?"

"Yes." Shay chuckled. The expression on Tassi's face resembled a child's when opening a gift Christmas morning.

"Great, I'll just run to Auntie's and grab a sandwich. Be back in a flash," she said, scampering out the door.

"She's in the back room," Shay heard Tassi tell someone and poked her head out of the back-room door.

"Oh, hi, Jen. I'm just finishing up back here. Come in."

"First off, are you okay?"

"Yeah . . . why?" Shay looked uncertainly at her. "Shouldn't I be?"

"Dean told me someone tried to break into your cottage," she said in disbelief and embraced Shay. "Oh, little sister, I was horrified to hear that." Jen held her out at arm's length and gave her the once-over. "You look fine, and I saw Spirit earlier, and he looks fine, but I guess . . ."

"Guess what?"

"It's just that all you've been through, and Bridget's chest and—" Jen turned away in an unsuccessful attempt to hide her tears.

"Hey," Shay said, rubbing Jen's arm comfortingly. "I'm okay, and Spirit's okay. He stopped the intruder from getting in. No harm done."

Jen sniffled. "If you say so, but wow." She braced herself. Her gaze fleetingly darted toward the window. "This has been some homecoming, hasn't it? I only hope that after everything that's happened, you've finally come to your senses and decided to take Julia up on her offer and sell this place," she said flatly, averting her eyes back to the window. "I mean, it's brought you nothing but bad luck since you first set foot in the place."

Shay followed the focus of her sister's attention, and narrowed in on the lanky blond figure sitting at one of Jo's patio tables. "Wait a minute." Shay grabbed her arm and swung Jen around to face her. "Did Julia send you in here today to make one last plea on Pierre's behalf?"

"What? No." She removed Shay's hand from her

arm. "It's just that she's right, and I happen to agree with her. Look, you innocently moved here because of what happened with Brad, but then got all *this* dropped in your lap." She swept her hand in the air. "Not to mention that a dead body was found right up there on the roof. Then your store in Santa Fe was robbed, and worst of all you found out that you're not who you thought you were. After yesterday, with your cottage getting broken into"—she swiped a tear from her cheek—"I don't think I can take any more." Her eyes finally met Shay's. "Don't you think there are enough signs to tell you this isn't what you want or need in your life?"

"Jen?" Shay looked at her in disbelief. "Do you really think those are signs that I should sell the shop, and then do what? Make jewelry on the beach?"

"It would be safer," she said meekly.

"But I'm not in danger. Can't you see that?"

"What about Bridget's warning?"

"Yeah, but—"

"No *yeah buts*. Don't you see this is your way out, and it would give you enough money to set you up for years?"

"Why the about-face? What happened to you being there to emotionally support me?"

"Don't you see, that's what I'm trying to do? It seems that no matter what properties Julia shows Pierre, the only one he wants is this location. They even went to Carmel, and he won't budge on this one." Jen took both Shay's hands in hers. "Please, please, for my sanity, at least, consider selling and leave all this behind and settle down to a nice normal life here."

"Jen, after what I've found out about my"—she gulped—"birth mother, you know I can't do that now. Besides, who's to say all those signs you're talking about don't point to Brad. If he found out about my inheritance, you know as well as I that he would stop at nothing to get his hands on everything I have. He did it before, and he'll do it again."

"Do you think Brad killed that guy?"

"No, well . . . I'm not certain because there are a few other likely suspects." Her mind flitted to an image of Burrows and Carmen. "But, I wouldn't put it past Brad since everything that's happened is something either he or a hired henchman would do on his behalf." She gazed closely at Jen. "But how do you know so much about Julia and Pierre's dealings, or have you, in spite of everything you said, been secretly courting her as a friend?"

"Of course not. I just happened to overhear a conversation."

"At Jo's? Where Julia still is? Tell me, Jen." Shay crossed her arms over her heaving chest. "Is she waiting for you to come back and give her a report?"

"No! I haven't even spoken to her about this. I just happened to overhear her and Karl talking when I met Jo for coffee on the patio. But, it got really busy, and Jo had to run off. By the way, I think she's really missing Tassi, but don't let on that I told you. It seems the girl she hired to replace Tassi has a worse attitude than Tassi did. Heavens, I hope that's not what I have to look forward to with Maddie in a couple of years."

"Jen, focus. What did you overhear? The impression you last gave me was that Jo didn't want Pierre right across the street from her either and was trying to convince him to look elsewhere."

"Yeah, well, she tried, but . . ." She shrugged.

"Let me get this straight. You overheard this conversation at Jo's?"

"Yeah, her and Karl were sitting at the table in front of me."

"That's the second time she's been there recently, which is interesting since she and Jo aren't friends anymore. You could cut the air with a knife between them."

"It seems they were waiting for Pierre to meet them, and as you know, Jo has a soft spot for . . . well . . . she tolerates Julia now but only because of Pierre."

"I see . . . Didn't they see you eavesdropping?"

"No, the umbrella was tipped, and they arrived just after Jo had to go back in. They had just sat down. It sounded like they were in the middle of an argument about her driving, and not really caring who was around to hear it. Of course, when Julia raised her voice, I had to move my chair closer."

"Of course." Shay knew how much her sister loved gossip, and if Julia and Karl were arguing in public, that would be enough fuel to bring hours of speculation to her next conversation with Jo. Shay didn't give two figs about Karl and Julia's marital issues or Julia's driving habits, but Jen had mentioned earlier that Pierre was still interested in the tea shop even after looking at property in Carmel. "So, after all that, what did they say about my shop and why Pierre is still so keen on it when Jo isn't?"

"From what I could make out, it seems that Pierre contacted Karl about possible investment property in Bray Harbor and told him he'd need some start-up funds as all his finances were tied up in Paris with his other galleries, and it would be a little while until he could free some up. Karl, of course, wanted to hook a big-fish client like Pierre and showed him a number of available businesses in the area, but he rejected all of them. However, they stopped in at the pub one day for lunch, and as soon as Pierre set eyes on CuriosiTEAS, he told Karl that was the exact location he wanted. Julia is furious now because you won't sell, and she can't get Pierre interested in anything else. She is going to lose a 'big sale,' and she emphasized *big*."

"That's their problem. I made it clear from the beginning I wasn't going to sell."

"Yes, but you also weren't a hundred percent certain until you got your back up with Julia. So maybe follow your initial instinct, considering every-thing that's happened since, and open that jewelry shop on the beach. For me?" She clasped her hands and tucked them under her chin.

Shay glanced around the recently painted shop. The tea and herb aromas hanging in the air still induced a calming state of mind. She shook her head.

"Come on, Shay, you don't even want to run it the way it was, and this town needs an upscale art gallery. Think of what it would do to make us a cultural capital of the peninsula. Besides, this deal has been months in the making."

"What do you mean by months? When did Pierre contact Karl?"

"About two or so months ago."

"Before Bridget disappeared?"

"From what I could gather it sounded like Julia and Karl tried to make a deal with her before she disappeared. When she rejected it, she told Pierre that maybe if he doubled his offer, she'd listen. Then Bridget disappeared, and they all thought the property would go to the bank, and he'd be able to pick it up then. In their minds, at that point it was a done deal."

"But Bridget had just gone missing and wasn't pronounced dead yet. Why were they even presuming he'd be able to buy it?"

"I guess Julia stepped in and volunteered to secure and maintain Bridget's properties until she came back. She still had a handle on it all, ensuring that if the worst had happened to Bridget, she'd automatically get the listing."

"That was nice of her."

Jen rolled her eyes. "Yes, the old Julia would have helped out in a pinch, but the new Julia wouldn't do anything unless money was involved."

"But if Bridget had only just disappeared at this point, no one except her killer or someone involved with her disappearance would have known she wasn't coming back and that her shop wouldn't go up for sale until she was declared dead, so why was Julia even negotiating with Pierre at that point? Bridget had turned down his offer."

"I'm pretty sure Mrs. I'll-Do-Anything-for-a-Dollar was hoping she'd be able to sell it either way. After all, it is prime real estate on High Street, but then Bridget's heir was discovered. When you claimed Bridget's property, it kind of put a wrench in all their grandiose plans. Don't you see? It's not too late for you to tell Julia you've changed your mind and—"

"Are you sure Julia didn't send you to try and convince me to sell?"

"Shay! I can't believe you actually suggested that."

"Well, it really seems like you're the one pushing this sale, even though you know your best *friend* doesn't want Caden's natural father right across the street from her and him."

Chapter 27

Shay's conversation with her sister haunted her long after Jen stormed out of the door of Crystals & CuriosiTEAS. It was so unlike Jen. Shay tried to put the about-face and pushing the sale down to her sister's mothering instincts, and that she only wanted the best for Shay. But what disturbed her the most was the revelation that the sale had been in the works for months. Only Bridget's killer, or at least someone involved with the killing, would have known that after she disappeared, she wouldn't be coming back and that her shop would be up for sale. That was, until Shay popped into the picture. Why were Julia and Karl pushing to have the sale with Mr. Fancy-Pants go through *before* Bridget was found and declared dead?

She gasped. Was her sister in fact unknowingly

advocating for Bridget's murderers? When Bridget turned down the first offer, had Julia or Karl made sure she wouldn't be around to turn down the suggestion of doubling the offer that Julia had dangled in front of Pierre?

The amulet around her neck warmed against her skin, and the image of Grady Kennedy's body on the greenhouse roof flashed into her mind. Was his murder connected to the sale? The amulet's warmth intensified.

Could Bridget Early have told Grady her plans to leave the building to Shay—and could Julia and Karl possibly have found this out? But how would they have found out? Shay wrestled with the possible scenarios in her mind until one made some sort of sense.

Unless after Bridget came back from Santa Fe, and according to Pearl, then really did disappear before her body washed up. Could Julia or Karl or both have held her captive in that time and forced her to tell them what was going on? Then under duress, Bridget *had* to tell them about Grady coming? Was he killed in the hopes it would make Shay change her mind about keeping the shop by convincing her—like Julia had tried to do that first day after they found the body—to accept without question the above-market-value purchase offer from the mystery buyer?

Erratic images ricocheted through Shay's mind's eye, and she struggled to keep them straight. Logically, she knew the information Jen shared with her shot Julia and Karl to the top of her suspect list. But she had known Julia since elementary school. Could she really be connected to murder, and the break-in attempt at her cottage? Was it all for show to scare Shay off, hoping it would make her leave town and relinquish the properties Pierre coveted just so they could make a buck?

The heat from the amulet made her skin prickle, and the fiery pain across her chest forced Shay to drop Bridget's leather-bound journal she'd held.

That was it, wasn't it? Bridget had been killed by the same person or persons who had killed Grady Kennedy. All she needed was proof. With that revelation, the amulet lost its heat, and the clarity she'd experienced seemed like nothing more than a kaleidoscopic dream.

"Sorry, I took longer than I thought I would," panted Tassi, sailing into the shop. "Auntie is having a heck of a time with her new hire and asked me to teach her a few tricks to serving that the girl doesn't seem to grasp." She rolled her dark eyes. "She's my cousin's girlfriend, and she thinks working there is a joke, like it gives her some kind of special privileges or something. I reminded her that I am Jo's niece and look at all the privileges it gave me. Now I'm working somewhere else. Like I said before, dumb, just plain dumb."

"Tassi, that's not nice. Everyone has to learn sometime. That's what first jobs are all about. Do you remember knowing *everything* when you first started working for your aunt, or did it take you a while to pick it up?"

"That's the thing, this girl worked at Styles Restaurant up on Fourth and at the Muffin Top Bakery before that. You'd think she would have learned simple serving skills by now, wouldn't you? Dumb, just like all of Caden's friends."

Shay studied the girl for a moment, contemplating her words. "Tassi, do you want to go back and work at Jo's? I'm pretty sure she'd—"

"No, never! I only said that to Breanna to shock her and maybe open her eyes that this is Jo's business and she needs to take her job more seriously and stop giving everyone the I'm-too-cool-for-you vibe." She glanced at the book Shay had dropped on the counter. "Is that one of Bridget's tea journals?"

"Um, yes. I thought it was a good time to start our first lessons, and as that ridiculous yellow police tape is *still* up, it seems we're in no rush to open."

"Goody." Tassi all but skipped around the table. "I've been dying to learn how it's done and what we'll need. This way I'll be able to assist you better during your readings."

"But having said that, Bill called from the furniture shop, and he's going to deliver the tables and chairs later this afternoon."

"That's great, and until then, we can practice." Tassi flipped the cover open and read the first page out loud. "*When you first start out, I recommend using regular loose black tea. Once you get surer of yourself, you can use herbal teas. The best herbal tea to start with is dried loose-leaf chamomile tea.*"

"That we have lots of," said Shay excitedly. "I know on the trips I've taken upstairs, I saw a whole section marked chamomile, but I do have to say, at

the risk of sounding corny, that the rest is all Latin
to me," she said with a giggle.

Tassi groaned.

"What? You know most people say it's all Greek
to me. Well, I changed it because some plants are
marked with their Latin—"

"I know what you did there. I'm not as dim-
witted as Caden's buddies."

"I know, I was just pleased with my little . . . oh,
never mind. I don't recall seeing black tea. Do you
know if we grow it?"

"No, that we do have to order. There're so many
types, and they all need particular growing condi-
tions, which is why so many different types are
grown around the world. I think Bridget had a list
of her favorites and used a distributor in San Francisco. The records should be up in the office."

"Okay, good to know. Now what else does she
have written here?" Shay slid her finger down the
page. "Bingo, now listen:

> *"There are many types of teas used in readings.*
> *But some work far better than others. The real trick*
> *is to find tea leaves that are similar in size and not*
> *too large or they won't cluster properly and not so*
> *small that they will become powdery in the bottom of*
> *the cup. You might need to try a few different grinds*
> *until you find one that works best for you.*
>
> *Here are the steps to take before you start the*
> *process:*
>
> *First you must clear your mind of any thoughts.*
> *Remember to trust your first impressions and do not*
> *second-guess yourself.*

Don't rush the process and let what you feel come naturally to you as you calmly study the shapes of the tea leaves and how they are distributed.

Don't ever force anything; let the answers to the client's questions come naturally as you pick out the shapes and figures of the leaves when they clump together.

Start by covering the table you're going to do the reading at with a clean cloth and then prepare the tea by letting it steep for a few minutes.

Have the client drink the tea and concentrate on the question they want the answer to. When they have drunk all but the last teaspoon or so from the cup, take the handle of the teacup in your left hand and quietly ask for help to read your client's future.

As the tea-leaf reader, you will be looking at the shapes and patterns left in the bottom of the cup and interpreting them to your clients. Remember that tea-leaf reading is an art and a skill and proper interpretation takes time.

Then swirl the cup in a counterclockwise direction.

Place a napkin on the saucer and flip the cup over to allow the excess liquid and tea leaves to drain onto the napkin.

Leave the cup on the saucer for about a minute so all the contents remaining in the cup drain away.

Then slowly rotate the cup three times and turn it upright, positioning the handle toward the client. You will see that tea leaves are now stuck to the bottom and sides of the cup in a variety of shapes and clusters.

Now, the leaves are ready to be read."

Shay rubbed the heels of her palms into her eyes and groaned. "That's all well and good, but how on earth do you figure out what it is you're seeing in the clumps and shapes in order to interpret them?"

"Keep reading," Tassi urged. "She goes on to say that *Generally, you'll see five types of symbols. Some will obviously be animals and other formations may remind you of a mythical being. Each carry their own meaning, but we'll start with what's obvious. For example, if you see something that reminds you of the wings of a bird, it can suggest freedom or a journey. Ask about that. There can also be very clearly distinguishable objects, letters, and numbers. Ask the client if they mean anything to them. However, if you clearly see a cross or an X, it might mean there is an obstruction or trouble ahead, so gently warn your client to be on the lookout and to take precautions. Just remember to focus only on the symbols that pertain to the client's question, or you'll feel overwhelmed by everything you see in the cup. But most important, use your intuition, and if need be, use the blue bottle to help guide your interpretation. It will show you the answers you seek. You only have to learn to read it and them.'"*

"Pfft, I don't think this is something I'm going to learn overnight."

Tassi closed the journal. "There's a lot more in here, but why don't we just focus on the first part now and get that down before you have to worry about the rest of it?"

"You're right. I'm letting myself get overwhelmed, and there is a simple question I want to ask, so I guess that makes me our first client."

"Great! This is going to be fun." Tassi clapped her hands excitedly. "I'll get the water on."

"Yes, and grab one of those teacup-and-saucer sets I saw in the cupboard. They looked perfect for a reading." Shay slipped one of the new linen tablecloths she'd purchased for the tearoom out of its plastic bag and flipped it over the round table in the back room. "There, space prepared," she called out and then muttered to herself, "Now I just have to clear my mind." Not an easy task since her mind was working overtime to put all the puzzle pieces of her new life in order. "Oh well, perhaps the leaves can help with that. Bridget seemed to think so."

"What did you say?" Tassi set a paper napkin alongside a white cup and saucer on the table.

"Nothing, I was just talking to myself. The white is perfect, by the way. It will make seeing the leaves a whole lot easier."

"Here's hoping." Tassi laughed and fetched the boiling kettle.

"Okay," said Tassi, "are you comfortable?"

Shay nodded.

"Now." Tassi held the journal and read the first line. "Bridget says to clear your mind."

Shay drew in a deep breath and slowly exhaled, forcing all the boxes in her mind to stay put and stay shut. Despite her efforts, one popped open and out jumped the image of her horrendous nonstop drive from Santa Fe to Bray Harbor in a compact rental car. The one that the knot in her stomach reminded her had drained every last cent she'd managed to save from Brad's betrayal. No good. She pushed that box back on the shelf in her memory files and sucked in another breath, slowly releasing it only to envision Liam's electric-blue eyes with that impish grin across his face exactly like the first morning she'd met him. Now, that one definitely had to go back into the box. If need be, she'd put a metal padlock on it to make sure it stayed closed.

"This isn't working," Shay said, her voice reflecting her frustration. "I just can't seem to clear all the clutter."

"Okay, breathe with me. In through your nose and count one, two, three, four, five, and hold and slowly breathe out counting one, two, three, four, five, six, seven."

Shay breathed along with Tassi and got back into a rhythm. Her mind began shoving all her memory boxes back in place until one tumbled down. The lid flew up, revealing the image of the body on her glass roof. "Nope, I just can't stop the chaos going on in there. It's been so much to take in, and clearly I haven't processed it all yet."

Tassi dropped down onto the chair beside her, tapping her black-polished nails on the table.

Shay swivelled in her chair to face Tassi. "How did you know about the 5:7 breathing technique? You're very good at it, you know."

Tassi focused on the hem of the tablecloth as she rubbed it between her fingers. "It's the exercise I use for my anxiety," she whispered.

"I had no idea."

"Nah, no one really does." She met Shay's concerned expression. "I'm doing better now though. It was really bad for a while, but the breathing really helps. So does being in the tea shop every day. Like you said, the smells in here are so comforting and relaxing." Her eyes widened. "That's it! That's how we can get you to relax and clear your head." She jumped to her feet.

"What are you talking about?"

"You said the smells in the store really made you calm and relaxed."

"Yeah, what are you thinking?"

"That back here it's not as strong. Why don't I make some dishes of the ones you really like and set them up around the room? That might help you focus, or we could try lighting some of Bridget's scented candles. She used those for lots of her readings."

"No candles right now." Shay waved her hand. "I don't know anything about them and would hate to conjure up more images like the ones popping into my head already. The herbal scent is good though." She glanced at Tassi. "The only problem is I don't know one from the other, so I have no idea which ones bring on that feeling."

"Maybe it's the combination of all of them?"

"We can try."

"Great!" Tassi seized three glass bowls from the cupboard and snagged a teaspoon from the drawer and dashed into the storefront.

Shay could hear the tinkle of the spoon on glass and smiled, wondering how she ever got so lucky when Tassi came to work for her. She was going to miss having her around all day once school was back in session. But she'd think about that later. She didn't need any more mental clutter.

With the scented bowls dispersed around the back room, Shay stretched out her back and shoulders and willed herself to relax as Tassi took her through the breathing technique again. When the image of Spirit covered in blood tried to make an appearance, Shay rested her hand on the warming pouch hanging from her neck and drew in a deeper breath, letting her belly expand out. The image disappeared.

Tassi continued to read the step-by-step instructions as Shay went through the motions of preparing the tea. When she had inverted the teacup and allowed it to drain, a whispered voice much like the one she'd heard before caressed her cheek. *Now clear your mind and trust what you see. There lies your answer.* Shay opened her eyes and gazed into the bottom of her cup.

She frowned. The image in the bottom of the cup was of a cat leaping across a squiggly line of leaves. She blinked and looked again. It didn't make sense. She glanced over at the sheet-covered table against the far wall and laughed. "What's so funny?" Tassi peered into the cup. "What do you see in there?"

Shay pointed to the table. "Those, I see those silly cats." She grabbed her belly, trying to hold her laughter in. "All I see is a cat jumping over a line or something. It's hard to tell, but the way it squiggled, it could be the air or an ocean. It doesn't make sense, and it has to be from spending all that time cleaning them, and now I can't get cat images out of my head."

"Why not try once more using the blue bottle? Bridget used it all the time with her readings."

Shay recalled what happened to her the last time she touched the bottle itself, not shielded by the leather casing. "No, I don't think I'm up to that right now." She rose from her chair and stretched out her arms and back. "Let's call it a day, and we'll try again tomorrow. It sure appears I'm going to need a lot of practice before I can charge people to read their tea leaves."

"Maybe you'll get lucky, and they'll all be cat people, so your reading would fit," said Tassi with a soft chuckle.

Shay stopped stretching. "What did you say?"

"I said—"

"I know." Shay waved her hand frantically. "Cat people, that's it. I have to find out if any of the suspects have a cat. Maybe that's the answer. Bridget did say to trust what you see and don't second-guess yourself."

"Oh, I guess that means we're finished for the day so you can go out and talk to people."

Shay couldn't miss the disappointment in Tassi's voice as she cast her gaze away and started to clear the table.

It was time for her to put on her big-girl pants. "No!" Shay placed her hand on top of Tassi's to stop her. "It means you win," said Shay, feeling invigorated by the new insight she'd had. "Let's try once more, but this time with the blue bottle."

"Really? Wow, this will be so cool. You *are* just like Bridget."

Shay looked warily at her. "I wouldn't go that far, but what can it hurt?"

Chapter 28

Shay hoped she wouldn't regret saying those words and settled in at the table again while Tassi rinsed the cup and brought another kettle of boiling water.

"Okay," said Tassi, "Bridget used to hold the blue bottle in her right hand, over the cup with the little bit left in the bottom. She'd have her customer ask their question, and then she'd go through the steps to prepare it with her left hand. By the time she flipped it back over to read the leaves, keeping the bottle over the cup the whole time, the bottle would be all foggy. That's where she said she saw her visions. In the fog. That's all I know about it." She shrugged.

That made sense. The boiling water in the cup would create steam and would fog up the bottle. Shay hesitantly slipped the blue bottle from the pouch. Her fingers tingled at the touch of the cool glass on her skin as she held it over the steaming teacup. She then closed her eyes to concentrate, and whispered, "Show me who is behind killing Bridget and Grady Kennedy and breaking into my house." She peeked at Tassi with one eye. "Too detailed?"

Tassi shrugged her shoulders.

Shay completed the tea ritual, drew in a deep breath, and flipped the cup upright, all the while keeping her eye on the bottle in anticipation of a repeat of the other night. She squinted and peered closer. Small bubbles really had developed inside the bottle. Her eyes weren't playing tricks on her, but that was all she could make out through the misty glass.

In the hope an image would pop into her mind, her fingers wrapped tightly around the bottle, and she closed her eyes. Even though she couldn't see if there was a glow radiating from the bottle, by the warmth emanating through her hand, she knew it was there. The last time she'd held the bottle it brought clarity to everything she saw, and she mentally crossed her fingers that this time she'd have the same outcome. She glanced down into the cup and groaned. "Another leaping cat!"

"You're kidding." Tassi peered into the cup. "Did you see *anything* in the bottle?"

"Bubbles, that's it." Shay shoved the cup away and purged her frustration by repeatedly banging her head on the table—might as well physically mimic what she'd felt like all afternoon after hitting one brick wall after another. "How am I sup-

posed to make a living off this?" She moaned. "I'll
be an embarrassment to the legacy of Bridget, and
the laughingstock of the whole town."

"Unless, of course, they have cats. Then they'll
love you."

Shay snorted a laugh. "Yes, cats, cats, and cats.
That must be the answer, but what it means beats
me." She rose to her feet. "This has been fun—
not—but I think it's time—"

A loud knock sounded on the front glass door.

Tassi peeked out of the back-room doorway.
"It's Bill and his son with the tables and chairs."

Shay sighed. "All right, I'll take care of it. You
go. You've put in a long enough day."

"No way! It *will* be fun to *finally* set up the tearoom." Tassi darted to the door to let Bill in.

There was a whirlwind of activity as the tables
were brought in. Tassi bellowed out instructions as
she skittered around, making sure they were placed
just so, as not to overcrowd the space. As quickly as
it had begun it was done. Shay couldn't stop the
grin that spread across her face. Everything looked
even more perfect than she had imagined. The
tearoom was finally beginning to take on a life of
its own. Her fingers stroked the bottle through the
pouch, and deep down she hoped that Bridget
would be pleased with the changes too. Now if she
could only learn to interpret the images she saw in
the teacup, she might be ready to welcome customers as soon as Burrows released the scene.

Burrows! Shay fished her phone out of her
pocket and quickly tapped out a text.

Do you know if Burrows has a cat?

In what seemed like an eternity but in reality was less than a minute, Dean replied.

He hates animals as much as he does people, why?

Thanks, just curious

"Okay, dead end there . . ."

"What are you doing?" Tassi quit fiddling with what apparently was an uncooperative table and placed a hand on her hip.

"Trying to solve the cat mystery. Hang on, I'll be there in a moment."

Shay tapped out another text.

Do you know if Carmen has a cat?

. . .

. . .

"Please answer." Shay glanced up at Tassi still arranging table placements, and then back at the blank screen. "Come on, Liam, this might be important."

"Finally . . ."

Not as far as I know, why?

Thanks, just a theory I'm working on.

Shay absently tapped her finger on the small screen and glanced out the window, trying to decide what her next move should be. Her chest constricted, forcing a gasp. In front of Jo's was Karl in his black SUV. His left arm, casually propped up on the edge of the open window, clearly displayed a light blue dress shirt with the cuff rolled up. She couldn't believe her eyes. His lower arm was wrapped in gauze bandages.

"Dean!" Her thumbs flew across the small keypad again, and she glanced out again to check

Karl's whereabouts just as Pierre hopped into the passenger seat and they drove off.

You have to question Karl about the attempted break-in at my cottage. His left hand is bandaged and he's wearing a blue dress shirt! He just left Jo's, driving south on High Street!

She pressed send, and she flew off another text.

Hi, sis, do Julia and Karl have a cat?

Laugh emoji . . . you have to be kidding. She's always said animals and kids would interfere with her career . . . rolling laugh emoji.

"Dang it!"

"What's wrong? Don't you like the tables this way?"

Shay glanced up from the screen and stared blankly at Tassi. "What?"

"You said something, and I thought you were letting me know that you didn't like the way I've arranged the tables."

Shay scanned the storefront. "I think it's perfect." She glanced down at her screen. No reply from Dean. She shoved her phone in her pocket. "I'm sorry. I was working on trying to solve the mystery of the cat image but reached a dead end. What you've done is great. Now we just have to see how soon Clara Wylde from Wyldeflowers can have her husband drop off those big potted plants I ordered." She glanced out at the yellow crime scene tape billowing in the wind. "Because no matter how hard Burrows tries to punish Liam, he can't keep us closed forever."

"Fingers crossed," said Tassi, "but from what I know of the sheriff, he'll try."

"That's what I'm afraid of." Shay's heart sank when she recalled what Dean had told her the day they'd discovered the body. She shoved her negative images aside and remembered that the sheriff was still one of the top suspects in the murder investigation, and a glimmer of hope replaced the sinking feeling in her gut. She checked her phone again. Still no reply from her brother-in-law.

"Do you want me to put the tablecloths on now?"

"Hmm?" Shay glanced up from her phone.

"The tablecloths?"

"Oh, right. Not yet. They'll need to be ironed first because they've been folded up in the plastic wrap. I'll do that tonight."

"I can do it. I'll take them with me when I leave."

Shay clicked her tongue against her teeth. "Come on, I know the readings today drained me. I'm pretty sure they did you too, and look at everything else you've done today." Shay waved her hand around the shop. "Let's call it a day. You go home and do something fun tonight, because I'll tell you, when I was sixteen, ironing definitely wasn't on my list of fun chores."

"I don't mind really."

"I know, and that's what I like about you, but . . . it's time to go home."

Tassi hung her head and nodded.

Shay's heart broke at the look of utter dejection on Tassi's face. *Was I this sensitive at sixteen?* She did the math and didn't like the number of years between her current age and sweet sixteen. She certainly was a lot older, but as for wiser? That remained to be seen.

Tassi's foot tapped on the wooden floor, bringing Shay back from the past. Ah, yes, teenage angst. She'd heard Jen say that she used positive reinforcement when dealing with a pre-hormonal Maddie. She needed to figure out what to say to Tassi. It would be horrible if she caused her to backslide on all the progress she'd made in dealing with her anxiety.

Shay closed her eyes and let the mixed aromas of earthy smells and seductive spice fragrances inundate her senses. The familiar tidal wave of calm rolled through her. The amulet pouch grew warm against her skin and an image danced through her mind's eye. It was like on a flickering, old-fashioned, black-and-white movie reel, and then the image on the screen became crystal clear. A black cat leapt through the air.

"No!" Shay cried.

"No what?" asked Tassi, staring at her. "Did you change your mind and want me to iron them now?" She set her backpack on the end of the counter, her hopeful gaze still fixed on Shay.

"No, it's that dang cat, and I have to figure out what it means because every time I try and clear my mind for guidance, I see it in one form or another. I just wish the images weren't so vague. I have no idea how I'm supposed to figure out what it means."

"Oh, I see," said Tassi, her voice taking on a dejected tone as she grabbed her backpack and started for the door. "Maybe try the blue bottle again," she said flatly. With a shrug, she left, letting the door bang closed behind her.

"Teenagers! Now I've offended her by not let-

ting her iron, of all things." Shay bristled with the
energy left in Tassi's wake and yanked on the cord
for the roll-up window shade to close it, but paused.
A patrol car pulled up in front of the tea shop, and
Dean hopped out, adjusted his police belt, and
marched through the door. The overhead bells an-
nounced his arrival.

"What's wrong?" he asked, taking one look at her
face.

She flapped her hands in frustration. "Teenagers! I sure hope you and Jen are ready for it. I
told Tassi I didn't need her to take the tablecloths
home tonight to iron them, that I'd do it, and now
it seems she's mad at me."

Dean let out a deep laugh. "Yeah, and if you'd
asked her to do it, she'd be mad about that. It's a
no-win situation when they get to a certain age."

"When did you learn so much about being sixteen?"

"I was the worst, if you remember. Plus, I run
into a lot of kids in my job. There is no right way or
wrong way at this age. You just have to listen to
them, and let them know you're there for them,
and never give up. No matter how bad it gets.
Those are the kids that eventually turn it around."
He pointed his thumb at his chest. "I'm living
proof of that."

"Hmm." She eyed him warily. "Yeah, I guess you
did turn out okay. Well, at least you've done right
by my sister, so I guess I'll believe you," she said,
fighting a smile.

"Just be patient. Tassi will come around. Some
days you'll be walking on eggshells around her,
waiting for her to throw a two-year-old-like temper

tantrum. Other days, you'll look at her and think she's a grown woman. The transition between childhood and adulthood is a tough phase and takes time and patience."

"Okay, but you didn't come here to talk to me about my staff woes. What's up? Did you talk to Karl about his hand? What did he say?"

"We did follow up, but we didn't talk to him personally."

"What do you mean?"

"I had a deputy follow him to see if there were any driving infractions he could pull him over on so he could question him then about his hand. Trying to keep it casual so as not to raise suspicion."

"And?"

"And nothing," he said with a shoulder shrug. "The deputy said he drove some guy to the marina and then went home. Didn't roll through a stop sign, didn't speed, did nothing he could write him up on."

"So that's it? Karl doesn't get questioned about the attempted break-in because he's a good driver?"

"Not exactly. I called the emergency department at the hospital, and they did treat him for a hand injury recently. At first the ER doc was leery about giving me information, but when I told him it had to do with a criminal investigation, he gave me a little history. Not much, but—"

"What did Karl tell them?"

"He told them it was crushed when the hood of his wife's car slammed down on it."

Shay frowned. "And the doctor believed him?"

"That's neither here nor there. The doc said the

injury sustained was consistent with a crush injury, and there was no indication of an animal bite, and that's all he would say."

"So now what? Do you question him to see if he was lying?"

"No." He rocked back on his boot heels. "I called an old friend of ours, Adam Ward. He's the—"

"Coroner, I know."

"And a pathologist at the hospital. He pulled up the file on Karl's emergency visit and said the X-rays showed a crush injury, and the doctor reported no abrasions or any indication of tissue damage other than extreme swelling to the knuckle area. He was fitted with a temporary splint until the swelling goes down, and then he'll be fitted with a regular cast as a couple of knuckles were involved."

"No dog bite. Hmm . . . then he's not our guy."

"It doesn't appear so, but Karl does have a lot of unsavory-type acquaintances, so he might have hired someone. I'll follow up on that."

"Yeah, that would be more like it because whoever tried to break in would have jimmied the door lock, and then they'd reach in with their right hand and—"

Dean nodded. "You're right. Otherwise, if it were Karl with his left hand injured, that means he—"

"Would have had to reach across his body to turn the doorknob and slide his hand inside."

"Which judging by all the blood around the door and on the porch is where Spirit attacked him—"

"Or her," Shay added.

"Yes, or her. In actuality, we're looking for someone with an injury to their right arm or hand, not their left."

Shay hung her head. "I'm really sorry to send you on a wild-goose chase with Karl. If I'd stopped for one minute, I would have seen that."

"Any lead we have at this point is worth following. Who knows, we might get lucky with one of them, and then all the pieces will fall into place."

"Speaking of leads . . ." Shay paused. What she asked next would make her seem as crazy as a bag full of cats, but someone once told her that the only dumb question was an unasked one. "Does anyone you know, who might be involved in Grady's murder or my break-in, have a cat? Any of the staff at the pub, or—"

"No, I already told you Burrows doesn't, but I'll ask Liam if Carmen does."

"Nah, it's okay, just a wild thought I had." *Yup, absolutely the dumbest question . . . ever.*

"I'll be off then. My shift's over, and Jen has dinner on. Want to join us?"

"No, thanks, not tonight. I think I'll just head home."

"Okay." He shoved his hat on and stopped at the door. "I almost forgot. Adam says hello, and he's sorry he hasn't been by to properly greet you, but this case has him as busy as the rest of us. Plus, I don't know if Jen told you, but he's just been promoted to district coroner and is trying to pack up and move to Carmel by the end of the month."

"She didn't tell me, but good for him. I do hope he stops by before he leaves. I'd love to see him again."

"Yeah, you two were pretty tight way back, as I recall."

"We were. Up until Jen married you, he was like the brother I never had," she said with a soft chuckle and squeezed his hand. "Wait. There's something that's been bothering me since I came back, and maybe you can enlighten me a little."

"I will if I can."

"It's something I tried to talk to Jen about, but she keeps brushing me off."

"Okay?"

"What was it exactly that happened between Jen and Julia? They were such good friends and now . . ."

"They're not, right? But I know why Jen doesn't want to talk about it." He shoved his cap back on his head. "The whole thing really hurt Jen. She couldn't believe someone who was her best friend could have tried to deceive her like that."

"What happened?"

"Jen's going to kill me for telling you, but maybe it's time you know since you're living here now and all. When Jen and I got married, she insisted we live in your parents' house. You were gone, and they'd left it to both of you, but after you told her you wouldn't be back, she thought it should stay in the family. However, we were newlyweds, and I wanted us to have a house that was both of ours. I didn't want to move into her childhood home and always feel like an intruder."

"But Jen would never have made you feel like that. She loved you so much."

"I know, but we were young, and I wanted to be the man of the house and not have your father's ghost over my shoulder all the time. Anyway, Jen eventually agreed, so we had Julia come in and do an appraisal. She was a relatively new real estate agent at the time and seemed eager for the listing."

"But you're still in the house."

He dropped his gaze. "Yeah, it seems Julia tried to lowball on a sale price, and overinflated the cost of the repairs it would need for her to bring the house up to code in order to sell it." His eyes narrowed as he recalled the story. "She offered to buy it from us to save us the hassle of fixing it up before we could sell it."

"And?"

"I was a relatively new police officer, but my gut told me something felt fishy. I called an old high school friend who worked at a real estate office in Carmel. He'd done some deals here in Bray Harbor and knew the market. Well, he came out and appraised the house at more than double what Julia had. He also brought in his father, who's a general contractor, and he told us that the repairs required were about a quarter of the cost Julia quoted. Apparently, they were mostly cosmetic, not structural."

"Oh my," wheezed Shay. "Everything Jen said to Julia that first day makes complete sense now."

"What did she say?"

"Just that she was money hungry and thought nothing about ripping off a friend or making money off her friends"—she waved her hand—"or something like that. But it all makes sense now. Did Jen ever ask Julia about it?"

"Yeah, and Julia laughed at her. She told her it was nothing personal, just business."

Shay's hand lingered on the door as she closed it behind Dean. If Julia could do something as underhanded as that to someone who was supposed to be her best friend, what else was she capable of when it came to just doing business?

Chapter 29

Dean's revelation of the history between Jen and Julia played over and over in Shay's mind as she pedaled back to the Crystal Cove Cottages. Why had Jen never, in all these years, told Shay about Julia's scam? Yes, she'd moved away and was busy with college, and then started her business and met Brad, but still. They were such good friends, all of them. Why would Jen have kept this from her?

She was still in the mindset of giving her sister a good tongue lashing but was also torn between that and letting it all go, when she arrived at the terraced staircase leading down to the cottages. After all, there were too many things between Julia and Karl that still didn't add up, and those made them number-one suspects in Grady's murder. But Liam had said it would take Miss Marple to figure this one out, and Miss Marple, she wasn't.

As she walked her bike along the sidewalk to her cottage, a white blur materialized and flew over the short fence surrounding her yard, and Spirit landed gracefully at her feet. His tongue hung out, giving him the appearance of smiling, and he danced on his back legs, yipping and twirling a greeting.

She laughed and scratched him behind his ear. "Yes, I'm glad to see you too."

He eyed the corner of her cottage just as Liam strolled around the side, a grin across *his* face. "Good evening." He hopped the fence with ease. "Your guardian here came to let me know ye were home." He scratched the large dog's head, but his eyes were firmly fixed on Shay.

"If I had known I would receive such a welcoming homecoming, I would have been here sooner." Shay eyed Liam warily. "To what do I owe this pleasure?"

He dug in his pocket and produced a key. "I thought ye might need this to get into your cottage. Andy, the locksmith, left it with me since I stayed and oversaw the installation of your new door locks."

"Right." Shay slipped it from his palm. "You know what, it's been such a crazy day. I completely forgot that you stayed this morning, and that after he came, I wouldn't be able to get in."

"I did too, so I guess it's a good thing your friend here thought of it then, isn't it?"

Spirit barked and wagged his tail.

"Yes, to both of you." She scratched Spirit's head and then swung the gate open, holding it with her hip as she guided her bike through.

"I was just making dinner, want some?" Liam shoved his hands into his front jeans pockets and looked very much like a shy little boy as he lingered on the sidewalk.

"After what you did for me last night and today, it's me who should be making you dinner."

"Okay!" His blue eyes sparkled.

"But . . . I haven't got groceries, so I was only going to have tea and toast tonight."

His face darkened. "Tea and toast? What kind of dinner is that?"

"It is what old spinsters eat, isn't it?"

"What are you on about?"

"You said I was like Miss Marple. Therefore, I thought I should live the part," she said with a teasing grin.

"Pfft. I meant the way your mind worked. It's like a steel trap, nothing else."

"I see." She could feel hot blotches erupting across her cheeks, and she dropped her gaze.

"Come on. Let's see what you have in the cupboards, and I'll make ye a real meal."

"I thought you said you'd started your dinner."

"I did. I looked in the fridge, but Spirit came to let me know ye were home, and that's as far as I got."

"I see."

"Come on. It will be fun. Me mum could always make a dinner to feed all six of us kids even when the cupboards were bare. You might be surprised by what we can find in there. Besides, we don't want you to pass out on the floor from malnutrition, which a diet of tea and toast will certainly bring about, do we now?"

Spirit sat back on his haunches and barked.

"All right, you both win. Come on in."

Spirit raced up the front steps and danced and twirled by the door.

"It looks like someone is glad to be back in his house today."

"Why didn't you just leave him in there after Andy left?"

"I tried, but he wouldn't stay. He wanted to do his guarding from the porch."

"He was out here all day?" Shay asked, slipping the key into the lock.

"Aye, I brought him over fresh water a few times and even shared my lunch with him, but it was a no-go about him going in."

"That's weird." Shay tossed her helmet and satchel on the end of the sofa. "I wonder what got into him."

"I even told him I'd drop the key off at the tea shop for you."

"And what did he say to that?"

"As ye can see, he'd have none of it. I think he planned for just this to happen."

"Just what?"

"Me coming in to make ye dinner." Liam gave her an impish grin over the top of her refrigerator door.

"Yeah, Spirit told you all that, huh?" She laughed and emptied her pockets onto the kitchen table. The key she'd found this morning in Bridget's storage unit thunked on the surface. She picked it up and turned it over in her hand.

"What do ye have there?" Liam eyed her hand as he dropped a small block of cheese on the counter.

"I don't know." She shrugged. "Another mystery, I guess."

He came to her side and studied the key she clasped between her fingers. "And ye have no idea what it fits?"

"None. I found it in a dress pocket of Bridget's when I went through her storage unit, where Julia had stored her personal possessions. It's not for anything in the shop." She tossed it on the table. "I don't recall seeing anything in here it would fit. So, I don't have a clue."

"Hmm, weird." He returned to the counter. "Now, ye have this bit of cheese and exactly two eggs. How about I make us fried-egg-and-grilled-cheese sandwiches?"

"Fried egg and grilled cheese! Is that an Irish thing?"

"I don't know, but that's what I lived on when I was at the police academy, and me mum used to make them, so maybe?"

"Okay." She eyed him skeptically as he broke the eggs into a pan and buttered the outside of the bread slices. "I guess you survived on them all these years, so I'll give it a try."

"Good, do ye have a grater?"

"I do. It's in that lower cupboard."

"Then ye can grate the cheese while I finish the eggs. Then they'll be ready to grill."

Shay pushed her plate away and sat back, absently stroking Spirit's head where he sat on the floor beside her. "You were right. This was so much better than tea and toast."

He grinned and popped the last piece of his sandwich into his mouth.

"It was such a crazy day, and even now when I think of drinking another cup of tea tonight"— her stomach gurgled in agreement—"I don't think I could."

He took their plates to the sink. "That is going to need a wee bit of an explanation, I'm afraid."

Shay relayed her day in detail, from the readings she and Tassi had attempted to her frustration over seeing the same image in the leaves each time she performed the ritual.

As usual, Liam sat back and intently listened to every word she said until she was done. He stroked his jaw in thought. "A cat leaping through the air, ye say?"

"Through the air or over water. With the way the leaves clump under the cat image, the squiggly line could be waves." She shrugged.

"Hmm." He pushed back in his chair and tapped his fingers on the table. "Do ye think ye'd be up for just one more cup of tea this evening?"

"Ahh . . . I don't think I can. Why?"

"As you know, me gran reads the leaves. I'm not saying I know how to also, but I've watched her enough over the years to have a bit of insight into the process. Maybe what ye need is fresh eyes on it. Maybe I can see something you're missing?"

"But Tassi saw it too, and she's had experience with Bridget when she did her readings."

"I know, but Tassi thinks the world of ye, and she'd be picking up on your confusion. Let's give it a try and see what happens. It can't hurt, can it?"

Shay rubbed her tummy. "I don't know. I was hoping to forget about it all and just relax tonight."

"Come on." He rose to his feet and filled the kettle. "Miss Marple never let a mystery dangle without finding the conclusion. Ye know deep down, ye can't either."

"Miss Marple, Miss Marple, Miss Marple. I'm really thinking you do see me as an old spinster."

The tips of his ears turned bright red, and he dropped his gaze. "Hardly," he whispered, and then muttered so it was nearly inaudible, "At least I hope not."

Not certain she had heard him correctly, her heart did a flip-flop in her chest. Then she thought about Zoey's forest-green eyes and her lithe body sashaying down Shay's front porch steps. Certain she must have misunderstood him, she glanced over as he switched the burner on. By this time, the red he'd had on his ears had transferred to her cheeks. She sucked in a deep breath.

"Okay, sure. I can stomach one more cup of tea today, but if it doesn't clarify anything the first time, I'm done. Tassi had me drinking it all afternoon, and I can't do that again."

"Deal." He flashed her a playful grin.

Her heart skipped and her mottle monster spread. "Why now?" she scoffed, retrieving the tin of loose-leaf tea and banging it on the counter.

His hand paused as he reached for a cup on the shelf and looked questioningly at her.

"Don't ask," she said and made herself comfortable at the table.

"Okay . . . I won't. Now, what else do ye need? A candle, incense?"

"I'm not ready for those yet." She shook her head. "Just the tea, a cup and saucer, and a napkin."

"Will a paper towel do? I can't find any paper napkins."

She nodded.

"Okay, where do ye want me?"

"Just have a seat and let me clear my mind."

Liam dropped into a chair as Shay did the breathing exercises she and Tassi had been through a dozen times before. This time, however, she was distracted by Liam's presence: the closeness of him, his musky, earthy cologne, and everything about him being an arm's length from her. She forced her mind to picture Zoey and was quickly able to shove it all into a box in her mind. She drew in another deep breath. When she envisioned the waves lapping around her legs as she had stood on the beach and the clarity that had come to her, she knew she was ready and began the ritual Bridget had given instructions for.

When she flipped the cup over and stared into the bottom, hot tears welled up in her eyes.

Liam frowned. "What's wrong, what do ye see?"

"The same thing I've seen all day, a dang cat leaping through the air!" She sat back and wiped the back of her hand across her cheeks. "I just don't get it. Bridget said to trust what I see and not second-guess myself, so I did. I called everyone who was close to any of the suspects and asked them about cats."

Liam nodded in agreement. After all, he had received one of her cat-inquiry texts too.

"I'm sure everyone thought I was nuts for asking about cats, but I could only think that the person behind everything had a cat and that's what the leaves were telling me, but now . . ." She pushed the teacup away. "I'm really starting to think I am nuts."

Liam peered into the cup and then back at Shay. "What did you say this squiggly line under the cat was? Water, air?"

"I don't know, either maybe. That's all I could think of."

His gaze remained focused on the leaves.

"Why, are you seeing something different?" She leaned forward and peered over his shoulder.

"Maybe," he said. "These squiggles are letters, not waves or air currents."

"What letters?" She pulled the cup closer and looked at the lines of leaves under what even he had identified as a cat, but frowned. "Letters, you say? Where?"

"These. This one rising above the line looks like an *a*, and—"

"The one next to it looks like it could be an *l*. See the way it's looped," she cried excitedly and continued reading. "Then there's an—"

"*I*," added Liam, "and another *a* and an *s*?" He looked at her. "That spells . . . *alias*?"

"That doesn't make sense. What in the world could a cat be an alias for?"

"You're forgetting. Bridget didn't always deal with things of this world."

"You're right." Shay snapped her fingers. "She lived with the belief in the fairy world." Her eyes lit up. "We have to do it again."

"Again, but you said—"

"I know what I said, but this time"—she pulled the blue bottle out of the pouch—"we're going to use Bridget's world to help us see what it really means."

Chapter 30

Shay followed Bridget's instructions, except this time she held the blue bottle over the steeping cup and concentrated on her question: *What does the image of the cat mean?*

When the leaves were ready, she drank the tea until only a small amount of liquid remained in the bottom. With her left hand, following the turning ritual, she covered the cup with the napkin and saucer, then flipped it over, allowing the residue to drain out, all the while keeping the bottle hovering over the teacup. She took a deep breath, righted the cup, and peered into the bottom.

It was the same message. However, this time she wasn't as certain the squiggly line spelled out *alias* or if it was because of the power of suggestion brought on by Liam's interpretation, so she focused on the blue bottle.

Tiny bubbles floated around inside the glass casing. She slowly turned the bottle over in her hand, and the bubbles danced and moved with her hand's motion.

Look beyond the amber veil. The whispered words caressed her cheek with a sense of urgency she hadn't felt before.

"Liam, can you get me one of those taper candles from the fireplace mantel and light it, please?"

"Um, sure." His chair scraped on the floor as he pushed it back.

"And another saucer," she called.

He set a lit candle on the table in front of her and set the plate beside it. "What are you thinking?" He took his seat again.

"I'm thinking that . . ." She slowly turned the neck of the bottle over the candle flame, and when tiny beads dripped onto the table, she grinned. "See, the neck was sealed with wax. There's something inside this."

She wrenched the stopper top until it slid out from the neck of the bottle and poured the bottle contents onto the clean saucer. "Look, it's an amber fluid."

"Do ye think it's tea?"

She sniffed it and shook her head. "I can't be certain, but maybe." She let the bottle slide through her fingers, and it hit the table with a clunk. "That's weird. It sounds solid, but it can't be." She picked up the bottle, held it in front of the flame, and squinted into the blue glass. "I can't believe it. There's something else in here." She turned the bottle upside down and jiggled it until an object slid through the neck and fell into her hand. Her chest deflated. She couldn't fill her lungs, and she gasped for breath.

Liam shot to his feet and to her side. "What's wrong?"

She gestured to the blue stone she held in her hand and struggled to find the words. "This, this . . ." She wheezed in a breath and filled her aching lungs. She darted to the window on the kitchen door, scratched the stone over it, and pivoted around. "If I'm right, which I think I am, it's a very rare and pricey uncut blue diamond and worth millions, and I mean *millions*," she cried and stared at the oblong stone in her palm.

"Ye're kidding, right?"

"No, it just cut the glass. Only genuine diamonds can do that, and given its deep vivid blue hue, it is the rarest of the rare. But, of course, I can't be certain without performing tests on it using some pretty advanced technological equipment. Although to my trained gemologist eye, I think it's the real thing."

Spirit crawled out from under the table and batted a paw across the table, sending the silver key to the floor at Liam's feet.

"What the . . . ?" Liam leaned over and picked it up.

"I think our wise friend here wants you to use your detective skills to figure out what that key fits."

Spirit yipped and wagged his tail.

"But how will this"—he waved the key—"tell us anything more than you've just discovered?"

"One thing I think we've both discovered about our friend here is he does nothing without a reason. We have to trust him and his instincts."

Spirit started his dancing-prancing thing, urging them into the living room. Liam shrugged in resignation. "After you." His hand made a sweeping motion, and he stepped back, allowing Shay to go first.

"The biggest question we have is who committed the murder and the break-in, right?" She scanned the room for anything that required a lock to open it.

"Yes, and what does the image of the cat and the word *alias* mean?" Liam paused and steadied his gaze on the coffee table trunk. He flipped up the tablecloth covering it and laughed. "Just like most evidence in any case, it is hiding in plain sight."

"You're kidding!" Shay scurried to his side. "Does the key fit?"

"Give me a second." He dropped to his knees, inserted the key into the old lock, waited for the click, and rose to his feet. "Care to do the honors?"

Shay breathed in slowly, counting one, two, three, four, five, and then blew out to the count of seven.

"What are ye doing?"

"Calming my mind," she said, kneeling in front of the trunk. "Okay, Bridget, not sure I'm ready for any more of your surprises, but if this gives us some answers, bring it on." She flipped the lid up and flinched back. When nothing popped out at her, she peered at the contents. Her racing heart quickly dropped to a normal rhythm. "It's only stacks of old newspaper clippings. Really, after all the lead-up?" She hated that her voice echoed the disappointment dampening her spirits.

"Something I learned about Bridget was that she also never did anything without a good reason, so these must have meant something to her." Liam picked up a handful of the papers, took a seat by the fireplace, and flipped through them.

"You're right. With everything I've learned about her so far, they are worth a look." Shay scooped up another stack, flopped on the sofa, and skimmed through the clippings in her hand. She sprang to her feet. "Do you see what I see?"

"These are all about jewelry heists. At least, mine are," said Liam, glancing up at her.

"Yes, mine too, and they go back over thirty years!" She read another article and gasped. "You know what they call a jewelry thief, a very good jewelry thief, one that gets in and out without a trace?"

Liam's mouth dropped open.

"A cat burglar!" they cried in unison.

"Look, here's one from a few years ago." She began reading it to him:

> "Although the main suspect in numerous gem and art robberies goes under several aliases, including Hanz Armbruster and Brucker Schmidt, it is believed these are all the work of one Louis Aubert, a French national and

one-time lone European cat burglar. Due to his razor-sharp mind and athletic ability, it is believed he has been recruited as one of the leaders in the crime group known as the Pink Panthers, an international jewel-thief network responsible for a number of robberies and thefts and believed responsible for what have been termed some of the most 'glamorous' heists in history. One criminologist even described their crimes as 'pure artistry.'

"The Pink Panthers have operated in numerous countries and on several continents, including successfully pulling off the heist at a Paris jewelry store in 2008, where they escaped in broad daylight with over 88 million euros, or over 102 million USD, worth of gems. The investigation is still ongoing.

"To this day, the apprehension of Louis Aubert remains a priority for Interpol; however, his identity has never been officially confirmed. Each time the police have a lead on his latest alias and move in on one of the businesses he operates as a front, Aubert is one step ahead of them. He vanishes, changes his name, and sets up shop elsewhere."

Liam steadied his gaze on her. "Do you think this Aubert could be Pierre Champlain? He has been desperate to get his hands on your tea shop and cottage, which makes me think now that he knows about the blue diamond."

"No." She recalled Caden's paternity and Pierre's history with Jo. "I can't see it being him. Joanne knows him and—"

"She knows him by one name though?"

"Right, but she had . . ."

"She had what?"

"Nothing. I just can't believe it's him." Shay remembered what Pearl told her about her own father and how he'd tried to take the pouch from Bridget's neck and hurt her, and Shay's grandmother, trying to get to it.

She sank into the sofa and relayed the story to Liam. "Don't you see? He followed her to San Francisco. She was scared to death of him and was on the run for over four years before she finally felt safe enough to come here to Bray Harbor where my . . ." She swallowed and whispered, "Where my other mother had taken me. It stands to reason he's the guy these clippings are all about. Why else would she have been following his criminal career so closely?"

"Hmm." Liam rubbed his neck. "Maybe you're right. If he's as good as these articles say, he's probably someone we don't suspect at all."

"Or one we do suspect, but he's got such a good cover that he's like you said earlier, hiding in plain sight."

Liam snapped his fingers. "Maybe he's not really a he, but a she, or has taken on the appearance of a woman. From the clippings I read, these

Pink Panthers disguised themselves as women more than once."

"Carmen!"

"What?"

"When Dean asked me about her reaction to the button I found, I realized she did say some pretty strange things to me that day about Burrows and the murder, and there was something off with her aura, it turned black and gave me the shivers. Plus we found out she *was* wearing a blue shirt when she went into the pub that night."

"Hmm . . . okay . . . maybe. She's only been in Bray Harbor for about six months now, but came highly recommended by her last employer in Las Vegas."

"References can be falsified and there's too many coincidences. Especially given what that article said about the thieves dressing as women."

"You're right, and she rarely talks about herself, but there's only one way I know to try and confirm any of this. I'll have to go to my cottage to do it though."

"Huh?"

"My father's old computer. It has access to Interpol *under an alias*. If I use his login information, I can still get into some of their older files and run a trace on her. Something, given my training, that in hindsight I guess I should have done more of a thorough job of before I hired her."

"Is that even legal, you know, hacking into the Interpol site?"

"Not exactly, but me da did a lot of work with them for years, and they never took away his access code. After he passed and the files he had access to were considered closed or cold, I'm sure they forgot about it."

"But what if it sends up red flags and you suddenly have a SWAT team at your door?"

"Then they can take over the internet search for this guy, and we have helped them catch an infamous jewel thief, one that's eluded them for years." He shrugged and rose to his feet. "I'll be back as soon as I have something that might link all this together."

Shay followed Liam and Spirit, who trotted along close on his heels, into the kitchen, and tossed her stack of clippings on the table. Something about all this had her senses reeling, but she couldn't put her finger on it. Was it the fact that Liam was about to commit cybercrime, or was the idea of Carmen, a man masquerading as a woman, too farfetched for her to wrap her head around? Her gut told her something was wrong with this picture.

"I don't think you should do it," she cried as he opened the door and stepped onto the small top landing.

"Why not? Don't you want to find out if this guy who seduced Bridget—who was a young girl the same age as Tassi, by the way—and then tried to kill her to get her pouch, is here in Bray Harbor stalking you?"

"Yes, of course I do, but it feels off. Something isn't right."

"Look, Spirit has made it clear that he's coming

with me. I'm pretty sure he'll protect me should the SWAT team show up."

"Liam, please . . ."

"What?" He flashed her that irresistible dimpled grin from the bottom of the steps.

She shook her head in disappointment and closed the door. "Just be careful," she whispered and rested her palm on the cool oak.

Chapter 31

Shay slowly rotated the blue bottle under the candle, making certain that the dripping wax sealed the stopper back into the neck. She set it on the table to allow the new wax to cool and with any luck, secure the contents. Given her science background, even though it had been in geology, there was no question in her mind that the liquid in the bottle had combined with the blue diamond, producing a chemical reaction of some sort. It was that reaction that had been responsible for what Bridget was reported to have seen in her readings and what she herself had witnessed. That had to be it. After all, that's the only thing that made sense to her.

She just wished she knew what the amber liquid was and hoped her opening it and some of it evaporating hadn't taken away any of the *magic* Bridget believed the bottle possessed. Even Shay's feeble attempts at a smell test yielded no results. She just didn't know her teas and plants well enough to replace the small amount that had been lost.

She picked the bottle up and inspected the neck seal. The wax had turned white, and she trusted that meant it was dry enough. She held the bottle in front of the candlelight and tipped it upside down. The tiny bubbles danced around the priceless stone, just as they had before, and a sense of relief swept through her. Until she knew what the amber liquid was, she couldn't afford to lose any more. Toes and fingers crossed that her DIY efforts would hold, she slipped the bottle back into the pouch and tucked it under the neck of her blouse.

Even this temporary distraction hadn't erased the edginess she'd felt earlier. Her skin still prickled, forecasting a fiery backdraft on everything she and Liam had discovered. She'd half thought that the bottle being back in the pouch and over her heart would calm her and wrap her in its warmth and closeness. But no. No warmth, no sense of well-being enveloped her. She was left cold and alone with a foreboding sense of dread haunting the shadows of her mind.

Shay hesitantly moved to the side window that gave her a clear view of Liam's cottage. A light glowed behind the closed curtains. A vision of him hunched over his computer flashed through her mind. He'd been gone for what felt like forever, and she was worried. It was clear that Spirit had sensed it too, or else why would he have been so eager to follow Liam home? Then she had a vivid image of handcuffs, and she grasped the window frame to steady her legs. Oh, why hadn't he listened to her? She knew in her gut that no good would come out of him poking around computer sites that he had no business accessing. Interpol of all things!

She craned her neck to try to see up the alley for any signs of flashing lights and realized that was foolish. The FBI, or whoever investigated these kinds of things, would just roll up in a big black SUV and not announce their arrival.

A knock sounded on her door.

She jumped. "Ooh, this is exactly how they'd do it too." She patted her hammering chest, willing her heart not to explode, and tiptoed to the door. A second, louder knock echoed through the house. As quietly as she could, her trembling fingers secured the chain lock on the door and she guardedly opened it a crack, expecting to find two men dressed in black. "Pierre?"

"Yes, can we talk for a minute?"

"Umm . . . is Jo with you?"

"No."

"Ahh . . ." She glanced at the clippings on the table and an uneasy sensation rushed through her. "Well, I'm kind of busy right now. Maybe you could drop by my shop tomorrow and we could talk then? But, if it's about buying my tea shop, then as I told Julia, it's not for sale."

"But, I think you're going to like what I have to say." His gray eyes sparkled under the porch light. "You see, my good friends Karl and Julia have kindly found me another property that would suit some of the requirements I have for the art gallery I want to open on the peninsula."

"Oh, that's wonderful. I'm glad they could help you out, goodnight now." She started to close the door when his hand flew up and pressed back hard against it, forcing it to remain open the crack that the chain lock allowed.

"I came to ask you to reconsider my most generous offer of the properties that you've recently come into possession of. You see, I am supposed to sign the documents on the other site tomorrow, but I wanted to give you . . . one . . . last . . . chance to reconsider."

Shay shook her head and pushed on the door in an attempt to counteract the man's pressure on the other side. "Yes, your offer was tempting; however, I have plans for the shop and—"

"I'll double what I offered previously. May I come in so we can talk?" He countered her increased thrust against the door, keeping their line of sight open.

"Look, I know the location of my shop is important to you. I heard about Jo and Caden, and I understand, but have you considered Jo in any of this? If the truth about Caden's paternity ever got out it could destroy the boy and their whole family."

"Caden? Pfft. A spineless boy showing no potential, too much like the man who raised him. The boy is of no use to me." He casually rested his right hand on the doorframe. "No, I'm after much more than that, and I think somewhere you might hold the key to what I seek."

"I don't understand. If it's not about Caden and Jo . . ." She glimpsed a piece of white gauze poking out from under his long-sleeved shirt cuff and danced a step backward. *Oh, Spirit, if ever you could sense something was wrong, now would be the time.*

He didn't wait for an answer and heaved his body against the door, snapping the chain.

"Hey, wait a minute." She stumbled backward and gasped. "You can't just barge in."

"I'm fairly sure you're going to want to hear the number I came up with. Why not accept it so we can both get on with our lives."

"Look," she said, backing up another step as his hot breath wafted across her cheek. She couldn't believe she'd done exactly what Bridget told her *not* to do. She'd second-guessed herself, and in this case, let her feelings for Joanne overrule her instincts and discarded him as a suspect.

Her eyes darted to the kitchen, looking for a knife, a fork—anything to arm herself with. She may have been caught off-guard when he arrived playing all Mr. Nice n' Friendly, but bursting through her door was another matter. Her fight or flight impulse kicked in, and she made a grab for Spirit's large metal dish beside the door. Pierre sprang in front of her, forcing her up against the table. The dish slipped from her fingers, clanged to the floor, and rolled on its rim under the table.

Now what? He'd also cut off any access she had to both doors and a way out. Panic coursed through her. *Stop and think, Shay. Think!* Then a whispered voice caressed her ear. *Keep him talking.*

She braced her knees. Fine, if he wanted to play cat and mouse, then she'd turn the tables and be the cat, not him. She glanced down at the newspaper clippings. One headline that Bridget had highlighted jumped off the page at her. She swallowed hard to squelch the bile forming in the back of her throat. "Well, Pierre . . . or should I call you Louis? Because that's your name, isn't it, Louis Aubert? You're the infamous cat burglar, and you *think* I have something you want?"

His gaze followed hers to the newspaper clippings, and he tossed his head back and chuckled. "Ah, *ma très chère*," he whispered, gently raising his hand to stroke her cheek.

She jerked her head and thrust his arm away, but not before his fingertips latched on to the cord around her neck, tugging her closer to him, rocking her off balance. "But I know you do. As you can see by those"—he gestured with his head toward the clippings—"I've had a very illustrious career and *always* get what I seek, one way or another."

The corners of his lips turned up in a mirthless smile. He gave the cord a hard yank, pulling it up to her chin. "See?" He triumphantly smirked when the pouch flipped up. "And look, I just saved myself a whole lot of euros by coming here tonight instead of buying your property. Who knew such an exquisite stone would not be better safeguarded and all this time was in plain sight?" A soulless expression filled his eyes as he tightened his grasp around the cord, pulling her closer, his hot breath wafting across her cheek.

"You're the one who strangled Grady Kennedy and broke into Madam Malvina's shop, aren't you?"

"Yes." His hand twisted, tightening the cord. "Who knew that Bridget had not hidden what I seek in one of her statues. As for the little Irishman"—he laughed—"I couldn't very well have him ruining everything I'd worked so hard to find, could I?" He leaned into her face. His rancid breath lashed at her nostrils as his grip on the cord tightened and squeezed.

She grunted under the pressure on her windpipe when his hand twisted again. She struggled to force air into her lungs. Her hands flew to the cord, fighting to get her fingers under it.

"Being a cat burglar, I do enjoy a good game of cat and mouse, and Grady and you have provided me with an enormous amount of amusement these past few months. But, alas, it's time for me to take my leave. But not without this!" he said, with another twist of his hand.

"Tell me . . ." Shay wheezed, and her fingers clawed at his hand. "Does Joanne know who you really are and the real reason you're here?"

He let out a mocking snicker. "I had no idea when I tracked Bridget and her priceless gemstone to Bray Harbor that little simpleton lived here. Just my luck I picked her coffee shop to stop at my first day, and she recognized me as Pierre Champlain—a name, by the way, I haven't used in over fifteen years." His eyes gleamed in the flickering candlelight from the table behind her as he tugged downward.

When he yanked on the cord again, she braced and anchored her back leg against the table. Her front foot thrashed out, and her toe clanged against Spirit's metal food dish. He started and looked over his shoulder. His grip loosened just enough that she managed to wedge a finger under his hand. "Then you were stuck using it again, right, Louis?"

Grip regained, he let out a mirthless laugh. "As much fun as this has been, *ma très chère,* remember, you brought this on yourself when you didn't accept my offer, and now you will pay even a higher price." He jerked her down toward the floor.

She flailed her arms out and grabbed for the table edge. *Stay upright!* her mind screamed. He wrenched on the cord again. *Not today, you son-of-a*—She kicked out hard with her foot.

A whoosh of air left his lungs, and he doubled over, his hands releasing the cord to cradle his groin.

I am not going to die tonight, not here, and definitely not by being strangled with Bridget's pouch.

Before he could regain his balance, she kicked him again, this time aiming for his knee. Another whoosh of air wheezed from him, and before he could regain his footing, she punched him across the chin. He staggered under the blow and crashed back into the wall beside the door, popping it open a crack. She seized the burning candle from the table, knelt beside him, one knee digging into his sternum, and held the flickering flame over his face. "If you move even an inch, I'll make sure the hot wax seals your eyes shut," she sneered.

The door flew open, and in a flash, Spirit stood snarling over Pierre.

"Freeze!" Liam burst through the door with gun drawn. He looked at Spirit and Shay. "Well, it looks like my work here is done." He rose to his full height and grinned. "Good job, you two." He leaned across Pierre sprawled on the floor, Spirit snarling and snapping over his face and Shay nearly sitting on his chest and hovering molten wax over his eyes. "Until the police arrive, I wouldn't move if I were you." Liam tapped the white gauze poking out from under Pierre's shirtsleeve. "Yeah, the throat wouldn't be as easy to hide, would it?" He winked, as he stuck his head out the back door.

"Just in time, boys," Shay heard him call out. "I'm not sure how much longer Shayleigh can hold Spirit off him or, truth be told, how much longer Spirit can hold off Shay."

Heavy boots thumped on the stairs, and Dean and four deputies marched into the kitchen with guns drawn. They took one look at the scene and holstered them. Dean replaced his with a pair of handcuffs, nudged Shay and Spirit off the criminal, flipped Pierre onto his stomach, cuffed him, and read him his Miranda rights.

Time went by in a blur as Liam and Shay gave statements as to what happened. A deputy gathered up the news clippings they'd discovered in Bridget's trunk and sealed them in plastic evidence bags. When the whirl of activity slowed to a manageable pace, Shay glanced at Liam.

"Mind telling me what took you so long in getting here?" she asked, rubbing her throat where the cord had cut into the skin.

His eyes scanned her throat. "I think we'll have plenty of time to talk about that later. First, we have to get ye to the hospital to get that"—he gestured to her neck marks—"treated."

"I'm fine, but I don't get Spirit's actions tonight. He has always had an uncanny sense of brewing trouble. Remember the day he wouldn't leave my house and someone—"

"Louis Aubert."

"Yes, Louis Aubert or Pierre or whoever he really is, tried to break in. Whenever he wanted you to come to me, he would do his dancy thing, so you'd follow. He did that with me at Pearl's so I would get the chest. I don't understand why his sixth sense failed him tonight and left me"—she touched her hand to her aching throat—"hanging until nearly the end."

Liam pursed his lips and cast his gaze down-ward.

"What? Did he try to get you to come back, and you ignor—"

"No, no, it wasn't like that."

"Then what was it?" Shay glanced down at Spirit. His tongue hung out, giving the impression that he was smiling.

"It was like he knew what was going to happen, but he wanted me to find more proof before he'd let me come back."

"I don't understand."

"He seemed edgy the whole time I was doing in-ternet searches. I knew you might be right about using the Interpol site, so I tried a few other searches and came up with basically the same in-formation that we found in Bridget's clipping. Like I said, Spirit was edgy. He would pace to the window, stick his nose between the drapes, whine, and then come back to my chair. After he'd been constantly doing this, I started to think that some-thing *was* wrong over here. So, I tried to get up, but he laid his paw on my lap and pushed me back down."

"You're kidding."

"No, it was so weird. He wasn't going to let me

leave. I didn't know what to do, and then I had a thought. Since every check I ran on Carmen came back clean and it appears she is exactly who she said she was—and a woman, by the way—I decided to check out our other suspects. I knew you had discarded Pierre Champlain, but my old police gut took over, and I ran a search on him."

"And? Did you find the proof then?"

"No, the only thing I came across was a news story from fifteen years ago about the mysterious disappearance of Pierre Champlain, the owner of two prestigious art galleries in Paris. He'd cleared out his galleries and was never seen again. According to the article, it was considered a pretty big mystery at the time, and officials thought foul play was involved, but the story was killed, and there was no mention of him again, anywhere."

"We know where he ended up, don't we?" She glanced down at Spirit. "Is that when he released you from custody?"

"No. I decided to throw caution to the wind and logged into Interpol . . ."

She flashed him a look of disbelief.

"I know, not very smart, but I searched a couple of names and related searches took me to Interpol's Most Wanted list and a man named Lorenzo Bonfanti. When I clicked on the name, guess whose photo popped up?"

"Pierre's?"

"Yes, and it was in that moment Spirit made his break for the door. By the time I got it opened, he was off and running. Trust me. We got here as soon as he wanted us to."

"Sorry to interrupt," said Dean. "But I think we

have everything we're going to get here tonight. As for him"—he gestured with his thumb toward Pierre—"anything else will come out in further interrogation."

"Will you be questioning him?" Shay glowered at Pierre, sitting stoic and unblinking at the table.

"I'd sure like this collar. It would be a nice notch on my career résumé, that's for sure. I have a feeling that because of his botched investigation, Burrows may be on his way out of the force, but—"

"You'll have to turn him over to the FBI," Liam said, shaking his head.

"Yeah, sadly I do. I've got a call in to the field director now and should be hearing back any minute." He waved at the deputy standing beside Pierre. "Okay, let's get out of here and let these good people enjoy the rest of their night."

The deputy seized Pierre's arm and guided him through the door.

"So that's it." Liam puffed out a breath, reached for her hand, and gently squeezed her fingers. "Tell me, Miss Myers, how does it feel, taking down one of Interpol's most wanted cat burglars?"

"Pretty darn good, I think. Although, I'm more relieved it's over." She laughed and absently stroked the pouch that had grown warm against her skin. A thought struck her. She sprinted to the parked cruisers. "Wait!"

The deputy paused, and Pierre glanced at her.

"Tell me something. Are you my father? Did you take advantage of a young girl in Ireland and then . . ." She steeled herself for an answer she didn't want to hear but had to know.

"Oh no, *ma très chère*, but I do know him well, and let's just say"—his gaze darted to the pouch around her neck and then locked on her—"he seeks to possess what you have as much as I do."

He winked, and then the deputy dragged him away and pushed his head down into the back of the patrol car. Pierre stared at her through the window. A slow smile crept across his lips. He blew her a kiss and laughed as they pulled away.

Chapter 32

"Jen," Shay called, "have you seen that wheelie thing I bought at Teresa's Treasures?"

Jen popped her head out of the back room. "You mean the tea cart?"

"Yes, that's it. Do you have any idea where Tassi put it?" Shay planted her hands on her hips and scanned the tea shop. "I don't see it anywhere, and how are we going to serve samples out on the sidewalk without it?"

"You gotta relax, little sister," said Jen with a laugh as she tossed a kitchen towel on the counter. She scurried to the window. "Just like I thought. She's already got the pre-steeped tea set up in vacuum carafes, and she's started serving tea samples."

"You're kidding." Shay raced to her side. "I thought things didn't get started until nine. I'm not near finished in here."

"Don't worry. There are always early birds at these sidewalk sales who are afraid of missing out on the freebies. My guess is none of them will actually come inside because then they might have to spend some money." She chuckled and surveyed the shop. "But it looks pretty done in here to me."

"It's not. Look at the flower vases on the tables. Don't they look off-center?"

Jen clicked her tongue against her teeth. "Like I said, relax. Your official opening is going to be great."

"I wish I had your confidence. It seemed to take forever to get to this stage, and now that it's finally here, I don't feel ready. There's so much left to do." Shay appraised the room setup. "But you're right. It *is* done, isn't it?" Shay grinned. "You know what my favorite part of all this is?"

"What, all the potted plants?"

"No. Seeing you wearing that red apron with *Crystals & CuriosiTEAS* embroidered on it. It's like it was made for you."

Jen tossed her blond head back and laughed. "It was, remember?"

"I know, but I'm just so happy you decided to come and work here part-time." Shay hugged Jen so tight she could feel her sister's heart beating in time with hers. "We're going to make a great team," she whispered, "you and me and Tassi."

Jen pulled away, swiping at her tears. "After what happened these last few weeks, someone had to be here to keep an eye on you," she said with a forced laugh.

"Come on, I doubt very much that stumbling across dead bodies or having it out with an international jewel thief is going to be an everyday event. You've been married to a cop too long, if that's what you're afraid of."

"That, little sister"—Jen bopped Shay on the nose with her fingertip—"is exactly what I intend to make sure doesn't ever happen again."

"Seriously? That's the only reason why you're here, to be my protector? Pfft," she scoffed, not able to contain her eye roll. "You're forgetting. I have Spirit." She glanced over at the sleeping dog beside the back counter. "And he's done a pretty decent job of that." She shook her head in disbelief that her sister would even think she'd become a magnet for murder, and gazed around the shop. A soft smile crossed her lips. "No, I have a feeling that Bridget has left me something very special here, and I'm excited to find out what it is, and I'm glad you'll be part of that journey too." She gently squeezed her sister's hand.

"That is a lovely sentiment, but"—Jen took both Shay's hands in hers and jerked her head toward the window—"I think one of us had better get outside and give Tassi a hand. It looks like browsers are rolling down the street in droves now, and we wouldn't want her getting overwhelmed and quitting on us, would we?"

"No, I'd hate to lose her."

"Good, then you go give her a hand. Let me put that interior design degree of mine to work, and I'll finish adding the final touches in here."

"Wait a second. I meant to ask you how Joanne is taking the news about Pierre."

"Well, as you can imagine, when she discovered that he wasn't here because of her and Caden, she was really hurt. But now I think a sense of relief has settled in, knowing her secret is still safe from her son. She's going to tell him about it someday, but when he's older, probably like Mom and Dad were going to tell you about Bridget on your eighteenth birthday."

"Yeah, but look at how that turned out."

"I know." Jen squeezed her hand. "But Jo's doing better now. She's almost back to her old self again."

"And Gary?"

"They had a heart-to-heart and he finally told her he'd known the truth all along, but it didn't matter because he loved her and Caden so much. It's all good," she said with a reassuring pat of Shay's hand. "But you'd better get out there and give Tassi some help. They're lined up at the cart now." She flashed Shay a celebratory grin and hustled back to the counter to retrieve her kitchen towel.

"Yes, it is all good now." Shay took one last look around. Her sense of satisfaction was reflected by the smile on her face. "I hope I've made you proud, Bridget," she murmured to herself before heading out into the bright morning sunshine and plowing directly into a hulking object. She shielded her eyes and gazed up. "Adam! I'm sorry. The sun, and—"

"It's me who should be apologizing. Can't talk and walk at the same time, it seems," he said with a soft chuckle.

"It's so good to see you. I've been meaning to drop by your office, but—"

"Don't worry. From what I hear, you've had a few more pressing things on your mind since you came back, and it's me who should have made more of an effort to come see you."

She waved him off. "Dean told me you got some big promotion and were busy packing to move to Carmel, so I understand. Life gets busy, right?"

"Yes, that was in the works, but then it all changed at the last minute."

"What do you mean? Didn't you end up with the promotion?"

"Yes, but the county coroner decided to save the California taxpayers some dollars by cutting my relocation expenses. So it appears, for now anyway, that I'll continue to work out of Bray Harbor. It all kind of went from sixty to zero overnight. But that's a good thing." He turned to a group at Shay's sidewalk table display and waved his hand.

A petite woman, whose hair dripped over her shoulders like amber honey, grinned and scampered over to his side. "I was wondering when you were going to introduce me." The woman thrust out her hand, taking Shay's in hers. "Hi. It's wonderful to finally meet you. As long as I've known Adam, well . . . let's just say he talks about you constantly."

Shay glanced curiously at Adam, recalling what Joanne had told her about his reaction to her leaving town after high school graduation.

"Sorry. Shay, this is Doctor Mia Harper . . . my fiancée."

"Your fiancée? That's great! I mean, I'm so happy for both of you." Happy wasn't the word for it; after what Joanne had told her about his behavior when she left town, she'd been afraid he hadn't dropped by to say hello because he still carried a torch for her. "And two doctors in the family, how wonderful."

"Ah no. I'm a PhD, not a medical doctor." Mia flashed a shy smile.

"Well, that's still great, and wow, this is great news. When's the big day?"

"I guess now that my life isn't going to be turned upside down"—he placed his arm lovingly around Mia and pulled her into his side—"we can start planning."

"Soon, I hope." Mia smiled up at him and then glanced at Shay. "You'll have to promise whenever it is that you'll be part of the bridal party."

"Um . . . You mean as a guest, right?"

"No, one of my bridesmaids."

Shay quirked an eyebrow so hard she feared she sprained her face. She hadn't seen Adam in years and didn't even know this woman. Was she crazy?

"I wouldn't have it any other way. You're Adam's oldest and dearest friend, and I can't think of anyone else better to stand up with us."

"Ah . . . well . . . thank you?" She glanced at Adam to see if he appeared to agree with Mia, but all he did was smile and look adoringly down at the petite woman. "I'm flattered, of course. But—"

"She's right, Shay, I never would have survived middle school, let alone freshman year of high school, without you as my best buddy. You have to accept."

"Okay . . . if that's what you both want, I'd be honored."

"Then it's settled," said Mia, glancing over at Shay's sidewalk sale table. "But it looks like you're busy now, so we'll chat later. Promise?"

"Yes, yes, I promise," Shay said, forcing a laugh, still trying to get a sense of whether this woman had taken leave of hers or was just genuinely a nice person who wanted to get to know an old friend of Adam's, or . . . what was that saying? *Keep your friends close but your enemies closer.* Did she think Shay's reappearance back in Bray Harbor threatened what she and Adam had? Shay opened her mouth to set the record straight.

"I'm afraid my soon-to-be-bride here might have an ulterior motive, though." Adam winked.

And there it was—the other shoe. Shay snapped her mouth closed.

"I told her about the greenhouse upstairs, and she's been dying to take a look since then."

"I do confess it's been on my mind," Mia said teasingly, "but that's not the only reason. I want to get to know your childhood friend. I'm pretty sure she's got some good stories to tell me about you growing up that I can use at our wedding dinner."

Shay breathed a sigh of relief. That wasn't even a house slipper dropping. "You don't need to have an excuse to come and see it, but . . ." Shay glanced over at Tassi. The crowd around the sale table and tea cart was now two-deep. "Maybe not today though. Any other time, and I'll be happy to give you a tour."

"Perfect! I'll definitely take you up on that." She grinned, and Adam kissed the top of Mia's head.

"I think," he said, "that you've just made this botany professor's day."

"Botany?" Shay stared at her. Maybe this woman wasn't the wackadoodle she'd first thought she was. "Yes, I think we do have a lot to talk about."

"I look forward to it." Mia gave her hand a light squeeze. "But we've kept you long enough. Go and enjoy your opening day."

"I will, thanks." Shay waved as they disappeared into the throng of people milling around on the sidewalk. A botany professor? *Wow!* That's exactly who she needed, to explain to her what the heck all that green stuff growing upstairs actually was and what she could use it for.

Maybe this day would turn out better than she thought it would, and to top it off, her little buddy, Adam, was getting married. She hugged her arms around her chest and squeezed. All-around good news, any way she looked at it. Shay couldn't stop smiling. She glanced over at the tables set up in front of Liam's pub and was stunned to see Zoey pouring sample glasses of beer and handing them out. Well, maybe the day wasn't all that perfect. She shored herself up and slipped in beside Tassi.

"Sorry, I tried to get out here earlier but got sidetracked. How's it going?"

"Great!" Tassi grinned. "Look what Auntie just dropped off for us to give out with the tea samples." She pointed to a tray of petite pastries. "There's two more trays under the table if we need them."

"Wow! Was that ever nice of her. I guess maybe that's something we should have thought of and pre-ordered. I'll pop in and pay her later."

"No, she said it was her gift to us on opening day." Tassi smiled at a tiny gray-haired woman as Tassi handed her a small paper cup filled with tea, and a tiny pastry. "Thank you for stopping by and don't forget to go inside and take a look at our brand-new tea shop."

"Thank you, dearie." The woman held up her cup in a toast gesture. "I think I'll do just that." The woman hobbled off toward the door of Crystals & CuriosiTEAS.

"Look at you"—Shay patted Tassi on the back— "up-selling the shop like that."

Tassi shrugged. "We gotta do what we can to get them inside because so far most are only interested in the free tea and the stuff on the clearance table," she added, pouring another cup of tea and giving the woman a smile worthy of an Oscar.

"You're right." Shay glanced at the long lineup of people waiting their turn for a free tea sample, and leaned into Tassi, whispering, "When things settle down today, there's something I need to talk to you about."

"Are you firing me?"

"What? No, definitely not."

"Then if it's what I think it is, I already know."

"You do?"

"Yes, I knew that first day when you came out of the pub and I was talking to you in front of the tea shop here. I swore I saw Bridget's reflection in the shop window watching us." She smiled and handed a tea sample to the next person in line. "You look exactly like her when she was younger, you know," Tassi whispered.

Shay blankly gaped at her.

"The photos, you know, the ones you found in the storage unit."

"Right, those."

"And like I said"—she shrugged and poured a

cup of tea for the next person in line—"I know I saw her that day, behind you, in the window."

Shay wasn't certain which one of them had the heightened senses, but—her gaze flitted to the gold lettering across the tea shop windows—if what Tassi was telling her was the truth, and not some school-girl fantasy, then the two of them would have no trouble picking up where Bridget had left off.

Tassi glanced over at the sale table and grabbed Shay's arm. "Look who just walked up."

"It's Madam Malvina and—"

"Orion," whispered Tassi breathlessly.

Shay gaped at Tassi and blinked, then blinked again. Was this starry-eyed girl the same one who barely noticed Orion's existence during their first meeting? "You go wait on them. I'll man the tea station if you like."

Tassi shook her head adamantly as a flush that rivaled Shay's usual mottle monster spread across her cheeks, and she quickly averted her attention to the two women trying to decide which flavor of tea they'd like to sample.

"Okay then, I will," said Shay, smiling knowingly at the girl, and trotted over to the table. "Madam Malvina, it's so nice to see you again." She extended her hand in greeting. The woman in black responded by clasping her slender hand in Shay's.

"When I heard you had more of Bridget's collection to sell, I just had to come and have a look." She glanced over the table. "I lost so many good pieces during the break-in, many of which had been spoken for by my customers, and I hoped I could find some more of her unusual statues to replace them with."

Shay took a shallow breath. "Yes, I heard about that, and I'm so sorry it happened to you."

"Pfft." She waved her manicured black-finger-nailed hand. "You had nothing to do with that, did you?"

Guilt seeped through Shay, but she couldn't very well tell Madam Malvina that the break-in was committed by an international jewel thief who thought she had a rare blue diamond, the very one Shay wore around her neck. "No, of course not," she said, hoping she was giving an Oscar-worthy performance and that the psychic couldn't read her true thoughts.

"Then, don't feel bad. These things happen." The woman in black shrugged and scanned the table. "You're not selling any of Bridget's stones or the amulet pouches she had. I missed taking those during my last visit, but since the thief cleared out my collection, I was hoping."

"No, I'm going to be selling those in the shop. I was a gemologist before, and they're something I know I can work with."

"I see . . . well . . . I will buy all the cat statues and the gargoyles, of course. Since that's what the intruder smashed and . . ." She picked up what was supposed to be a magic wand, and then gathered up a collection of bottles labeled Spiritual Oils. "I'll take all these too." She scanned the table again. "Oh, and these." She grabbed the mysterious-looking palm-shaped incense holders.

"Look, I feel so bad about what happened to you that there's no charge for any of this. Take it as my gift."

"Hmm." The woman eyed Shay skeptically. "I get the feeling there's something you're not telling me."

"No, of course not." Shay bit out her words. "But, please, I know Bridget would have wanted you to have them, and you can see by them being on my clearance table, I have no use for them. Please, take them as a gift."

The woman studied her face then slowly nodded. "Your heart is true even though your words may not be, but I always trust my instincts about a person. So, why not." She leaned into Shay and whispered, "I think you and I have a lot to talk about one day, right?" She didn't wait for Shay to answer and snapped her fingers. "Orion, take these to the car."

Shay scurried behind the table, dug out a box from under it, and filled it with all the items Madam Malvina had claimed. Then the two of them left as quickly as they had arrived. Shay sucked in a deep, cleansing breath. "Wow, she's good," murmured Shay. "I really thought I was a better actress than that."

Chapter 33

Shay glanced over at Tassi. Even though she was still smiling and chatting with everyone who stopped by, Tassi's blush had yet to recede. Was Orion the reason or was she getting overwhelmed?

An idea flashed in her mind. After dashing into the shop and around the back of the sales counter, Shay fished out a small leather pouch. Even though she planned to use them as gemstone pouches, one would work perfectly for what she had in mind. She filled it with an assortment of the teas and herbs she recalled Tassi mentioning she loved. After tugging the tie tight, she offered Tassi the pouch. "Here, why don't you take this? I filled it with some of your favorites, but if you want to change them out, feel free."

"What's it for?" Tassi asked, taking it from her fingers.

"Because you said the scents in the store really

helped with your anxiety, and I don't want you getting overwhelmed." Shay pointed to the cord. "You can hang it around your neck. That way, when you're not in the shop and you ever feel anxious about anything, you can open the top and take a whiff. It might help, along with your breathing exercises."

"Wow, thank you." She tied it around her neck, patted the leather, and tucked it under her T-shirt. "This will really come in handy when I go back to school." She softly smiled, gazing down at it. "Now, I have my touchstone, and you have yours."

Shay's hand went to the blue bottle in her pouch. "Yes, and we both have to learn how to use them, together."

Tassi's eyes glistened with tears, but before one could fall, she straightened her shoulders, put a smile on her face, and served the next customer, reminding them to check out the new shop inside.

Yes, this had turned out to be a great day. She cast a quick glance in Zoey's direction. Well, in spite of what was happening in front of Liam's pub. But her thoughts were interrupted by a familiar musky scent wafting over her shoulder.

"Hi, neighbor."

She swung around. "I was wondering when you'd drop by." Her breath caught in her throat when his blue eyes lit up and he flashed her that dazzling smile that turned her knees to jelly.

"I see ye've been busy today."

"From what I can tell, you haven't done too shabby yourself." She gestured to the table in front of the pub. "I see you recruited Zoey to give out samples."

"Yeah, I'm trying out a new craft beer, and it seems to have been a hit because we got slammed inside today. I needed all hands on deck in there. She was off and volunteered to help out."

Shay stared directly ahead. "That was nice of her." She knew her tone came out a bit cooler than planned, but she had already proved today with Madam Malvina that she wasn't very good at hiding her true feelings.

"Yes, it was," Liam said with a strangled chuckle.

She grabbed his arm. "Is that the sheriff's car pulling up in front of Jo's?"

"It looks like it."

"But I thought Burrows was suspended?"

"Take a look at who's driving."

"Dean?"

"Yeah, it was made official this morning. Apparently, with the full internal investigation ongoing regarding Burrows's handling of not only this case, but other things that recently came to light about the way he's been conducting himself, he's been fired."

"*Other* things coming to light?"

Liam shrugged his shoulders, but she didn't miss the impish sparkle in his eyes.

Dean marched across the street toward them, weaving around the festival goers, tipping his hat and nodding at everyone he passed. By the time he reached them, his grin seemed like a permanent fixture.

Liam gestured with his hand toward his friend. "Shay, I'd like to introduce you to Bray Harbor's newest sheriff."

"I'm so happy for you." She hugged her brother-in-law. "Jen never said a word about this today."

"She doesn't know it's been made official yet. Is she inside? I gotta tell her before she hears it on the street. It means I won't be working shifts anymore, which she'll be happy about, but it also means my days could be a whole lot longer with the added responsibilities." He took an uneven breath.

"Jen didn't know you were after the promotion?"

"She knew I wanted it, but like me, she assumed it would be years away—after Burrows finally retired and the kids were older and we weren't running the mom-and-dad taxi service anymore."

"Knowing the two of you, I have faith that you'll figure out a way to make it work." Shay laid a reassuring hand on his arm. Even though *reassured* wasn't exactly how she felt. It meant Jen wouldn't be available to work during school holidays because Dean would be on straight day shifts. Her only hope then was that Tassi continued to behave, and her aunt and parents didn't make her return to Carmel.

"I hope so." His hesitant steps toward the door gave evidence to his nerves. "And by the way"—he paused in his tracks and came back, glanced around and whispered—"I thought you both would want to know that it seems Pierre's never been caught before, and this arrest has really rattled him, so he's confessed to everything, mumbling something about being bewitched, which was the only reason why he got caught."

"Bewitched?" Shay recalled the whispered messages in her ear. "Did he say if he killed Bridget, or was that an accident like it was reported?"

Dean pushed his hat back on his head and steadied his gaze on Shay's. "That's another weird thing that happened. If Grady hadn't been killed, then I never would have thought about asking him about Bridget's death because it *was* ruled an accidental drowning. But, apparently, Pierre was only trying to get her to tell him where the diamond was by using the old water dunking interrogation method."

"He drowned her?"

"He said that part was an accident. He didn't mean for her to die, but the last time he let her up for air, she was . . . So he left her body where it was, in that little cove around the rocky outcrop, at the end of the beach by your cottage. The current must have swept her up and, well, that's how she ended up under the pier."

"And why there was no evidence of foul play," said Liam. "It's a well-known fact, in some circles, that waterboarding or dunking leaves no physical trace—except the drowning part, of course."

"Oh, and he said during the dunkings she said some pretty strange things to him."

"Like what?" asked Shay.

"Like, when she stared him straight in the eye and asked him what darkness had entered his life to turn him into a killer. And then something about, 'Do your worst. I've made sure everything will turn out like it's supposed to.'"

Shay shivered and hung her head, recalling the words Tassi said to her that first day when they'd met outside the tea shop. *Promise me you'll find out who did it.* Shay winced with the heat emanating from the amulet on her chest. Now they all knew the truth and Bridget had, in her way, made certain of it.

"Did he tell you why he killed Grady? Anything, a hint about what the man was here to tell Shay?" asked Liam. "Did he give a reason for killing him or was it another *accident*? I mean, looking through his files, and like Bridget apparently told him, murder wasn't one of his methods of operation before."

"No, he said he had no idea why Grady had been summoned by Bridget, only that after Bridget died, he knew he'd gone too far, but had too much invested in this whole thing. There was no way he could chance that Grady would mess it up for him by talking to Shay, in case Grady had also figured out Pierre was behind Bridget's death."

"But why did he kill him on my roof? He could have done it in countless other places that wouldn't have drawn so much suspicion, like the B&B in Carmel. It never would have linked any of this together."

"You're right, but remember that because Grady was killed, we managed to figure this whole mess out before anyone else died. He said your rooftop was the perfect place, because it might send a message to you, and you'd sell."

"But how did he manage it? No one saw him up there."

"He said that night he'd left a message at Grady's B&B to meet him on the patio at the pub, saying he was a friend of yours and had some information for him. Then Pierre used a rope and grappling hook to gain access to the greenhouse roof from the alley—"

"I bet that's why one of the bolts had scratch marks on it."

"Most likely. Anyway, he then sat and waited until Grady was alone on the patio. Then he hung the rope down over the edge where Grady was sitting, and due to his practiced precision as a second-story cat burglar, he managed to easily loop it around Grady's neck. After that, he gave it a sharp tug and hauled Grady onto your roof, breaking his neck in the process."

Shay's stomach twisted with the violent image of Grady's murder burned in her mind. "The poor man, and to think he was only here to help me."

"Yeah, but Pierre was going to stop at nothing to get his hands on that rare stone. After years of tracking it and Bridget down, he was convinced that she must have it hidden somewhere in the shop or her cottage and was going to do whatever it took to get his hands on it. Never in a million years did he think it was hiding—"

"In plain sight." She glanced at Liam and shook her head. "Yeah"—she rubbed her neck—"and, obviously, neither did we."

"Yeah," said Dean. "It's too bad you got hurt in the process, but on the bright side, we did get a guy who authorities have been chasing for over thirty years. So, it all turned out in the end, and now you won't ever have to worry about him again. Because I get a feeling that he'll be going away for a long, long time." He glanced into the tea shop. "I guess it's time."

"Wait," said Liam, glancing around. He leaned over and whispered, "Whatever happened with the Brad thing and the jewel theft?"

"Ooh," said Dean. "Brad's a slippery character, that one. I guess it helps when you have the most prestigious law firm in New Mexico handling your cases."

"Yeah," jeered Shay. "With everything he's put me through, he reminds me of the Teflon man."

"Yup, it seems nothing sticks to that guy, does it? But as it turns out, he didn't have anything to do with the break-in. Through our interrogations we discovered it was Pierre. When he couldn't find the jewel here in the tea shop, which he had searched on his supposed frequent viewings of the property, he took a chance that Bridget took it with her to Santa Fe and hid it in the jewelry store."

"But I saw him and Karl that same evening. How did he get to Santa Fe and back so quickly? Because then I saw him at Jo's the morning right after the break-in."

"It seems Pierre might have had access to a private plane and airport so could have managed to get in and out undetected. He's also very well connected, so had inside help with the security system. The FBI are following up on that."

"Wow," said Shay. "I can't believe the lengths he went through to get his hands on the diamond." Her gaze darted from Liam to Dean. "Maybe it's worth much more than I thought it was?"

"Not necessarily," said Dean. "It might have ended up being more of a pride thing for him than anything else. Remember, he'd committed two murders, but still had nothing to show for it. He was getting desperate and was afraid he'd have to leave empty-handed, which for him had never happened before. His last visit to your cottage, well, that was a last-ditch attempt, which nearly paid off."

"And very likely would have," chuckled Liam. "That is, if he hadn't run into our very own *young* Miss Marple here."

"I doubt very much she ever physically kicked anyone's butt," laughed Shay.

"Oh, I heard she was a feisty one back in her younger days." Dean winked. "But maybe, Shay, you can enlighten me on something?" He tugged a notebook out of his jacket's inside pocket and flipped it open. "Not much was stolen in that robbery, considering all the gemstones in the shop inventory, so I found this interesting." He flipped through his notepad and stopped. "This is the list Brad's assistant reported as missing to the police, and I'm not sure what they all have in common: aquamarine, turquoise, some sapphires, blue jadeite, moonstones, blue Akoya pearls, azurites—"

"They're all blue stones."

"Which means if Pierre hired someone else to commit the robbery in Santa Fe, then someone else knows what's in there?" Dean said, gesturing to her neck.

Shay's eyes widened. "Who else besides the three of us knows about the diamond inside the bottle? Do the FBI?"

"Not as far as I know. I don't think they've made the connection to the stolen blue gems and anything like that, and Pierre certainly isn't telling them about it."

"Probably hoping when he gets out he'll get another crack at it," snarled Liam through his clenched jaw.

"I think he's going away for a long time, but you can't take any chances with someone else knowing about it."

Shay's thoughts flashed to what Pierre had said just before the deputy sheriffs drove him away: *He seeks to possess what you have as much as I do.*

"So," Dean added, "I suggest that you never let anyone aside from us know about the diamond in there either, not even Jen. Just the knowledge of it could put people at risk from a would-be thief."

Shay nodded in understanding and clasped her hand around the pouch. "I'm sworn to keep the Early family legacy safe, and that's exactly what I'm going to do."

"Good, we can't take any chances in the future." Dean braced his stance, adjusting his sheriff's utility belt. "Okay," he said, drawing in an unsteady breath. "Time to tell my beautiful wife that there's a new sheriff in town." He pivoted on his boot heel and strutted off toward the shop door.

Shay smiled. She sensed his nervousness as he stepped inside. He knew this promotion would bring big changes to their family, but she also knew her sister well enough to know that she only wanted the best for the people she loved. Shay had a feeling they'd be just fine.

She contentedly lingered beside Liam where they stood on the redbrick sidewalk beside her clearance table, her fingers absently playing with the cord around her neck. The pouch it tethered grew warm against her skin, and the air around her crackled. Every day since she'd discovered the blue bottle, she'd felt her senses heighten, stirring her to her core. As she surveyed the festive scene on High Street, the colors took on that now-familiar crystalline vibrancy, and she could feel their different textures against her skin. Yes, her little town had changed over the years, but then so had she, and in more ways than she'd ever imagined possible.

She looked over at Tassi, whose face glowed as she chatted cheerfully with customers at the tea cart. Through her shop window, Shay spied her sister wrapped in her husband's arms. A tsunami of love coursed through her.

"You know," she said, glancing up at Liam, "when I first came back to Bray Harbor and saw what I inherited, I wasn't sure I could make a go of it. But now, I can't imagine a better life. Maybe Bridget knew what she was doing after all."

"You know there's a quote that I think says it all. I don't recall who actually said it, but it goes something like 'Change can be difficult and painful. Ask the caterpillar, and then ask her again if it was worth it when she becomes a butterfly.'"

She chuckled softly. "Thanks, but I'm afraid I'm still very much at the caterpillar stage and have a lot to learn before I become a butterfly."

"Aye, that might be true, but also remember Shayleigh means fairy princess in Gaelic, and from where I stand, ye live up to the name well." He leaned over and whispered, "Besides, I think I can see ye wings starting to break through. At least, that's what me gran said when I told her about ye." He flashed her that toothy grin of his, the one that highlighted the dimples in his cheeks.

She sighed as he casually strolled back over to the pub display. However, she didn't miss the radiant glow on Zoey's face as he approached her at the table. Yes, bad timing, if only . . . A smile formed on Shay's lips as she gazed up High Street, taking in the happy faces of all her new neighbors and some new friends as they took in the day's festivities. "Thank you for my new future, Bridget," she whispered.

Visit our website at
KensingtonBooks.com
to sign up for our newsletters, read
more from your favorite authors, see
books by series, view reading group
guides, and more!

Become a Part of Our
Between the Chapters Book Club
Community and Join the Conversation

Betweenthechapters.net

Submit your book review for a chance to win exclusive
Between the Chapters swag you can't get anywhere else!
https://www.kensingtonbooks.com/pages/review/